# The
# Dark
# Brotherhood

**A NOVEL OF SUSPENSE**

**PAUL A. CLARK**

**C.L. FORBES**

**Dedicated to**
*The Comte de Saint-Germain*

# Acknowledgments

The authors' wish to thank Michael Clark, JoAnn Jones, Dee Morgan, Gary Fisher, and Dion Fortune for their assistance, support, and inspiration.

# Prologue
# Northern England

Merrick finally had the ritual in his hands.

*The one that was going to change his life.*

Normally such manuscripts are warily guarded by private collectors or locked away in dusty vaults of scholarly libraries. In either case, their contents are generally deemed *secret* and are restricted from examination by the casual or curious dabbler in occult arts.

But Merrick didn't consider his interest casual. He'd searched for a ritual like this one for years. After numerous unsuccessful attempts, he finally found a young library assistant at Oxford who thought that old religious ceremonies were full of unintelligible nonsense. She had no idea why they were considered confidential, or why anyone would care who saw them. She succumbed easily to his charming flirtation and within minutes he had a copy of the pages he wanted.

Now, while trying to hide his impatience from the others, Merrick walked briskly up the moss-covered hill. The path was obscured in the darkness, but he decided not to turn on his flashlight. The entire area, while uninhabited and normally unpatrolled, was privately owned and trespassing was strictly prohibited. Or so the sign on the gate they passed through moments ago warned. But it didn't matter. He had walked this trail countless times since he was a child, and he knew every inch by memory.

The hill was unusually silent. Often the sounds of crickets unified in song, or small animals scurrying through the bushes, accompanied Merrick on his midnight excursions. Tonight, he could hear only the *crunching* noise that his feet, and those of his team, made on the pebbled gravel of the narrow path as they walked single file.

The air was still, and a steady stream of mist drizzled from the cloud-filled sky, covering the midnight adventurers in a shimmering layer of moisture.

For years, Merrick had visited the small stone henge, and each time he returned, his desire to discover its mysteries grew. He often felt as though the stones spoke to him, urging him on, pleading with him to release their hidden power. He knew that this particular circle had been constructed several thousand years ago to channel unknown universal forces. All he needed was the right key to unlock its secrets.

Most people who visited the area had no knowledge or understanding of the latent power of the site. Even the locals considered this particular ring to be nothing more than an archeological curiosity of minimal historical value. Merrick knew otherwise. The mystical pattern was exact, and had been created for a special purpose.

Throughout his school years, while friends played soccer, chased girls, or diligently studied for future entrance to elite universities, Merrick spent most of his time combing through used bookstores looking for the means to activate the energy of the stones. For hours, he pored over volumes on the early rites of the Celts and Picts and read through the ceremonies of the medieval occultists and alchemists. He even tried out a few of the more promising rituals he found. None so far had been successful.

Not yet anyway.

Usually Merrick performed his little rites at the site by himself. He was too afraid that if he shared his passion, he would be laughed at. He was also jealous and protective of the stone circle, and he didn't really want anyone else to know about its power. This ceremony was different. It called for seven members, and there was no way around it. Any change at all could damage the outcome. Equilibrium must always be maintained. Cosmic force needs stability.

Building a team had been difficult. With few options available, Merrick had been forced to select his officers, or so the ritual called them, from among a local occult group. Most were semi-interested college students who seemed more into impressing their friends than really learning or doing anything of value. They had very little experience and he had to train them quickly. According to the instructions of the manuscript, the ceremony must be performed at the autumnal equinox, which was tonight. Waiting another full year was not an option for Merrick, he had waited long enough.

While he reviewed the procedures of the ceremony in his mind, he heard a stifled giggle come from somewhere near the back of the line, and for a moment he found himself questioning his decision to prepare so hurriedly. *What if they're not ready?*

But as Merrick made the next turn through the growing mist and cold, the mystical henge slowly came into view, and all his thoughts of doubt were instantly dispelled. Incredibly, the carved boulders looked

2

much as they had centuries before. Most had eroded slightly, and a few were chipped or broken, but overall the original pattern remained intact, and he inwardly reaffirmed his pledge to discover their secrets.

Asserting his new and somewhat tenuous authority, the self-proclaimed occultist directed his officers to lay out the various daggers, cups, and incense burners they had carried up the hill. While he situated each ritualistic implement according to the directions of the manuscript, his team clothed themselves in their homemade robes and capes. He then instructed the six new members of his team to join hands and form a circle at the center of the stone ring.

With great intention Merrick then walked the perimeter of the site, and with a silver dagger in hand, drew a large five-pointed star in the air at each of the four directions. Every step he took was filled with purpose as he intoned the words of power directly from the pages before him. When his rotation was complete, he settled himself in the East next to the largest stone. There he raised a long iron sword high above his head, and using a loud theatrical voice, began reading a formula of summoning.

*Thee I invoke, the Bornless One; Thee that didst create the Earth and the Heavens. Thou art Osonophoris; Whom no man hath seen at any time. Thou art Iabas. I am thy prophet unto whom thou didst commit thy Mysteries, the ceremonies of ancient days.*

His booming speech sliced through the air while his team stared with adoration at their leader. As Merrick spoke each word he felt the strength of the rite growing. He could actually feel each syllable vibrate first in his vocal cords and solar plexus and then down his spine and out through his feet. The sensation was amazing. He felt as though he had been plugged into a giant generator and every cell in his body had been turned on for the first time in his life.

While the vibration increased, Merrick observed things inside of the circle that he had never seen during his many other visits. It was almost as though he had grown a second set of eyes, and this pair could perceive things of an otherworldly nature, ones he never imagined existed. Using his new vision, he saw his own arms and legs growing in size and soon he was looking down from a lofty height high above ground.

He looked around expectantly, as a green shimmering light formed around the edge of the circle. It started as just a faint outline around the larger boulders, and then the light expanded and enveloped the entire area, including his officers. It throbbed and pulsated, as if it was alive, and Merrick relished the feeling of a long-sought victory.

3

But as the radiant beams continued to swell, their color gradually turned murky and he became concerned. *That's not supposed to happen.*

Soon the light transformed into darkness and every tingling cell in his giant body suddenly felt agitated and out of place. It actually felt like the atoms in his flesh, muscles, and organs were now battling and repelling one another.

He looked at his officers, and their terror filled expressions confirmed his suspicions. They felt it too. Confused, they looked at each another and waited, expecting the sensation to pass.

Soon it did. Seconds later the officers began to hallucinate. Fear radiated through their beings as Merrick appeared to them as a demon, horns replacing ears, fangs in place of teeth, glowing red eyes full of malice.

Screams poured from their mouths as a horrible, evil current of energy surged through their bodies. Panicked, they tried with futility to break the human ring and run from the site. But the more they struggled, the stronger the current flowed, and their hands remained locked together as though fused into place. Helpless, they exchanged pleading cries that faded unanswered into the somber night.

Merrick fumbled through the manuscript looking for a way to stop the errant ritual. As he desperately scanned each page, he soon realized that in his rush to perform the ceremony, he hadn't noticed that the all-important *license to depart* clause was not included.

*Fear gripped his soul.*
*Merrick was unable to stop it.*
*The gates of chaos unlocked.*
*The demon of the abyss advanced.*

# Introduction

There were four books: incredibly old, incredibly evil. In the time of beginnings, each was constructed painstakingly by dark adepts who lived in lands now drowned beneath the waves of unforgiving oceans. Transmitting the ancient knowledge into these books was perilous and sometimes fatal to the *Brothers of the Shadow*, and many who composed these works were sucked into the outer darkness that borders our island of time and space.

The origin of these evil teachings remains unknown, but rumors abound that four chaotic entities known as the *Lords of Imbalance* spread the information early in humanity's evolution to bring about the eventual annihilation of our species.

All four books, or *Grimoires* as they were known, bore one of the seals of these creatures of chaos. Each seal was an intricate combination of letters, colors, and geometric figures designed to subconsciously control the mind of whoever possessed the book...with one exception.

Anyone with sufficient knowledge of the unique symbolic system, and the ability to interpret its hidden meaning, could instead use the power of the Grimoires to command an Army of the Shadow. Thus, the books became the secret keys to open the Cosmic Gates of the Outer Darkness, and possession of one brought unimaginable power to the knowledgeable operator.

It would be better if these Grimoires had remained unknown, locked away in forgotten rooms, or perhaps exiled to other non-cosmic dimensions where their forbidden contents would be unavailable to ignorant men and women seeking power for avarice or selfish dominion.

Unfortunately, this is not to be the case. For one of these books, exercising its sinister power, is about to reemerge into our world.

# Chapter 1
## Somewhere in the
## Carpathian Mountains

Lightning flashed like the bright sparking of magnesium in a fire, temporarily blinding the driver of the small sedan. Seconds later, a crash of thunder pierced the sky and violently shook both the car and driver. In response, Marty the Magnifico, cursed to himself as he squinted through the rain-soaked windshield.

"Be a big star, build your reputation on an international tour," Marty mocked aloud as he scanned the darkness in search of a place to pull over.

A month ago, his manager Arnie, suggested doing a series of shows through countries that had at-one-time been behind the Iron Curtain. The magician had thought the idea was crazy, but Arnie had been persistent.

"They'll love your act Marty. You'll be an overnight success," he had promised.

"Yeah, right," Marty muttered as he reached for his phone in a vain attempt to contact the man responsible for his current situation. But as he started to dial Arnie's familiar number, he saw that he had no signal, and instead threw the useless device onto the passenger seat.

Almost in reply to his growing frustration, the chill-you-to-the-bone Carpathian wind whipped around the sides of the car, and pushed it over the faded-yellow dividing line. Reflexively, Marty swerved back into the far right lane while he wondered if he was close to the border.

So far this road had been practically deserted, but he hoped he might find some place to stop once he crossed out of Slovakia. If he didn't, the strong winds might soon push him over the edge of the high cliffs. Then his career would be over even faster than it would if he continued to let the critics slowly crucify him.

*Maybe not such a bad idea.*

Feeling dejected after the reviews of his last performance, Marty had decided that what he needed was to spend some quality time alone. On impulse, he rented a car to drive to Ostrava in the Czech Republic, while the rest of his entourage and props made their way by train. It never occurred to him to check a weather report before he left.

The storm started two hours into his trip, and for the last fifty miles or so, rain poured from the sky without a break. Early on in the drive, Marty had considered turning around, but he knew if he did, he would miss his matinee the next day in Ostrava.

As he stared sightlessly through the windshield, unwelcome thoughts weaved in and out of his mind. Repeatedly, he flashed back on yesterday's show, where he had performed many updated versions of tricks first introduced by his lifetime idol, Harry Houdini. Sadly, his act had lulled the audience into a hypnotic state, more akin to sleep than awe.

These days it seemed like even his best escape tricks bored the audience. Most people are too used to the impossible stunts that appear in just about every Hollywood blockbuster. Of course, in reality, no one is capable of jumping 200 feet out of a helicopter engulfed in flames, onto the roof of a van traveling 70 miles per hour, and then immediately putting the karate moves on the driver. Yet, over and over, the modern-day audience accepts these exploits without question, and they even expect the same kind of magic in person.

"Maybe if I could train a bear to escape from a water tank the audience might be satisfied," Marty thought amusingly to himself.

When he and his wife had visited a marine-life water park last year, he was amazed that the audience would erupt in applause simply because a dolphin could wave hello with its tail. "I need a little bit of that," Marty speculated.

Feeling utter frustration, he tried to clear his mind of the unwanted memories by squeezing his eyes shut for just a split second. Unfortunately, Marty picked the wrong time to indulge in his own self-pity. Had his eyes been open at that very moment, he might have seen the wall of water that came rushing down the steep rocky slope to his right in time to avoid the flood in the road in front of him.

Instead, his lids flew open as he felt the car slide uncontrollably toward the far side of the highway. Instinctively, he turned the wheel in the opposite direction and slammed his foot on the center pedal. The saturated brakes groaned under the strain, and the car fishtailed back and forth. Marty reached for the gearshift, and with all of his strength jammed the resistant clutch into first gear, and then pulled up the emergency brake.

Mercifully, the vehicle skidded to a stop just short of the highway's edge, as the tumultuous waters swirled around the tires and then retreated down the mountainside. Stunned, he tried to slow his rapid breathing while sweat streamed down his forehead and his heart felt like it was going to beat out of his chest.

He sat there for a time after that, listening to the rain pelt the roof of the car until slowly he recovered his senses.

Marty then tried to re-start the car, but nothing happened when he turned the key. He tried again several times with no success. The magician wasn't much of a mechanic, but he assumed that all of the water must have temporarily flooded the engine. At least, he hoped that was all it was.

For now, he resigned himself to the idea that he wouldn't be going anywhere for a while, and he pulled the key out of the ignition.

*Not a big deal, at least I'm alive.*

Except that without the heater on, it was cold inside of the car, *really cold.* He clasped his arms tightly around his chest, and rocked back and forth in an effort to stave off the invading sensation. He then tried rubbing his hands together vigorously, but soon numbness spread through every part of his body. Fearfully, he looked around at the barren hills and prayed for a miracle.

Unbelievably, as the next crash of lightning lit up the surrounding area, the stranded driver saw something in the distance he hadn't noticed before. At first, he thought it was just a natural rock formation, until another bright flash streaked through the sky, and he saw that it was some kind of building. It seemed big and didn't look like a house, ranger station, or any other place one would expect on an isolated roadside. In fact, it seemed oddly out of place with its long, narrow windows set at regular intervals.

"Maybe it's a medieval castle?" Marty mused to himself humorously. Visions of Dracula and the old B-class vampire movies he had seen on the late-night film fests when he was a kid flashed through his mind.

But as the cold continued to seep through his clothing, Marty decided he better go check it out, even if it meant taking a long walk in the rain.

He reached for the door handle, mumbled a few choice words, and pulled his coat close around his waist to prepare for the inevitable deluge. Then, remembering he left his umbrella back at the last nightclub, he decided to use his jacket as a makeshift rain-fly and pulled his arms free from the sleeves.

Ignoring a fleeting feeling of trepidation, he forced the car door open against the wind, jumped out, pushed the automatic lock button, and banged the car door shut.

And then he remembered.

Immediately alarmed, Marty pressed his face against the glass and saw his keys sitting on the seat, right where he left them.

*Damn it!*

In disbelief, he kicked the silver door just as a loud peal of thunder exploded nearby. He closed his eyes and let out a long defeated sigh.

The defeated feeling however, was short-lived. Soon the freezing water soaked his boots and pants to the knees, and he begrudgingly turned toward the structure on the hillside.

After slogging through the mud for what felt like miles, although really the distance was much less than that, Marty found himself standing in front of a large, iron-studded door made of what looked like oak. A large knocker was affixed to the roughly hewn timber, and directly beneath was a matching engraved plate. As he narrowed his gaze to take a better look, he heard the sound of chanting muffled through the walls.

*Chanting? What is this place, some kind of monastery?*

In preparation for the European tour, Marty had read several history books on the area. When playing in a new country he felt it was important to understand the local customs, and cultural past of the citizenry, in order to maximize interest and avoid any embarrassing mistakes. He knew from those readings that monasteries had at one time littered the countries of Eastern Europe and that some had survived to this day.

Shrugging, Marty lifted the heavy doorknocker and sounded three rapid thuds while he continued to look questioningly at the plaque. As the next bright flash streaked through the dark night, he saw that a perfect inverted pentagram had been etched onto the shiny brass plate. In the center of the down-turned star was an equal-armed cross overlaid by a budding rose. Around the edges of the entire design was some kind of lettering.

*Strange emblem for a monastery.*

After a minute passed with no response, the magician raised the handle and prepared to knock again. Before he had the chance, the door opened and almost pulled him across the threshold. Surprised, he jumped slightly.

As light spilled from the interior, he noted that the letters on the engraved plate were in Arabic.

Only then did he realize that an imposing figure was holding a lantern and staring down at him. As he looked up, he almost jumped for a second time.

# Chapter 2
# Southern California

The completely refurbished 1938 Jaguar purred contentedly down the tree-lined street as a late-afternoon breeze wafted through sun-streaked sky. As the driver maneuvered down the familiar street, he gazed at the Spanish-style homes, neatly trimmed hedges, colorful roses, and signature bougainvillea of the old suburban neighborhood as if he were seeing them all for the first time.

Reaching his destination, Arthur Alexander turned into a brick-lined, circular drive and stopped in front of a seven-foot copper fountain topped with the archangel Michael, a refreshing anomaly to the surroundings.

The recently oiled hinges of the classic coupe opened noiselessly as he glided from his seat and made his way to the entrance. As he reached the front step, the giant rustic doors opened, and Odelia, his housekeeper and personal manager, looked up at him with her perpetual bright smile.

"You always beat me to it," he said as he stepped onto the huge woven rug that covered the floor of the majestic foyer. She nodded in recognition, and without a word, took his jacket and disappeared somewhere toward the kitchen.

Arthur turned and headed down a long high-ceilinged hallway. The heels of his shoes made a light *clicking* sound on the imported ceramic tiles as he walked past tastefully framed photographs, oil paintings, and sketches. Many of the pieces boasted breathtaking landscapes as he had a penchant for nature in all of its forms.

Today, he paused for a moment to glance at one in particular. It was a mountain range, probably somewhere in Asia or the Far East, and though it was simple, the arrangement of elements was stunning. A deep, still pool of indigo water, snow-covered peaks, and an endless azure-blue sky all combined to create an artwork that induced feelings of peace in its viewers. The painter herself was generally unknown, but at the bottom right-hand corner of the canvas, the name *Lynette* was written in tiny scrawl.

Arthur stared at the painting for a moment, and then turned away and continued down the corridor.

Arriving at the hallway's final door, he reached for the bronze handle just as a lone streak of light filtered through the glass of a nearby window, briefly illuminating the gold ring he wore on the index finger of his right hand. A tiny Calvary cross superimposed over an equilateral triangle shone for just a moment, until his full body moved into the glowing beam and he stepped into his place of sanctuary.

Inside, Arthur strode by neat stacks of books, papers, and ancient artifacts, until he reached a large cedar desk. Taking a deep relaxing breath, he slid into the high-back leather chair he used routinely to prepare the many seminars and lectures he conducted.

As usual, Arthur was dressed in the best of taste. His choices were always classic and appropriate, and not necessarily dictated by current trends or the styles of the leading men in Hollywood. He did, however, have a proclivity for designer suits and his personal tailor was skilled at creating designs that fit his frame perfectly.

His most striking feature, though, was his eyes. They were light gray in color and gave the impression that they could see into the mystical heights of the misty future, or penetrate into the arcane depths of one's soul.

As he shuffled through various files in search of something specific, an ornately carved letter opener slipped from the side of the large table. With cat-like reflexes, Arthur intercepted its journey to the floor, and then he gently returned it to its place.

In silent concentration, he then reviewed the found document while scribbling notes in the margin.

Until his mind began to wander again.

For the second time that day, Arthur was unable to shake an inner feeling of discontent.

*Something is wrong.*

Searching his inner sensorium for answers, he tried to recall a dream he had the previous night. He knew it had been important, but for some reason he was unable to summon the details, which was unusual. Typically, Arthur could remember his dreams in vivid detail, and this particular mental block had him puzzled. While still lost in thought, several knocks echoed on the library door.

Not waiting for an invitation, Michael Richardson, his friend and colleague, confidently entered the room. "Screwing around as usual I see, Dr. Alexander," he offered mischievously.

Coming to full attention, Arthur rose from his seat and enthusiastically greeted the six-foot-five male with a firm handshake and a friendly hug. Michael then plopped himself down on an embroidered overstuffed chair while his host returned to his place with a smile.

"So what is it today?" Michael inquired. "The analysis of yet another deranged psychopath prepared for your eager pupils?    Or is it a mysterious alchemical formula to be delivered at one of those secret societies you frequent?"

"Nothing quite as exciting as that," Arthur retorted in good humor. "I'm just reviewing some documents I found on my latest trip."

Michael knew exactly what he meant. In his spare time, the professor was either traveling the world or rifling through libraries, bookstores, or research institutes. Arthur was known affectionately by his friends and associates as a "bibliophile" as he read dozens of books monthly. He loved books, and the more ancient and obscure, the better.

Michael could press for more details, but he knew he wasn't likely to get any straight answers. While always friendly and social, Arthur was also a very private man.

"So what do you hear from your comrades around the globe? Are there any new adventures afoot? Since our visit last month to the haunted vacation home of that eccentric couple in Ontario, my life has been rather dull and routine."

Arthur let out a low laugh as he glanced inquisitively at his clever friend. "I'm sure," he replied with the appropriate sarcasm.

Michael, an associate professor of both religion and physics at a nearby college, did not lead a routine life.  His father was a devout man of religion and his mother, a scientist by profession, believed exclusively in empirical data.  Michael had spent most of his life trying to reconcile to himself, and his students, the seeming conundrum between religion and science, a pursuit that generally filled much of his free time.

But since his breakup with his fiancée two months prior, Michael's unscheduled visits had become more frequent.  Arthur understood, and did his best to provide his colleague with both comfort and distraction.

"Actually," the older man continued as he sat up, crossed the room, and picked up a golf putter he used almost daily, "I think perhaps that once again you have managed to show up just as something intriguing is brewing on the horizon."

"Like what, watching you putt every single ball into the can without a miss?"

Arthur chuckled as he effortlessly shot the second ball toward its target. A slight telltale ping sounded within the receptacle as the little white sphere hit its mark.

As he prepared for another go, the phone in the pocket of his tan pants began to play his favorite tune. Without missing a beat, Arthur reached for it while continuing to swing at the next ball.

While he conversed with the unknown caller, Michael noted with irritation that Arthur again hit the can with amazing accuracy.

The two often played golf together, and Arthur had beaten Michael almost every time. Just once in the last few months Michael had clung to a narrow victory and he longed for the day that he could repeat the act. Reliving that glorious day with a wistful sigh, he glanced back at Arthur and tried not to be too nosy while he listened to the conversation.

"Do you need my help? Yes, I understand. I can be there in about an hour."

As Arthur prepared to hang up, he looked over at Michael.

Seeing through his friend's obvious attempt to look uninterested he added, "I have a colleague with me who has some experience in this area, would you mind if he joined us?"

With a few affirming nods, he then said goodbye and looked back at Michael who was trying hard to look innocent.

Boiling with curiosity, Michael was first to speak. "Well?" he asked simply.

"Are you free tonight, Michael? I am engaged to meet up with someone I think you might enjoy meeting."

"Kind of a coincidence, don't you think?"

"I guess so," Arthur answered with a smile, "If you believe in coincidence."

Michael quickly agreed, and Arthur shot off the last ball before heading toward the door. As he reached for the light switch, he received the internal message again.

*Something is not right.*

As they stepped from the room and shut the door, any observer, had there been one, would have seen that the final white dimpled ball lay five inches from its intended mark.

14

# Chapter 3
# The Carpathian Mountains

At first he thought he was seeing a ghost.

As Marty looked up, he saw that the form hovering over him had exceedingly pale skin and two huge, dark, sunken eyes. He also thought the man was one of the tallest, thinnest, sickest looking men he had ever seen. Speechless, the magician simply stood and stared until the monk rasped out a question, his mouth twisting beneath a hooked, at one time, broken nose.

Marty could not understand a word he said, but he thought it sounded like some form of Czech.

Many of the people he had met while traveling in these European countries spoke at least a little bit of English. Apparently this monk was not one of them. Searching his recently acquired vocabulary of the language, Marty managed to stammer out, "Do you speak English?" in a passable Czech accent.

To Marty's surprise, another voice answered in his place.

"He asked you if you plan to come in or just stand there and let the rain soak us all?"

Snapping his head to the side, he looked down and saw that another, much shorter, monk had joined them. As he looked now at the newcomer, he noticed that the top of the man's head had been shaved to form a perfect circle in the center of a thick mane of brown curly hair.

Without replying, Marty quickly stepped inside while wondering what sect of monks still wore a tonsure as a show of sacrifice.

The magician then glanced around the substantial entryway and was immediately struck by its austerity and overall lack of ornamentation. Both the walls and floors were made entirely of cut stone, and he saw no lamps, lights, or anything else powered by electricity. The room was lit only by candles and torches.

As Marty's eyes scanned beyond the threshold to search for a phone, computer, or some sign of technology he could use to get out of this place, his attention was drawn to the floor beneath him. There, a steady stream of water was trickling from his rain-soaked coat and fueling a growing puddle.

The *drip, drip* sound seemed unnaturally loud as it echoed through the room, and he became conscious of the fact that he was ignoring his hosts. Before he had the chance to apologize, the shorter man broke the uncomfortable silence.

"You must forgive Brother Grigor. He does not mean to be inhospitable. He doesn't speak much English, although he is fluent in Czech, French, Greek, and Hebrew. I think you startled him," explained the shorter man.

"Well, Father, I certainly appreciate your help."

"No, no," answered the monk. "I am not a priest, merely a humble brother," he said with a flurry of hands. "You may call me Brother Viktor. And it is we who should thank you. We have not had a visitor for a very long time."

Then he added under his breath, "although, you were, somewhat expected."

Marty responded with a confused, unsure smile.

"Come, you are shaking, we must get you some dry clothes," Viktor commanded with no further reference to the unusual comment as he beckoned Marty to follow.

Obediently, Marty trailed the monk down the passageway while various thoughts assailed his mind. Questions like "What in the hell is this place? And why isn't there anything here from the 21st century?" were foremost as his eyes roamed the unvaried stone through every corridor. Interestingly, Marty noted that the general layout and architecture of the building reminded him of sketches he had seen of the interior of the Great Giza Pyramid.

With growing curiosity, he glanced over at his two escorts and realized that they made quite a humorous pair. The tall, pale monk was so thin that his robe flapped and swayed as he walked. In contrast, Viktor's robe was stretched tightly across his ample belly. Marty also noticed that the brown garment was so short, that the monk's sturdy, tree-like legs were poking out from below the hem.

"Perhaps, when you have changed, you could join us for a late supper? It is a modest fair of onion stew and bread, with some of our wine. I think you will enjoy it. Our cellars were once famous, you know."

"No, I didn't know, does anyone?" Marty thought to himself as he wondered if anybody ever visited this peculiar and isolated place.

16

After turning the next corner and walking down another series of halls, they finally arrived at a very plain eight by ten monastic cell furnished with only a wooden cot, a small chair, and a stand with a washbasin. Again, there was no ornamentation, religious or otherwise. On the cot, neatly folded, was a dark habit, similar to the ones the monks wore.

"We will dry your clothes. Until then, if it will not offend you, you may wear one of our robes," Viktor suggested, as he gestured toward the dark folded garment at the foot of the bed.

"Please, meet us at the refectory, uh, that is the dining room, when you are ready," Viktor said as he smiled and motioned for the tall monk to light the candle on the wall.

Once Grigor's task was complete, they stepped back into the hallway and disappeared down the corridor.

Only after they left did Marty reflect on how they had not asked him a single question about who he was, or how he ended up at their doorstep in the middle of the night.

*Although you were somewhat expected.*

As Marty glanced around the room, he noticed there was a high window on the far wall. He dragged the chair close and then took a look around outside. Nothing much had changed, it was still pouring down rain. He tried to catch a glimpse of his car, but this side of the monastery faced away from the highway.

"Oh well, there won't be much traffic on a night like this one," he mumbled to himself. "My car should be safe. Only an idiot would be driving in the mountains during this storm," he admitted with a dry, self-depreciating laugh.

He looked down to the other side of the pass, and saw a few twinkling lights of what he guessed was a small village. "Surely they must have a phone," he thought to himself. He would have to ask Viktor when he saw him at dinner.

Marty then undressed and placed his wet clothes just outside the door. As he walked back across the room to retrieve the monk habit, he impulsively sat down on the small cot.

He was amazed by how comfortable the thin lumpy mattress was, and unable to resist, Marty slipped under the single woolen blanket. Feeling fatigued from the stressful drive and the long walk through the rain, Marty decided it was alright to shut his eyes for a few moments.

*Surely the monks won't miss me yet.*

But within seconds his tired body fell into a deep, silent sleep. So deep that he didn't hear the whisperings in the hall as the tall monk, Grigor, gathered his wet clothes. He also didn't see the monks who passed by his door and gestured excitedly. Or hear their hushed exclamations, "věštba, věštba!" Which in English, meant *prophecy*.

# Chapter 4
# Burbank, California

Josh Erskine stared back blankly, as the four impatient eyes bored relentlessly into his.

He couldn't believe the chain of events that had unfolded today. Being Saturday, his intention had been to sleep in, watch football for hours, and then take a long, hot sauna. Various edible delights and intoxicating spirits were, of course, part of the entire scenario. "What went wrong?" he asked himself now.

It all started well before dawn when the piercing shrill of his volume-turned-up-to-max cell phone in the adjacent room rousted him from a sound sleep. He tried to ignore the unwanted intrusion, but whoever it was, kept calling back.

When the annoying song his niece had downloaded for his ringtone played for the third time, he reluctantly resigned himself to the idea that it was time to get up. Half asleep, he then shuffled to the study to find that his associate Stan Myer was responsible for the calls.

Without taking the time to listen to the messages, Josh dialed the International Institute for the Research of Psychic Phenomena directly. Stan was the night manager there at the Institute, and he answered on the first ring.

Before Josh could say a word, his associate began reciting a long list of concerns in a hurried, virtually unintelligible manner.

*Why is simple conversation often so difficult?*

It never ceased to amaze the IIRPP chief how much trouble the average person had in getting his or her point across. In fact, given the complexity of suggestion, body language, and internal filtering systems Josh thought any successful communication between two or more humans was a miracle.

After nearly five minutes of rolling his eyes, tapping his feet, and running his hands through his hair, Josh finally pieced together the story. Apparently, several of the full-time psychics at the Institute had experienced disturbing dreams or episodes during the night, and they needed him to come in right away.

"So much for my day off," he thought wistfully as he staggered to the shower.

Just as the rising sun peeked over the nearby mountains, Josh arrived at the IIRPP's familiar six-story building. The structure itself was nestled among the many television studios that populated the neighborhood, and yet, even in that high-profile location, visitors often commented that they never realized the Institute was there. As he turned into the parking lot, he looked up at the long reflective glass panes, and mentally prepared himself for the day.

Still feeling sleepy, Josh slowly exited his car and walked through the downstairs security doors, coffee cup in hand.

Before he even made it to the elevator, the entire gang swarmed him.

Everyone was anxious to relay his or her personal story, and patiently Josh ushered everyone into the fourth-story conference room. One by one, he then listened to the events of the night.

Hours later, just as things were settling down, the CIA arrived. Not just the CIA, which would be much too simple. No, agents from the CIA and the FBI had both made an appearance in the early afternoon.

"What are *they* doing here?" an annoyed Stan muttered under his breath as they escorted their new arrivals to Josh's office.

"How should I know?" Josh returned mystified.

He *did* know from his many years in the field of parapsychology that the government had a keen interest in occult phenomena, more than most Americans were aware. Except, up until now, they had paid very little attention to the work of the Institute, and their presence today was certainly unusual.

Once seated inside his office, Josh asked his unexpected guests how he could be of assistance. Both operatives were very reserved and revealed little of why they were there. The CIA agent did, however, press Josh firmly for all the details of the night's events.

Josh had no idea how she knew about the episodes, but he was very reluctant to share what he knew.

"Where is Dr. Alexander? I need him to get me out of this mess," he thought anxiously.

Josh had risen to his current position because he was both brilliant and psychically gifted, not because he was great at negotiation.

By the age of three, Josh had known he was different. When he asked his mother, a devout African-American church-going Southern Baptist, about the *visitors* he frequently saw, she dismissed his experiences as those of an imaginative young mind. But as he grew in age and his guests grew in number, so did his mother's concern. She first took him to see her church pastor, then a private therapist, and finally to see a psychiatrist.

Fortunately for Josh, his Aunt April came to stay with his family one summer when he was seven. April worked for an international company, and she traveled extensively through countries in Asia for her job. She often sent his family exotic post cards from places like Tokyo, Shanghai, Kuala Lumpur, Mindanao, and even New Delhi, but she rarely visited in person and Josh had not seen her since he was a toddler.

April's visit changed Josh's life.

She quickly recognized his abilities and showed him how to work with them, and how to allay the fears of others. She explained to him that most people are uncomfortable with things they do not understand or experiences they themselves do not have, so it was up to Josh to put those around him at ease.

For most of his childhood and teens, Aunt April was his only confidant, until he graduated high school and found that there were others like him. Eventually, after college and nearly a decade as one of the IIRPP's subjects, Josh was promoted to Director of the Institute.

Yet, while Josh worked well with the subjects of the IIRPP's research, he was not always great at negotiation. He sometimes even had difficulty interfacing with the many private donors that kept the Institute in business. Josh was adept with things of the *inner world*, but he often felt as though he was out of his element when dealing with other members of the human race. And collaborating with the government was definitely not something he felt equipped to handle alone. For this encounter, he needed Dr. Arthur Alexander. His good friend was skilled at blending the outside material world seamlessly with the unseen one, and his calming demeanor usually put everyone at ease. Put simply, Alexander knew how to handle people, and Josh needed him, *now*.

As he looked back at the agents, Josh tried to steer the conversation toward a lighter topic until Arthur arrived.

"Did either of you happen to hear the football scores on the way here?"

No response.

"Surely you guys can get any information you want?"

They were not amused.

Just as Josh felt his temperature rise, he heard footsteps in the hall and then a knock on his office door.

"Thank God," he whispered as he bolted from his chair.

# Chapter 5
# Burbank, California

With a big smile on his face, Josh Erskine ushered in his two new arrivals and then made the appropriate introductions.

"Arthur, this is Agent Analia Arias from the CIA and Agent Bill Stone from the FBI. Agents, this is Dr. Arthur Alexander and his colleague…" Josh skipped a beat unable to remember Michael's name.

"Dr. Michael Richardson," Arthur finished with polite charm.

The four shook hands, sat down, and then wordlessly summed each other up.

Agents Arias and Stone looked like hunters sniffing out their prey while Arthur seemed unaffected and returned their looks impassively. Michael, on the other hand, was able to see the agents with a less serious eye. Allowing his gaze to roam freely, he observed that Agent Stone was wearing an immaculate dark-gray suit adorned with a sky-blue silk tie. He also noted that it was tied so tight that it appeared to be choking him. *Probably not much fun at a party.*

Conversely, Agent Arias was much more pleasurable to look at. She seemed observant and intelligent, and Michael had the distinct feeling that she was very good at her job. She also happened to be quite beautiful, in an appealing *Dirty Harriet* sort of way. Her legs were shapely, and the white silk blouse she wore beneath her tailored jacket accentuated her curves nicely. The features of her face were angular and her red-brown hair, which she had pulled back into an attractive twist, shone under the bright office light. Michael soon found himself fantasizing about what she would look like if she unhooked the clasp and let her auburn locks cascade to her shoulders.

Just as his vision started to get good, Arthur decided to break the silence.

"Josh, it's obvious that something important is going on here. For the benefit of everyone, perhaps you could start by telling us what it is you do here at the Institute.

Josh nodded and sat forward in his chair.

"Here at the International Institute for the Research of Psychic Phenomena, we believe that human beings possess an array of inner senses that function well beyond the limitations of our five outer ones. While seeing, hearing, smelling, and so forth are integral to our daily existence, and of course necessary for navigating the world we live in, we are particularly interested in other capabilities we believe all humans possess. Ones that most people discredit or ignore."

Out of the corner of his eye, Arthur could see that Agent Stone was becoming more uncomfortable with every word Josh spoke, while Agent Arias was leaning closer as though committing to memory every word.

"Here at the Institute we work with hundreds of subjects who either live here or commute in daily who are engaged in a range of on-going experiments, ones that we attempt to reproduce and measure just as any scientific researcher would."

"What kind of experiments?" Agent Arias questioned.

Taking a deep breath, Josh continued, "It's hard to explain given that abilities vary incredibly from one subject to the next, but I can say that we conduct studies in telepathy, telekinesis, astral projection, and prediction, to name a few."

Josh let that little piece of information hang in the air before he proceeded.

"I know what you're thinking. Most people consider the sending of telepathic messages or mental manipulation of objects to be the stuff of fiction. But human beings *are* capable of such things. Some people are born with these abilities. Others intentionally develop them by performing specific practices and exercises. Here, we teach people to nurture and harness these inner abilities, which come in a variety of forms."

"Like what?" Agent Arias inquired.

"Well, without going into too much detail, some of our psychics are clairvoyant, they see things that most people do not, while others here experience clairaudience or clairessence. In the latter cases, these individuals hear an inner guiding voice or simply feel or know things of particular value. In whatever form it takes, our subjects are able to tap into a huge storehouse of knowledge, one that links them to information that most of us can only dream of having access to. In other words, they are able to make day-to-day decisions based not just on what they have read, or learned or experienced in the past, but on the data they receive *internally* from a kind of universal supercomputer."

"There even are those," Josh continued after clearing his throat, "that believe these inner abilities are an important next step in the evolution of humankind and that they need to be explored and expanded. And that is our purpose here. Our donors are acutely concerned about the many challenges facing humanity. They believe that these inner abilities may play a significant role in solving the problems currently facing our world."

Agent Arias said nothing while Agent Stone looked at Josh with unmasked cynicism.

Feeling the need to move things along, Josh decided it was time to focus back on the situation at hand. "Many of our subjects reside full-time in the upper residential section of our building, and last night several of them experienced an unsettling psychic event."

"What kind of event?" Arthur asked.

"Some of them had disturbing dreams while others received messages during meditation or trance. Nothing all that unusual, except in each case the person was visited by someone they consider a "guide" who warned them that there has been a breach on the astral plane."

"Wait a minute, before you continue," Analia interjected, "Mr. Erskine, what exactly is the astral plane?"

"Many places exist that are currently beyond our detection through modern means Agent Arias, although science does postulate that our world is only one among many alternate dimensions. The astral plane is a parallel dimension that directly affects our world of matter."

"Some people believe the astral is a place where souls go when they die and that it is populated by spirits, angels, or disembodied entities. Others profess that the astral is a realm where all possibilities exist simultaneously, and that thoughts and images are the modus operandi. Still other belief systems assert that the astral plane serves as a 'matrix' for everything in our material world."

Agent Arias nodded and Josh continued.

"Since last night, we have been trying to put together the details and to make sense of the experiences. I have no idea if the events are valid or not, but I think we should take them seriously. I asked Dr. Alexander here today with the hope that he might be able to recommend a course of action, given that he has quite a bit of experience in this area," Josh explained.

"What kind of experience?" Stone asked as he looked over at Arthur with renewed interest.

"Let's just say for now that Dr. Alexander is a prominent figure in both the psychological and para-psychological worlds," Josh answered.

"Mr. Erskine," Michael spoke up. "May I ask a question? Exactly why are the CIA and FBI interested in all of this?"

Josh looked around the room, hoping that one of the agents might decide to respond.

"Maybe I can answer that question," Arthur offered in their place.

"The United States government has been conducting their own research into psychic phenomena for decades. It is my understanding that recently their investigations have turned toward something that is termed *remote viewing*. This particular psychic skill is important to them because their subjects are able to project their *consciousness* out of their body to any location around the world. Once there, they are able to observe all proceedings and interactions as though physically at the locale, completely undetected. It's sort of a low-tech way of monitoring the covert activities of those the government considers enemies of the free world. Of course, it's not something they advertise."

Neither agent confirmed or denied Arthur's explanation.

"I assume, therefore, that some of *their* in-house psychics have experienced something similar to those here at the IIRPP and they are here trying to validate the information they have received."

"Well, now that we all understand why we're here, gentlemen," Agent Arias interjected, "what I would like to know is if you have any specific information as to the possible cause of all of this?"

"No, we have no specifics," Josh answered, "but...," he looked over at Arthur for support.

Seeing Josh's reluctance, Arthur gestured encouragingly.

"Our psychics report that the disturbance appears to be brewing somewhere in Europe, most likely in the vicinity of the United Kingdom. They believe some incident there is feeding the astral breach."

Arthur shook his head slightly as though this particular piece of information made sense.

"Well, Dr. Alexander, hopefully you can use your *expertise* to guide our next steps," Stone challenged.

Arthur paused while he inwardly decided how much to say. "Ironically, while we were driving here tonight I received a phone call from one of my contacts in London. Apparently, they've had some kind of negative psychic happening there, and they have requested my immediate assistance in the matter. It seems like too much of a coincidence to be unrelated. I think it would be best if I went to the UK immediately and reported back to Mr. Erskine as soon as I am able."

Agent Arias immediately objected. "That is totally unacceptable, Dr. Alexander. My instructions are to find out exactly what is going on, and I have been assured that time is of the essence. I have no intention of sitting around and waiting for you to give us a call."

"I will take Dr. Richardson with me, and Agent Arias you may accompany us if you like."

Josh was stunned by Arthur's invitation and his easy-to-read face showed his surprise.

"I will stay in close contact with Mr. Erskine and share new information as it arrives. He can then pass on everything to you, Agent Stone."

"No matter what your credentials are Alexander, I don't believe it entitles you to decide how this situation is handled," Stone argued. "This is a matter of national security, and you are not qualified to make that kind of decision."

Arthur sensed that Agent Stone approved of the plan even though he was very vocally protesting. His response was therefore confusing and Arthur could only assume that Stone was worried about saving face in front of the CIA. Perhaps all he needed was a suitable excuse to remain at the IIRPP while still appearing to be in charge.

Arthur decided to test his theory.

"Agent Stone, any number of things could happen in the next few days. Psychic events are unpredictable and can change with no warning at all. We need someone like you working near Mr. Erskine, in case something comes up that he isn't able to handle alone," Arthur explained.

Stone looked back and forth between Josh and Arthur before replying. "I guess I can do that. But I better get some answers soon or you'll be hearing from me, Alexander."

"Agent Arias, can you leave this evening?"

"No problem. I can leave right now. My luggage is downstairs in my car."

"Then it looks like we have a plan. Josh, I will keep in touch," Arthur promised as he stood up.

Josh reluctantly agreed and Arthur, Michael, and Agent Arias exited his office. The IIRPP chief then looked over at Agent Stone and prayed silently that Arthur would make quick work of this.

As he sank back in his chair despondently, he reflected on Arthur's behavior.

*Why did Arthur agree to bring Agent Arias with him?*

In all the years that Josh had known his friend, he had never allowed any stranger to interfere with his work.

26

# Chapter 6
# The Carpathian Mountains

*The cloaked shadowy figure approached.*
*A pungent primal smell filled the air.*
*Long, spindly, icy fingers opened and closed rhythmically.*
*They grasped impatiently.*
*Closer. Closer.*
*The scent became stronger, putrid.*
*The darkness surrounded him.*
*He couldn't breathe.*
*Pain exploded through his pliant, yielding body.*

Marty's eyes flashed open and he gasped for breath. He strained to remember where he was, and a feeling of panic coursed through his body. His questing eyes searched the darkened room for answers, until he saw the simple washbasin, the plain wooden chair, and the walls made of stone.

*I'm still in the monastery.*

As he threw off the meager blanket and struggled to the side of the small cot, Marty rummaged through his short-term memory, until eventually the events of the night came rushing back. Then he wondered what woke him so suddenly.

He remembered cold, intense cold seeping through his defenseless skin and penetrating right to the marrow of his bones. And pain, so much pain.

Looking down, Marty realized that his body was virtually naked.

While shaking, he reached for the cast-off blanket and tried to pull the thin cover over his hunched shoulders. He soon realized that his frozen fingers were unequal to the task as he fumbled around unsuccessfully.

*I should have put on the robe Brother Viktor offered me.*

Marty's eyes darted to the foot of the small bed where the dark robe lay rumpled in a pile. Suddenly, the garment seemed much more appealing. As he reached greedily for it, he saw out of the corner of his eye that his newly dried clothes lay folded just inside the cell door.

*I must have been asleep for hours.*

Not waiting for further invitation, he crossed the room and willed his fingers to clothe his body, pausing periodically to cup his aching hands around his bluish lips. Long streams of heated air slowly brought his stinging digits back to life as a thousand tiny pins poked relentlessly at the warming flesh.

"I guess I missed the onion stew," he whispered while his empty stomach echoed a long angry growl in protest.

Marty pulled his cotton sweater over his out-stretched neck and jumped into his pants as fast as he could. After tying his boots, which were still a little damp, the magician quietly opened the cell door. The hall was silent, and not a single monk was in sight.

Confused, he looked back and forth down the corridor, trying to decide which way to turn. Everything looked the same in this place, and he had trouble remembering which way he had come, or which way he needed to go to find the dining hall.

He mentally tossed a coin and then turned left, hoping he was heading in the right direction. As he moved down the otherwise-empty hall, the monks began to chant. The sounds were faint, but clearly coming from somewhere behind him.

*That's why no one is here. They must all be at midnight mass or something.*

Marty continued moving forward, still determined to find something to eat, when he realized that the intonations of the monks weren't like any Gregorian chant he had ever heard. Rather than the heavenly choruses he generally associated with the church, the notes of this hymn sounded odd and flat. And the more he listened, the more discordant the off-beat syllables sounded.

*Is there anything about this place that isn't weird?*

Not only was the hymn inharmonious, but the monks were obviously not chanting in Latin, or anything that sounded like Czech.

Not like he was an expert or anything. Marty's exposure to foreign languages was primarily limited to the neighbors he knew growing up in a small cosmopolitan suburb of Toronto. Many of the people he lived near as a child were recent immigrants who mixed their native speech with English and French. Marty enjoyed picking up phrases when he could, and much of what he learned stayed with him to this day.

"Didn't Viktor say that Brother Grigor was fluent in Hebrew?" he said aloud.

*Yeah right, Marty, that's what it is, Catholic Czech monks chanting in Hebrew.*

Marty could actually speak a little Hebrew thanks to living down the hall from the Bernsteins. His best friend Arnie, the very same Arnie Bernstein who had grown up, become his agent, and ultimately got him into this mess, had taught him the basics of the ancient language years ago.

He listened closely to the chanting again and soon he was able to rule out Hebrew, or even Yiddish. The intonation was different, and he was unable to recognize a single word.

*My Hebrew can't be that bad!*

Momentarily shaking off the endless string of questions his inquiring mind continued to ask, Marty tried to relate what he heard to some memory filed away in the endless vaults of his mind. He loved puzzles, he just had to know how things worked, and he was determined to find out what these monks were up to.

The Bernsteins kept coming to mind, but he knew that the chant wasn't in Hebrew. Then finally he remembered the old man from Yemen who ran the second-hand store across the street from his apartment building. Marty used to work for him sometimes when school was out. Akmed always treated him well, usually referring to him his as his "little Canadian friend." Memories of the Arabic phrases the old man had taught him slowly came floating back.

*The monks are chanting in Arabic.*

Once he had that figured out, Marty was easily able to recognize the basic inflections and he even picked up a few words here and there.

*Now this is bizarre. Why are the monks chanting in the language of Islam? And why are the notes so discordant? Arabic doesn't generally sound so jarring.*

The Arabic inscription on the monastery door resurfaced in his mind and the magician wondered at the connection. Food now seemed less important as the wheels in his mind turned rapidly. Almost unconsciously, Marty twisted around and moved briskly down the hall in the opposite direction.

Reaching the end of the passage, he came to a set of large double doors. Hesitantly, he pushed them open, and cringed as the hinges squeaked in protest. While holding his breath, Marty stepped inside and noted with surprise that although the chanting came from this direction, the room was empty.

*Where are they? This place looks like the chapel. Why aren't they here?*

Tentatively, Marty strode down the narrow aisle toward the high altar at the other side of the room. As he drew nearer, Marty saw a comforting crucifix hanging from the wall. He gazed at the reassuring religious ornament, expecting its presence to calm his nerves, when he noticed that an unusual corpus hung from the cross. Rather than the traditional humble, suffering Christ, perpetually atoning for the sins of humanity, this hand-carved representation had a cynical smile on his face, as if he were enjoying a private joke.

Marty's mind was quick to rationalize what he saw. *Maybe whoever carved it was just a really bad artist?*

But he was no stranger to the church, and this *thing* in front of him was no careless mistake.

His father, who had served as a deacon in a local parish before Marty was born, walked him through every step of the Sunday service when he was a child. He insisted that Marty commit to memory all of the symbolism of the ritual from the meaning of the words the priest uttered, to the significance of each church-adorning artifact.

As he stared at the disturbing corpus, Marty's mind wandered back to the sounds of his father's beautiful tenor voice resonating through the little church that he and his family had frequented on Sundays and holidays. He remembered feeling so proud of his father and those songs would follow him throughout the day and night.

His father's favorite hymn, "He Will Lift You Up on Eagles' Wings," resonated through his head.

He had once said to Marty, "How that song lifts my soul. If you ever feel the need for God's protection just remember the words. They have always been there for me and they will be there for you, too, son. I guarantee it."

Marty wondered why that particular song was coming to mind. For some reason, it seemed important. And then the thought drifted away as smoothly as it had entered.

While he considered his next move, the chanting stopped and the recognizably high voice of Brother Viktor took its place. The monk's words were unintelligible, but it seemed logical to assume that he was reciting some kind of prayer. As the sonorous Arabic syllables rolled from Viktor's tongue, Marty realized that his voice was coming from somewhere behind the high altar.

The magician moved closer and noticed that on the far wall, a large hanging tapestry rippled rhythmically. There were no windows in the room, and the chapel was unlikely to have central air or heating, so Marty was at a loss to explain the movement.

"They don't even have electricity for Chrissake," he muttered aloud as he tried to remain calm.

*What do I have to be afraid of?  After all, these monks have only been hospitable.*

Determinedly, Marty walked behind the altar and slowly lifted the aging sour-smelling drapery.

# Chapter 7
# The Hills of Hollywood

In the tangled streets of the Mt. Olympus district, just above the Magic Castle in Hollywood, stands the Mount Abiegnus Foundation.

The Tudor-style mansion, erected in 1923, houses a variety of rare and ancient artifacts, most of which have been collected and protected through untold millennia by a dedicated group of select individuals.

The Foundation itself exists as a modern-day repository for countless, priceless pieces of work, and also as a living monument built to honor the enlightened masters of humanity.

Alongside its one-of-a-kind relics, the Foundation's numerous libraries are also home to a host of unknown writings from a diverse array of spiritual, mystical, philosophical, and scientific teachers including Socrates, Newton, Descartes, Bacon, Einstein, and even Abraham Lincoln.

While the Foundation's primary purpose is to preserve a somewhat secret and guarded record of the past, its grounds, buildings and furnishings are all designed and arranged to stir the emotions, and fire of the imagination of its numerous and assorted guests.

In particular, a sharp-eyed eagle and a graceful swan stand guard over the gated entrance of the protective nine-foot iron fence, which runs the perimeter of the Foundation.

———

As Arthur pulled the black hybrid SUV up to the familiar gates, he made a silent salutation to the pair of creatures before heading purposefully up the long cobblestone drive.

Simultaneously, from the back seat, the very attentive Agent Arias perceived Arthur's ever-so-slight nod toward the striking beasts and with curiosity, wondered what he was doing. "He's certainly an interesting man," she commented quietly as she shook her head and reflected on the events of the day.

She had no idea why her new boss, Assistant Director Banes, had given her this as her first assignment. She had zero experience in this kind of phenomena and she didn't really want any. She spent her first two years with the Agency working in Information Management, and then the last three in a covert division that monitored the movement of arms and weapons across international borders. Both had been desk jobs and she had never been out in the field.

All that changed last week when Banes requested that she transfer to his office. After only the briefest of introductions, he informed Analia that she would be his personal assistant, and would be working on any project he assigned her. He never explained why he recruited her, and Analia chose not to ask. Director Banes was a high-profile member of the Agency and this job could open many future career doors. She was excited about the position and looking forward to life in a new city.

That was until Banes described this case to her.

There she had sat, in quiet astonishment, as he explained psychic visions and telepathic messages. She had no idea that the CIA seriously investigated such matters, and she was stunned that she was going to be a part of it.

In truth, Agent Arias did not believe a word she heard this afternoon. She had little doubt that this case was some kind of elaborate hoax or scheme designed to make somebody either more rich, more powerful, or both. Long ago she reasoned that just about everything evil in the world had to do with one or the other, and at a young age she had decided to spend her life personally combating greed and oppression.

Nevertheless, Agent Arias was no saint. She had always been, and still was, full of ambition. She constantly felt the need to move forward, to seek, to gain, to search for more. *Content*, was not a word in her vocabulary and this assignment, however weird, was going to take her career to the next level.

Analia also trusted her instincts, which told her emphatically that Dr. Alexander was the man to follow in this case. Whatever the outcome, she felt certain that Arthur was going to lead her right to the action.

Reaching their destination, Arthur stopped the vehicle in front of the impressive edifice, and the newly formed trio exited the car.

Analia's trained eyes immediately searched the area, critically taking inventory of everything she saw. The landscaped grounds were extensive, a fact she considered unusual given the overall premium on land in the area. They were also immaculately groomed, and Analia found herself appreciating how much work it must take to keep the dozens of flower beds and hundreds of plants, shrubs, and hedges neatly trimmed and healthy.

When they reached the majestic portico, Arthur sounded a special series of knocks on the front door and then waited patiently. As someone approached from within, Arthur looked up and smiled at the scanning security camera while Michael raised his right hand and gestured with a friendly little wave.

Within moments, a middle-aged man in a formal butler's uniform opened the door. Arthur gazed directly into the man's eyes and without the exchange of a single word, the uniformed man politely ushered the visitors inside.

As they stepped across the threshold, Analia's probing gaze settled on a three-foot ivory statue. The figure rested gracefully on a green marble table and featured the face of an androgynous youth. Its left index finger was placed elegantly on its lips, and as the door closed, Arthur turned and bowed his head toward the unconventional piece of art. After briefly hesitating, Michael followed Arthur's example and made a similar gesture.

Unable to resist her growing sense of curiosity, Analia decided to ask Arthur why, for the second time since their arrival, he had made some kind of greeting to a piece of statuary.

"I'm sure this must seem strange to you, Agent Arias, but I assure you this is not an exhibition of idolatry. It's actually a reverential acknowledgement to the meaning ascribed to the figures both in and out of this establishment," Arthur explained while he reflected on the fact that Agent Arias had noticed his earlier salutation.

"And what meaning is that?"

He paused as though trying to decide what to say, while exchanging an amused grin with Michael.

"Here it comes," Michael thought to himself. "We've only known this woman for a few hours and already Arthur's going to lay it on her."

"The statue represents a disciplined and dedicated personal pledge to unselfishly serve humankind, both silently and anonymously. It also represents an inner promise to safeguard a variety of ancient secrets."

"Ancient secrets?" Analia repeated before nodding.

Agent Arias was anxious to hear all about Dr. Alexander's *ancient secrets,* but for now there was no time to pursue the subject. They were due at the airport in less than two hours and finishing their task here was her top priority. She would have plenty of time on the airplane to grill Dr. Alexander while they flew over the Atlantic.

Arthur then turned back to the man who had opened the door and asked, "Is Frater Jacob here yet?"

"Yes, he just arrived and is waiting for you in the main library."

The butler then motioned for Arthur and his guests to follow, and they all crossed a large inviting reading room, replete with Italian recliners and a huge brick fireplace. As they passed, Analia looked at the carved mantelpiece and wondered if ever got cold enough in Los Angeles to light a fire. While they walked down a wide hallway filled with paintings and more statuary, Analia's eyes roamed appraisingly over busts of Pythagoras, Akhenaton, and Thales, as well as paintings honoring Pope John XXIII, Cardinal Richelieu, Leonardo da Vinci, Sir Isaac Newton, Cagliostro, The Count de St. Germain, and even Victor Hugo.

Halfway down the hall they turned and walked through an open set of doors and entered an expansive two-story library. In the center was a long, walnut table, surrounded by another cheerful fireplace and comfortable-looking furniture.

To their right was a set of dual-paned French windows, designed to shed ample light on the well-positioned personal writing desk of Frater Jacob. Recently oiled, built-in bookcases, carved from a dark cherry wood, lined the other three walls. On these, thousands of expensively bound books were interspersed among beautiful objects.

Peering closely, Agent Arias recognized dozens of golden figurines shaped to look like Buddha, Jesus, Moses, Mohammed, Krishna, Hermes, Lao Tzu, and others.

"I wouldn't want to know the price tag of this place," Michael remarked with awe while Agent Arias continued her inspection with growing incredulity.

Arthur meanwhile crossed to the desk near the windows and shook hands warmly with a knowledgeable-looking man.

"I retrieved it from the vault right after you called. It's right over here."

Jacob motioned to the end of the long table, and everyone quickly made the journey to the other side of the room. There, lay an old black leather case that looked like it had seen a lot of action. A golden cross was embossed on the lid and in the center was a five-petal red Tudor Rose.

Very gently, as though it might break, Arthur opened the case, removed a red silk scarf, and exposed the inner contents. Inside was a slender rod that appeared to be just over a foot long and about two centimeters in diameter. It was made of a honey-colored wood and wrapped from end to end with three equal-length pieces of fine silk cord, one colored white, one red, and the other black.

Intrigued, Agent Arias bent over the case to take a better look.

On closer inspection she noted that a clear, flawless quartz crystal, shaped into a perfect tetrahedron, was affixed to the tip of the rod. At the other end was a similarly shaped piece of volcanic obsidian. Two brass rings separated the three segments of the rod, and carved on each were letters of an alphabet unfamiliar to Analia.

The object was impressive looking and almost without thinking, she reached out to touch it.

Arthur's fingers nimbly intercepted hers.

"I don't think you want to touch that. The rod is much more dangerous than it looks. A copper wire is coiled underneath that delicate silk cord and a needle made of magnetized iron runs under the wood and connects with the crystals at each end. When exposed to certain types of energy, all the pieces work together like a superconductor and the rod often carries a residual charge."

"Jacob, maybe you could share its colorful history with my friends? They seem rather interested in it," Arthur suggested with a gleam in his eyes.

Jacob lighted with enthusiasm. He always enjoyed telling a story, especially to someone new.

# Chapter 8
# The Hills of Hollywood

"No one knows for sure who made this extraordinary piece of occult craftsmanship or for what purpose it was originally constructed. The information we have regarding its history comes mostly from legends. Our oral tradition attributes the rod's existence to a person known as Narada, who is believed to have constructed it over 12,000 years ago in a temple on the mythical island of Atlantis."

Confused, Analia looked back toward the case. "How can that be thousands of years old? That silk cord looks brand new."

Arthur and Jacob again exchanged amused grins. "Yes, Agent Arias, the silk is new, as is the copper directly beneath the cord. Over the centuries, its various caretakers have replaced some parts as needed, but the crystals and staff, are original and perfectly preserved."

"It is believed by some," Jacob continued, "that Narada assembled the rod in order to guard the Elemental Gates of the Universe. Unfortunately, a group of dark adepts got a hold of it instead, and tried to use it to open the Gates of Chaos. The same account alleges that the resulting dispute had something to do with the cataclysm that drowned the island."

Michael and Analia looked at each other quizzically.

Oblivious to their reaction, Jacob continued.

"After the sinking of Atlantis, the same source explains that Narada entrusted the rod to a young priest, a man by the name of Helios. Narada instructed Helios to take the rod and journey with the Seed Bearers to a large continent far to the East. When he arrived, he was to present it to Narada's handpicked successor, Melchizedek, who is more popularly known in scholarly circles as Thoth Hermes. Presumably Narada must have given Helios instructions on the use of the rod to pass onto Melchizedek, or at least have explained how important it was to keep it out of the wrong hands. Any other reason for not destroying the rod would have been unconscionable, given what had happened in Atlantis.

There is however no record of that part of the transaction, if indeed it ever even existed, so we will never know for sure."

"Once Helios delivered the blasting rod, Melchizedek continued to travel with the Seed Bearers until they reached a region of the Giza plateau, where he lived out the rest of his life. Many years later, after his death, his family and followers placed the rod into his tomb somewhere deep in the deserts of Khem."

"Why would they do that?" Michael questioned. "I mean, I'm surprised none of his students wanted to use the rod themselves. Why would they bury it forever?"

"I suspect that Melchizedek put the fear of God in his followers. He probably knew just how dangerous the rod was and emphasized the point to the few people in his confidence. They were probably too afraid to keep it."

"Excuse me, Jacob, may I ask what a Seed Bearer is?" Analia asked enthusiastically, hoping that some part of this story might make sense.

"Yes, Agent Arias, the seed bearers were a select group of individuals who were chosen by the priests of Atlantis to take secrets and technology to safe places across the Earth. Some of them travelled west into North and South America while others ventured east toward the United Kingdom and even beyond into areas of the Middle East and Asia."

Analia nodded, carefully masking her thoughts, while Jacob continued.

"Anyway, the rod is said to have been buried for thousands of years in Melchizedek's tomb until Alexander the Great successfully located the burial site in the fourth century BC."

"Again, according to oral tradition, when the conqueror broke the seal to Melchizedek's antechamber, he was so shocked by what he saw, that he almost fainted."

"The small chamber was lit by mysterious glowing lamps, ones that must have been burning since the tomb was erected. On either side of the crypt, two laser-like beams of light shone from the eyes of two full-sized statues of Anubis. The beams converged in the middle of the room, and where they intersected, the blasting rod floated in mid-air."

"As Alexander inched forward, he inadvertently moved in front of one of the statues and his body broke the connection. The rod immediately fell to the sandy floor and all of the lamps went out. Alexander was left standing in the middle of a dark chamber, lit only by the small flame that still burned at the tip of the torch he held in his hand."

"Cautiously, he bent down and picked up the rod. As his hand clasped the slender shaft, a glowing figure materialized three feet in front of him. The ghostly vision was dressed in the shadowy robes of a High Priest of Thoth, but Alexander could clearly see through the man's form. He thought about running for the exit, and then instead summoned his legendary courage and saluted the apparition with a sign Aristotle had taught him years before. Aristotle had also taught him to use the gesture whenever confronted by something, 'supernatural.' Alexander decided that moment qualified."

"The transparent form smiled at Alexander and handed him something that would later be known as the Emerald Tablet. Soon after, it vanished and left Alexander standing in the dark."

"After the young Macedonian's death several years later, both the rod and the tablet were carried to Alexandria and were buried with the conqueror for centuries. It is rumored that the rod then surfaced briefly during the late-15th century in Toledo, Spain, only to again disappear during the expulsion of the Jews in 1492. Next, it is reported to have arrived in Florence with the Diaspora where it was later one of the many artifacts brought back to Paris during the sack of the city by the Grand Army of Napoleon."

"It remained there until the mid-1800s, when it somehow came into the possession of Eliphas Levi, a famous 19th-century occultist. Levi then passed it to his fellow Rosicrucian chief, P.B. Randolph. *And* by a series of circumstances, the custodianship of the rod passed to our organization last year."

Agent Arias looked back and forth between Arthur and Jacob to make sure his narrative was complete before she responded. Once she was satisfied, she decided it was time to let her sentiments be known.

"Dr. Alexander, Jacob, forgive my skepticism, but Atlantean priests, apparitions, and occultists? Do you really believe all of this?"

Jacob, Arthur, and Michael all nodded affirmatively.

"It's alright, Agent Arias. It doesn't matter if you believe the stories or not. All you need to understand at this point is that we need this device in order to solve our little problem in the UK."

"Wait a minute. No matter what I believe, Jacob here has implied that this blasting rod thing was used to sink an island. Why then do you need it for our trip?"

"Because, Agent Arias, the rod is a very powerful psychic tool and it can perform a variety of occult techniques. Ones that we will most likely need to rectify the problem there."

Without further comment, Arthur reached down, snapped the case shut, and grasped the leather handle. "Oh, and I guess you should also know," he continued, "there are many beings, human or possibly otherwise, that would love to get a hold of this, so we'll have to do our best to protect it. That and given how old it is, it's priceless," Arthur finished with a wink in Analia's direction.

Arthur then thanked Jacob warmly and quickly headed back down the hall before Analia had the chance to decide if he was kidding or not.

As she and Michael fled back down the corridor to try to catch up with Arthur, who Analia thought moved incredibly fast for a man of his age, the phone in her pocket vibrated for the third time that hour. No doubt it was Banes again, who was still waiting for an update on her activities.

As she followed Arthur back through the foyer and outside, she resigned herself to the idea that she would have to text Banes on the way to the airport.

The problem was, she had no idea what she was going to say.

# Chapter 9

The recently manicured, masculine fingers tapped at regular intervals on the etched-glass desk, emitting an eerie clicking sound with each successive pass.

A tanned pinky finger was first to fall, followed rapidly, by fluttering middle digits, and culminating with the light drum of a jeweled index finger. The monotonous pattern then repeated after a slight, deliberate pause.

A sultry, female voice broke the concentrated silence via the intercom connected to the next room.

"I have him on the phone, sir. I'll connect you right now."

The long, well-formed fingers temporarily ceased their activity to switch on the silver gadget attached to the right ear of their master.

"Do we have it?"

"Yes, I received confirmation a few minutes ago. It's on its way."

"Are you sure it's the one I require? The *exact* one I specified."

"Yes, it will arrive in approximately 10 hours."

"How did you get it so quickly?

"You know me, I don't believe in wasting time."

# Chapter 10
# The Carpathian Mountains

Hesitantly, Marty lifted the molding tapestry.

Underneath he found a half-open doorway and another empty passageway. *Obviously this chapel is used for something other than prayer and benediction.*

"These monks should be a little more careful or someone like me might discover their secrets," he whispered as he stepped across the threshold. The corridor was dark and lit only by the occasional candelabra.

As Marty quietly made his way toward the chanting he noticed that the candles in this hall gave off a terrible smell. He first detected the strange odor when Grigor lit the small candle back in his room, but then he had fallen asleep before giving it much thought.

Now the pungent scent assaulted his nostrils, and Marty realized that these candles smelled much worse than the one in his room. He knew that during the middle-ages, candle wax had been made of tallow or animal fat, which gave off a very unpleasant odor when burned. *Are these monks still using candles made of tallow?*

While various ideas ran around his monkey mind, a term he fondly used to describe his overactive imagination, Marty looked up at the ceiling and noted a generous display of cobwebs. "I guess they don't come here much," he joked to himself, trying to stave off the increasing uneasiness he felt in his bowels.

He then navigated a series of snaking turns, each he assumed, bringing him closer to the chanting monks as he heard Brother Viktor's words grow steadily in volume.

The last narrow hall opened into a large gallery that overlooked a circular arena where Viktor and a group of monks were performing some kind of ceremony.

Marty looked down at the spectacle while carefully placing himself so that he could not be seen from below. From his new position, he was unable to make out all of the details of the proceedings, but he could see that the faces of the brothers looked distant and trancelike.

All, except the face of Viktor.

He looked very much awake and his eyes were shining the way one might picture those of a suicide bomber just before cashing in his ticket to paradise. It even seemed to Marty that Viktor was grinning maliciously while he hovered over a stone table.

As the monk continued to recite words in Arabic, the circle of brothers drew closer to him, clearly interested in something Viktor was displaying there. As the zombie monks circled the altar, they blocked Marty's view and he couldn't quite see what it was.

After craning his neck and almost falling over the gallery guardrail, Marty was finally able to see what he assumed to be a large book. Next to it was something that appeared to have hair.

Brother Viktor then drew a huge ancient-looking broad sword from the thick belt he wore around his waist. He raised the weapon high above his head and abruptly ceased speaking. The other monks stared expectantly at Viktor as he reached down, retrieved the hairy item from the altar, and lifted it up for the viewing pleasure of his idolizing minions.

And then Marty saw it.

With jubilance Viktor held the prize for all to see.

*This can't be real!*

Slowly a glowing green light enveloped Victor's body. His corpulent form rose from the floor and hovered just above the heads of his fellow clerics. As he floated in mid-air, blood streamed from what Marty could now clearly see was a severed human head, while Viktor's eager disciples rushed forward, anxious to be baptized by the macabre crimson lustration.

Viktor lowered his sword, bringing it parallel to the floor, and then resumed his repetitive incantation. Rapidly, something began to materialize in the air just in front of him as a circle of flame erupted around the altar, forcing the monks to push back.

Marty stared down, eyes wide open, as some kind of *thing* appeared out of nowhere. It had finger-like protrusions jutting out from a spherical ghostly body and he had no idea what to make of it.

As the outline of the ghoul came into full focus, Marty's eyes glazed over, his knees buckled, and his body crumpled to the gallery floor.

From somewhere deep within, he fought for control of his useless limbs, but his head swam and he began to lose consciousness. Just before Marty slipped into darkness, a large clammy hand clutched his shivering arm and pulled him back down the hallway.

43

# Chapter 11
# The Carpathian Mountains

"What kind of fool are you?" hissed a familiar voice in his ear.

Marty opened his eyes to find Brother Grigor, the tall lanky monk, looming above him. "I thought you didn't speak English," the magician whispered as he slowly dragged his body to an upright position.

"It's lucky for you that I do," answered a very angry Grigor. "You were about to be ensorcelled, my American friend. Put under a fatal spell. The quicksand was pulling at your feet, and you were willingly walking into its depths!"

"Actually, I'm *Canadian,*" Marty corrected before he responded to Grigor's warning. "And what do you mean? What were they doing in there? How could Viktor rise off the floor like that? Man, I've seen all kinds of tricks, but that show was unbelievable."

Grigor clamped his hand roughly across Marty's mouth, and pulled him further down the passageway. "Quiet. Do you have any idea what would happen if Viktor knew you were up here? At the very least, your head would serve as his next altarpiece. Or worse yet, he would send out his creature of darkness to feed upon your soul!"

"What are you talking about," Marty responded while he pressed his lips tightly together to control his rising anger.

"What you saw was not the illusion you think it to be," Grigor warned as he pulled Marty closer, his eyes boring deep into the magician's.

"That's impossible."

"Not when the book of Azarelis is atop the altar."

Marty flashed on a mental picture of the large leather- bound book he had seen in the arena.

"Whoever possesses the Grimoire commands the Forces of the Shadow, but unfortunately it comes with a terrible price."

Grigor turned back toward the gallery and loosed his grip on Marty's shoulder. With despair in his eyes, he took a deep breath and then looked directly at Marty. "Viktor wants to possess both your body and soul and then give your life to that creature."

As Marty reached to wipe the dust from his pants, he wondered if the pale monk might be mentally unbalanced.

Grigor responded to Marty's thoughts as though he had spoken aloud. "You think me mad after seeing what was on that table? No, my naïve friend, it is not I who is crazy!" He then looked back and forth down the hall.

"You cannot return to your room. They already know you are not there and have two brothers stationed to apprehend you when you return."

"Here," Grigor gestured as he moved down the corridor and pointed toward the wall. "Push that stone, the one with a smooth finish."

Not quite sure why he was taking directions from an obviously disturbed monk, Marty did as instructed. As he pushed the indicated stone, he heard a snapping sound as a section of the wall moved back about a foot to reveal a small opening.

"It's an assassin's hole," Grigor explained in response to Marty's inquisitive glance, "the perfect place to slip out and stab an unwanted guest in the back. I don't think any of our current brothers are aware of its existence. Long ago, a trusted friend showed it to me. See if you can squeeze in."

"You've got to be kidding me! Why should I trust you? How do I know you won't trap me in there and turn me over to Viktor?"

"You don't," replied the confident monk in his thick Czech accent, while a teasing smile played at the corner of his lips. "But if I wanted to expose you, why didn't I just call out for Victor when I found you in the Chamber of Conjurations, spying on the ceremony of summoning?"

To emphasize his point, Grigor pushed his face to within inches of Marty's while he reached for something at his side.

Marty tensed and prepared to defend himself as Grigor grabbed the magician's right hand and slid a silver stiletto dagger into his now sweating palm.

"I could have buried *this* in your back at any time."

Marty grabbed the sharp knife and looked murderously into the tall man's eyes.

After a stare down that lasted nearly a minute, Marty finally nodded and then moved toward the hole.

"There is a small opening on the back wall, close to the ground," Grigor explained. "If you crawl through it you will find a narrow tunnel that leads to a place concealed by bushes just across from the main

45

entrance to the monastery. Once outside, run to your car and never look back. Do you understand?" he said coldly.

Marty nodded.

"Good. Make haste now, my friend, and remember me in your prayers." With a strange look on his face, Grigor then withdrew his pale head from the opening and the wall slid back into place with a low, grinding thud.

# Chapter 12
# Ostrava
# The Czech Republic

"Where the hell is Marty?"

"We've been through this, Arnie. He hasn't contacted me or anyone else since he left yesterday," Jackie answered, her voice a mixture of apprehension and irritation.

"If he doesn't get here soon, the manager has promised to cancel today's matinee and also the next two shows."

"What do want me to say, Arnie? I can't just make him appear at will. He certainly wasn't himself when he left but I can't believe that he would do this on purpose. It's just not like him. You know Marty, he's *always* on time."

"Then why hasn't he at least called us? He had his phone with him when he left."

"I don't know. It must have been the storm. Something must have happened to him. I hope he's alright."

Arnie let out a long, frustrated sigh. "I guess I can try to negotiate with the guy."

While Arnie tried to think of a convincing argument, he thought about the manager's mouth, the one that looked like it hadn't smiled in decades, and realized that any attempt at an explanation would be pointless. "I knew it was a mistake for Marty to try to make it over those mountains by himself."

Arnie stopped when he saw the look on Jackie's face. She was genuinely worried about Marty, and Arnie's interrogation was obviously making her feel worse. Feeling guilty, Arnie lapsed into an uneasy silence while Jackie's mind creatively conjured up various disaster scenarios. And her imagination was easily stirred into action. Marty had not been *right* for a long time.

When Jackie first met Marty, he knew what he liked and he knew what he wanted. He had a passion for life, for fun, and for illusion and he planned to rock the world of magic just as Harry Houdini had over a hundred years ago. Back then, Marty had been confident, arrogant, and self-assured. He had even been Jackie's savior.

Growing up in the city of Toronto as a petite, pretty, and popular teen had been both a blessing, and a curse to Jackie. She was admired by many and had difficulty dealing with all of the attention she received. She never quite knew how to handle it, and sometimes she got into trouble.

One night at a party hosted by one of her distant cousins, an older man approached her. They talked for a while and she soon found that he was polite, funny, and apparently quite rich. Still though, she felt that something about him wasn't quite right. She started to get up and walk away a couple of times, but the cloud of smoke filling the room relaxed her and she never quite got around to it.

Much later, when she went to the bathroom, Jackie innocently left her drink behind. Ten minutes after her return, the room started to sway.

The next thing she knew, she was in the back seat of a car parked in the underground lot of the apartment building, and her tight black skirt was pushed up to her waist.

And *he* was on top of her.

Jackie tried to push him off, but her arms and legs felt paralyzed. She tried to scream, but her vocal cords resisted her commands. Feeling panicked, she squeezed her eyes shut and tried to clear her head.

It was no use. All Jackie could feel was his heavy, sweaty body pressing hard against her. All she could smell was the strong odor pouring from his unclad chest.

His rough hands roamed her body, as he pushed his tongue deep into her mouth. The taste of smoke and alcohol overwhelmed her and Jackie felt her stomach lurch. She fought back the vomit, but the bile slipped through her defenses and into his mouth.

Jackie thought he might actually stop then.

When his fist hit her face, she knew she had underestimated him.

What happened next was like a scene from a movie.

The rear driver's side door jerked open and there stood Marty and Arnie. Marty yelled something Jackie was unable to hear while they both grabbed an ankle of her attacker and yanked him out of the car.

He never saw it coming.

Powerless to grab hold of anything in time to break his fall, her assailant's face smacked down on the cement floor, instantly breaking his nose. Outraged, he got up and tried to fight. Marty grabbed the creep by the collar and struck him hard across the face. The older man reeled back and almost fell to the ground again.

Marty's face was full of rage as adrenaline pumped through his veins. Jackie was now able to sit up slightly and as she stared out the window, she saw murder in his eyes. Marty grabbed the man's shirt collar and drew back his now- throbbing fist, ready to take him out with a second blow.   Then, just as suddenly, Marty pulled back, and told Arnie to call the police.

Jackie never really knew what Marty thought of that night to make him stop, and he would never talk about it whenever she brought it up. She had always just supposed that he had mercy on the guy.

Whatever the reason, Jackie was just thankful that Marty and Arnie lived in the same building as her cousin.

After that night, the three of them had been inseparable.  Four years later, a very happy Jackie and Marty married and then the trio set off to pursue Marty's dream.

Unfortunately, nothing went as planned.

Marty would have one successful show, and then receive a bad review the next night. Maintaining equilibrium was difficult for the magician, and he had trouble finding his comfort zone.

And then the accident happened.  Several years into their marriage, Marty and his father were coming back from their annual father-son hiking trip. Marty was full of energy and insisted on driving.  On one of the twisting turns of the Angeles Crest Highway, a motor-cross racer leaned a little too far around a tight curve. The peg of his bike caught the pavement, and both rider and motorcycle flew end over end into the windshield of the truck. Marty jerked the wheel and inadvertently plunged the vehicle down an embankment.   The truck rolled several times before it crashed headfirst into a tree.

The accident killed his father instantly.

Marty never forgave himself.

He took some time off after that, but when he returned, his earlier fire was gone. His tricks were good, as good as they had always been, but something was missing and the audience felt it.  He started to isolate himself and pull back emotionally. His confidence faded and he stopped sharing himself with Jackie as he always had.

Jackie in turn had been reaching out more frequently to Arnie. They spent more time together, and Marty seemed oblivious. A few months ago, Arnie decided that they needed a change and he convinced Marty to launch the Eastern European Tour.

Now, forcing back a tear, Jackie turned toward Arnie. Her face was strained and the tiny, almost invisible, lines around her eyes were creased with worry.

Arnie tried to assure her that Marty would be fine.

Jackie was unconvinced as she walked back toward her dressing room and whispered to the walls, "Marty, where are you?"

# Chapter 13
# The Carpathian Mountains

The cold woke him, *again.* "Damn, is any part of this monastery warm?" Marty questioned aloud as he rubbed his arms vigorously.

He had sat in the hole for a while after Grigor left, trying to decide his next move while he recited the pros and cons in his head. Marty had first played the game he called, *devil's advocate,* when he started performing simple magic tricks as a child. Arguing the merits of a trick in his mind was his way of imagining what the audience would think.

Later in life, he found himself using the same technique to solve routine daily problems. Sometimes he had full-blown conversations with himself. At times, he even voiced them aloud.

His indecisiveness had lasted for a while before he finally made up his mind. And then he had fallen asleep while he waited.

Marty stood up and peeped out of the spy hole. The hall was empty and the chanting had stopped. As he stepped into the corridor, he paused.

*Maybe I should trust Brother Grigor.*

Marty had thought hard on the brother's words before he fell asleep. Eventually, he decided that Grigor was sincere, but probably deluded. Either he had spent too many years secluded in the monastery or his religious fervor had clouded his objectivity.

Marty believed nothing he had seen tonight was real. He had spent his whole life deceiving people, and he was sure that Viktor was doing the same. No doubt he wanted to control the other monks. And what better way to do so then to allegedly possess supernatural powers?

What he couldn't understand was how Viktor had risen so high off the floor. As far as Marty could tell from the gallery above, Viktor had used no traditional devices to accomplish the feat. No mirrors, no wires, no electronics.

As an image of the monk flitted through his memory, Marty lapsed into a heady vision of himself floating above a large cheering audience. The fantasy was so seductive that Marty knew that his choice to stay had been right. He *had* to find out how Viktor was doing what he was doing.

So rather than making his way down the tunnel as Grigor instructed, Marty left the assassin's hole and crept back to the Chamber of Conjuration, reciting rationalizations the whole way.

*After all, I can hold my own against any monk, even one with a sword. And I still have the dagger that Grigor gave me. I can just slip in and slip out and I probably won't even need to use it.*

Arriving at the gallery, Marty looked down at the deserted arena below. Thankfully, the head was gone, but the book was still on the altar.

*What had Grigor called it, a Grimoire? That has to be it. That book must contain Viktor's secrets. What other explanation is there?*

Marty crept down the staircase and made his way across the stage and through the dying flames of the burning circle. Up close, he could see what he hadn't been able to from the gallery above. A complicated series of words and designs were painted on the floor and as he neared the altar, he saw that the same patterns were drawn on its sides. The book itself was larger than it had appeared from above, and it was resting on a carved disc made of hardened wax.

Marty looked down at the large volume and squinted curiously at the strange diagram painted on the cover. Fascinated, he reached down and moved his fingers across the unusual design. As he did, he experienced a feeling of inexplicable revulsion. He quickly lifted his hand, and the feeling faded away. Undeterred, Marty slid his hand down the right side of the book and palmed the edges of its pages, enjoying the feeling of the aged parchment paper. He then ran his fingers over the brass guards that protected each corner of the book before he returned to the cover. This time he just *looked* at the golden inverted pentagram and single black rose.

Feeling a little nervous, Marty slowly opened the cover. Inside, on the first page, was another diagram. This one was circular and labeled with Arabic letters. As he looked down at the intricate pattern, he noted that it seemed almost three- dimensional. Marty blinked his eyes a few times to clear his vision and then reached down to touch the page.

"Don't touch that seal!"

Marty whirled around to see brother Viktor emerge from the darkness on the other side of the altar. He was holding his sword again, and he looked ready to use it.

"You have no idea of the forces you would have released if you had touched it," he hissed.

Marty's stomach dropped as his eyes roamed the very sharp-looking tip of the sword.

Viktor laughed.

*How dare you laugh at me you!* Outraged, Marty snatched the book from the altar and smashed it into Brother Viktor's face.

The round monk howled in pain and grabbed his nose protectively. The broadsword dropped to the floor with a *crash*.

Marty stared for a moment, unsure what to do, and then reached down, grabbed the heavy book, tucked it under his arm, and ran like a fullback up the gallery stairs. Without looking back, he pounded through the dark twisting hallways until he reached the assassin's hole. As he pushed the smooth stone, he saw Viktor rounding the corner, sword in hand.

As the wall rolled back, Marty ducked into the opening and then bent down to find the secret hole at the back. As his hands roamed searchingly across the solid walls he felt a moment of panic. *Did Grigor lie to me?*

Viktor cursed as he squeezed his body through the entrance, just as Marty finally found the small opening. He crawled through and scooted on his knees until it opened out into a very narrow low-ceilinged tunnel. Anxious, Marty stood up so quickly that he almost tripped over himself. As he fled down the passageway several thoughts assailed his mind. *What if this tunnel leads to a dead end? What if Grigor has given me up and 30 deranged blood-thirsty monks are waiting for me on the other side? What if Viktor cuts me to shreds with that sword of his?*

*He won't. After all, you still have Grigor's dagger and Brother Viktor doesn't seem like he's in very good shape. What if you outsmart them all and the book guides you to years of international success?*

The last thought renewed Marty's determination and he plunged down the corridor as though death himself was chasing him. After a few hundred yards, the tunnel opened into a group of overgrown bushes, just as Grigor had promised.

It was still raining outside, but fortunately not as heavy as it had been before. Without stopping, Marty sprinted toward the highway. When he reached his abandoned car he realized with dread that he had forgotten the key was locked inside. As expletives poured from his mouth he looked back down the path and saw Brother Viktor making his way through the mud.

Frantically, he searched the ground nearby for something to break the car window. Not immediately seeing anything, Marty absently reached into his coat pocket and couldn't believe it when his wet hand curled around what felt like a key. He pulled it out and looked down unbelievingly.

*How did this get here? I know I left the key on the seat.*

With Viktor closing fast he decided not to question his good fortune and quickly unlocked the car and jumped in. Much to his surprise, the small sedan started on the first try. While thanking God profusely, Marty backed it out onto the rain-soaked road, and then headed down the only clear lane.

To his horror, there, illumined in his headlights stood Brother Viktor, his lips framing the words of some kind of curse.

As Viktor raised his sword high above his head, Marty slammed the gas pedal to the floor. He was not about to let Viktor stop him and he felt sure the monk would move.

Relentlessly Viktor howled what sounded to Marty like "abracadabra" in a foreign language while he stood his ground.

Marty jammed the clutch into second.

As the magician sped toward Viktor, a blue-white streak of light burst from the sky and exploded in a blinding flash just beyond the hood of the car. Marty slammed on the brakes and braced for the impact that never came.

When the smoke cleared, Marty saw Viktor several feet away, covered in bright orange flames and screaming his head off. His tonsured hair stood on end, pointing in every direction like a ridiculous circus clown as sparks and smoke streamed from his ears. The monk grabbed at the air and ran in circles.

As his burning form neared the edge of the cliff, Marty reached for the door handle. He had no idea how he could help at this point, but he felt strongly that at least he should try. But before he could pull himself from the car, Viktor tumbled down the steep slope and rolled down into the canyon below.

Shocked, Marty waited for a moment, trying to figure out what had happened. And then he realized that Viktor had been foolish enough to raise an iron sword in the middle of an electrical storm.

"God one, evil monk, zero," Marty muttered he sped away, kicking up dirty water, gravel, and mud the whole way.

# Chapter 14
# Somewhere Over the Atlantic

The jet aircraft took off smoothly, shuddered on and off for a few eye opening minutes, and then leveled out to a steady 35,000 feet above the Earth.

Now, many hours into the flight, the plane cruised peacefully above the endless black abyss of the Atlantic Ocean. All of the lights, except one faint strip, were off in the interior of the luxury aircraft while most of the passengers slept, or at least attempted to. Agent Arias and her companions sat in the business-class seats just behind the first-class section.

Wide awake, Agent Arias' eyes roamed appraisingly across an apparently sleeping Dr. Alexander. As she watched his chest slowly rise and fall, she found herself wishing she knew more about him.

Everything about Arthur seemed a contradiction. His body was lean and fit and he moved like he was in his twenties. Conversely, his mannerisms were formal, and he spoke as though he had lived a hundred years. He was obviously very intelligent, but probably a fanatic of some kind. She also felt certain they had never met, and yet, he seemed so familiar. Feeling frustrated, she decided to shift her attention to his friend Michael Richardson. He, on the other hand, *was* young. He was also either a fool or an indiscriminant adventure seeker. *What is his interest in all of this?*

She knew he found her attractive, as she had caught him looking at her several times. She often had that effect on men who knew her only casually. Most backed off quickly once they found out that her only real interest at this point in her life was her career. Dr. Richardson would likely follow the same pattern.

"So you two are colleagues?" Analia questioned Michael. She was still somewhat annoyed that Arthur had chosen to fall asleep rather than discuss their plans, and her voice reflected that sentiment.

"We are," he returned, a characteristic boyish grin playing at the corners of his upturned mouth.

"Where do you work?"

"We're both instructors at a small university."

"You're college professors?"

"Yes, although I don't always use that term. I consider myself a teacher. Arthur is the head of the Psychology Department and I teach classes in Scientific Theory and World Religion."

"Interesting combination," Analia returned with a slight raise of her left eyebrow.

"Yeah, that's what my parents think."

"You say that as though they don't approve."

"No, not at all, I'm actually a kind of synthesis of their life work."

"How's that?"

"My mother is a researcher specializing in viral diseases and my father is an accountant and part-time minister at a church near their home. She believes in science. My father believes that God influences most of our day-to-day experiences."

"It doesn't sound like your parents have much in common."

"Actually, they've really made it work, probably because they really love each other."

Resisting the urge to poke fun at Michael's sentimentality, Analia continued to ask questions. "And you've decided to remain loyal to both and not choose sides?"

"No, I just don't believe they have to be mutually exclusive."

"So am I to understand that you believe both points of view are valid?"

"I do. I believe that perhaps God created the universe using measurable scientific laws and means. I try to teach my students to open their hearts and minds to the possibility that someday science and religion might live together in harmony, one reinforcing the other. I even believe that current scientific theory is beginning to support the idea that the universe is governed by a pervasive intelligent force, or omnipotent creator."

"Really, how is that?" Analia asked as she crossed her arms.

Many people viewed Michael's beliefs as extreme, and so he was unaffected by Analia's apparent doubt. "There are several really."

"How about just one professor?" Analia suggested. She had no desire to listen to multiple scientific theories.

"OK. Take M-Theory, for instance. In response to the microscopic gravitational inconsistencies present in Einstein's Theory of Relativity, scientists have recently developed a revised blueprint or map of the universe."

"Is it going to be important that I understand what you just said?"

"No," Michael responded with a smile, "all you need to know is that there are some problems with Einstein's famous theory, at a sub-atomic level, and that M-Theory successfully unites General Relativity and Quantum Mechanics. It also draws on many variations of what has been termed String Theory or Super-String Theory. Essentially M-Theory postulates that the entire universe is permeated by tiny invisible strings, all of which are identical."

"What does that prove?"

"Well, if the theory is accurate, then everything in the universe is created equal, at least at a sub-atomic level. Basically, every substance or manifestation in our universe is composed of flat or looped strings. And, just like the strings of a musical instrument, they vibrate at different rates. When combined together, they create the heavy particles of an atom as well as particles that have no mass, such as those that carry light."

"How does that prove the existence of God?"

"Well, if the theory is correct, then we know the universe is teeming with microscopic intelligent organization."

"Intelligent?"

"Yes, the rate at which the strings vibrate determines the substance that is created. What M-Theory doesn't adequately explain, is why the strings vibrate at different rates. I believe it's possible that they are consciously responding to some kind of omnipotent instructions."

"I'm confused. Are you saying that these strings are behaving as though directed by something or *someone*?"

"In a very over-simplified sort of way, yes, that would be correct."

"And you think this someone is God."

Without directly replying to her inquiry, Michael continued with his explanation. "Think of it this way. Is there anything on our planet that humans have created without thought? Everything we build or grow begins with reason and creative imagination. Every building ever constructed, every domesticated crop, every artistic masterpiece was a creative thought in the mind of its maker before it was a physical reality. And, all of the materials we use for our designs and creations are either native to our planet or manufactured in a laboratory. We simply reorganize existing matter to fit our needs and desires. Is it possible then that similarly these strings vibrate and arrange themselves according to the thoughts of a higher being for the purpose of building our universe?"

"Let me make sure I understand your point. You believe that M-Theory suggests that there is some kind of omnipotent presence manipulating our world through these things called strings, and you believe that intelligence is actually what most people term God?"

"Precisely."

"Interesting, Dr. Richardson, totally un-provable, yet interesting," Analia responded in a patronizing tone.

"Actually, I believe it is completely provable, just not by using the tools of a modern day scientist."

"Don't tell me, this is the part where your father's religious convictions come into play I suppose?"

"You learn fast, Agent Arias. You ought to take one of my classes."

"I'll be sure to put that on my to-do-before-I-die list," Analia responded drily.

Agent Arias was bright and quick-witted, and Michael was thoroughly enjoying the conversation, even if she was also a cynic.

"My father has always been a man of faith. He believes there is a God because inside his heart he knows it to be true. I have spent years studying this concept of faith as it appears in religions across the world, and I have found that devout people of any religious denomination generally agree with my father."

"That conviction could be just cultural influence or wishful thinking."

"It could be, or perhaps it's something else."

"Like what?"

"Take, for example, our five senses. We apprehend our entire existence through sight, smell, touch, hearing, and feeling. However, when we are limited to only these faculties, life is rather restricted. In order to expand what we are able to see and know, humankind has created artificial means for doing so by inventing devices such as the telescope, microscope, and the microchip. Through their use, we now know that so much more exists in the universe than that which we can see and hear without aid. Consider for a moment the possibility that we are unable to scientifically prove the existence of God because we aren't using the right equipment."

"If, for a moment, we accept the possibility that we are creatures produced by a higher intelligence, wouldn't it make sense that our creator would want us to know of his or her existence? Can you conceive of an intelligent parent who would not want to make themselves known to their offspring? What if there is a definitive way to know and feel the presence of this higher intelligence. Perhaps most people simply don't understand how to use the powers God has given us?"

"You're saying that we might all possess the ability to know God, we just don't use it?"

"Yes, exactly."

Agent Arias knew how easy unproven theories can be twisted into whatever shape desired, just as any set of data can be subjectively interpreted to prove almost any point. She admired Dr. Richardson's conviction, but also thought his ideas bordered on the outrageous.

"I believe, as do many, that we are not just physical bodies composed of matter, but that we are also spiritual beings outfitted with an array of inner senses that need only to be utilized to comprehend things unknown to most."

"I also believe that we might even have the innate ability to comprehend multiple realities. According to M-Theory, in addition to the four dimensions we are familiar with, three of space and one of time, there exists, seven other distinct dimensions of reality. In fact, the theory hinges on a basic assumption that the only way certain electrons can be charged, is if they move between dimensions."

"Perhaps by using our as-of-yet undiscovered *internal antennae* we might even someday be able to personally experience a multi-layered universe."

Michael paused there, waiting for some kind of response from Agent Arias.

"So am I to understand that you believe that people possess the innate ability to comprehend God, and also transcend time and space in order to experience various levels or dimensions of reality?"

"Yes."

"Sounds more like the makings of a great science fiction novel than a legitimate theory. Perhaps you've missed your calling?"

Just as Michael readied his reply, the captain's voice pierced through the quiet cabin via the internal intercom.

"Ladies and gentlemen, we are now approximately 45 minutes outside of London's Heathrow Airport and will begin our descent shortly. Local time is one o'clock a.m. and the temperature is a brisk seven degrees Celsius."

"I guess you'll have to continue your fascinating explanation later, Dr. Richardson. There's something I need to do before we land," Agent Arias commented as she picked up her carry-on valise and headed toward the bathroom.

Still keyed up from their discussion, Michael let out a long sigh.

"And you said I really laid it on her."

"I knew you weren't really asleep. Did you hear everything we said?"

"More like I heard what was unsaid. You really like her, don't you?"

"I don't even know why. It doesn't appear like we have much in common."

Arthur let out a low laugh before turning back toward the window and closing his eyes again.

Yes, he liked her, too, but his mind was busy reviewing the facts of the case and he needed to stay focused. He knew that he had only heard half-truths so far and that there was a lot more going on here than anyone had led him to believe.

After returning from the back of the plane, Agent Arias asked Dr. Richardson one last question. "So assuming for the moment that your theories actually have merit, not that I am saying they do, just suppose. What do you call these people who use these alleged inner senses?"

"There are many groups of people who use them, especially in the East, but the few people I know, call themselves initiates."

# Chapter 15

This time as Arthur closed his eyes, he slipped into a state of unconsciousness, somewhere between waking and deep sleep. Memories, daily experiences, and other dreamy images raced one after the other in rapid succession across the inner screen of his mind, until finally he was aware that he had awakened onto the plane of imagination.

*Arthur looked around and saw that he was standing at the base of the Tor in Glastonbury, England, a place he had physically visited many times.*

*Ritualistically, he requested permission of the dragon, the guardian of the ancient and holy site, before he ascended the mystical path. After intuitively receiving admittance, Arthur started to climb.*

*As he gazed at the nearby countryside he realized that his imagination had cast him back to a time more than 2,000 years ago, when lowland seas washed right up to the base of the small conical hill.*

*Arthur took pleasure in the historical view as he circled toward his destination. From his elevated position, the surrounding hills appeared to be tiny symmetrical islands, and he knew instantly that he was looking at the land once known as Avalon.*

*In the distance, one apple-tree covered mound caught his attention. There, he could see a large wooden structure he knew was used in millennia past as a training school for druidic priestesses.*

*Turning his attention, he looked down on the gentle swell of Wearyall Hill. Its orchards marked the spot where Glastonbury Abbey would exist centuries in the future. In this time, Arthur could see the familiar mud-and-wattle thatched hut he knew housed the earliest Christian church in England. He also knew that the little building was home to Joseph of Aramithea, the uncle of Jesus, the Nazarene.*

*Continuing his short journey, Arthur then topped the crown of the Tor and saw the standing stone circle of ages past.*

*He blinked his eyes, and the hillcrest transformed into the modern-day ruins of a 14th-century church tower. A gray-bearded man in hiking clothes leaned against the doorway. Arthur involuntarily took a quick breath, for he had seen this man before.*

"Hello, my son," he smiled in greeting to Arthur. "It took you long enough to climb this little hill. Are you getting old already?"

"No, Master," responded Arthur, "I just wanted to enjoy the view."

"Ah, you are learning. I have a message for you. Your immediate assistance is required. Azarelis is knocking on the doors of the watch-towers, and soon they will open for him. You and yours must seek the quarry in a cave on the coast, so as to neutralize his mischief and chaos. Come closer, and I will impart the location."

Arthur stepped forward and the wise man placed his hand on his forehead. Images of a sea cave, miles up the coast of England, formed in Arthur's mind along with all the details of how to find it, and how best to approach.

The vision then faded deep into Arthur's subconscious.

"When you need this information, your mind will make the link. For now, you must continue to rest. Soon you will need all of your strength and power."

"May you rest beneath the shadow of His wings whose name is peace," spoke the old man to Arthur. The Master then turned and silently walked through the tower and down the hill. As the man's diminishing figure disappeared on the horizon, his body transformed to that of an eagle and he flew gracefully away.

When Arthur woke to the sound of the flight attendant's voice, he remembered nothing.

# Chapter 16
# The Carpathian Mountains

As Marty sped along the snaking, twisting turns of the mountain pass, the sun shown gloriously down, illuminating the residual raindrops on every bush, tree, and shrub. They sparkled like jewels and Marty found himself wondering if it had all really happened.

But of course it had. The proof was sitting right there next to him.

On the passenger's seat, Viktor's cherished book lay innocently basking in the early-morning light. Marty longed to reach out and touch it, discover its secrets, and yet ever since he left the monastery, and fled past Viktor's sizzling corpse, he had doubted his actions.

*What was I thinking? What if it wasn't all an illusion? What if that severed head wasn't a fake? At the very least, Viktor used this book to cruelly bend the minds of the other monks. How could I take it?*

Marty knew that he had to find a way to revitalize his tired show. If he didn't, his career would be over. This book was the key to a new life, one full of success and money and feelings of self-worth. He had been letting Jackie and Arnie down for years, and it was time to take his life back.

*You can't Marty. The Grimoire is evil. Viktor came running after you with a sword for Chrissake! He's crazy. Do you want that to happen to you? Something isn't right here, and you don't need to be a part of it!*

"You're right," he said aloud, "I'll just get rid of it. It isn't worth it." Marty reached over, grabbed the leather book, and rolled down the window.

*No, you have to take the book back. If you don't, its power will enslave you forever!*

*What?*

This voice sounded different from the one he normally wrangled with in his head. Unsure what to do, he wavered.

*Do it. Get rid of it now while you can!*

For a second time Marty prepared to toss it when the strange voice in his head again protested.

*It's not safe. You have to take the Grimoire back. It's is more powerful than you realize. It must be returned.*

# Chapter 17
# The Carpathian Mountains

Hours later, Marty was once more driving the stretch of road that he had so anxiously departed from while it was still dark. Everything looked different in the bright light, and he found himself wondering how close to the monastery he was.

When he reached the washout in the road, he stopped the car. "I must have driven right past it," he said aloud while his head whipped back and forth in confusion. *So where's the monastery?*

*It's there, you just can't see it with your eyes.*

*What?*

He knew he must be in right place. He saw the familiar gap in the pass, but where was the huge stone structure? Feeling frustrated, Marty opened the door, grabbed the book, and started marching in the direction that he had before.

Soon, the confused magician realized that he was walking on the exact spot where the monastery was last night. Except that today the hill was practically barren. All that remained was a pile of blackened rubble and an unstructured mound of stones.

For the second time in 24 hours, Marty felt like he was starring in a bad horror film. "Shit like this just doesn't happen in real life," he yelled aloud. "Where the hell is the monastery?"

Desperate, he started walking in a circle, examining every inch of rain-soaked earth. Finally, on the third pass, he saw something sticking out of the mud and he reached down eagerly to pull it out. His blood turned to ice as he realized what it was.

There in his hand was the same brass plaque he had seen the night before as he pounded on the monastery door. He could clearly see the Arabic inscription and the same inverted pentagram that adorned the cover of the Grimoire in his hand.

Last night it had gleamed as though recently polished. Now it appeared rusted and corroded like some kind of excavated artifact.

"Oh God," Marty whispered as he stumbled back a step.

"Hey. What are you doing?" called a voice from behind him.

Marty jerked his head toward a tall figure approaching him from the road.

"Grigor," Marty gasped.

"How do you know my name?"

As the man moved closer, Marty realized his mistake. This man was dressed in a work-coat and pants and was not quite as tall as the pale-skinned cleric. His hair was also different. The Grigor Marty knew had white hair. This man had a full, brown-colored mane. But his *eyes*, his eyes were the same as the ones he had stared into just the night before. The resemblance between this man, and the Grigor Marty knew, was uncanny.

"I'm sorry," Marty blurted, "I mistook you for a friend of mine, also named Grigor, I guess," he said with a shrug. "He was a monk here," Marty continued while gesturing vaguely in the direction of the ruins.

"You must be confused, sir. There have been no monks or a monastery here for centuries."

"How do you know?"

"My great, great… well, my distant ancestor was a brother here long ago. Time moves slowly in this part of the world. We never forget our family history."

Marty stared at the man through unblinking eyes, temporarily at a loss for words.

"He was killed the night the monastery was destroyed. All the monks were. They say lightning never strikes the same place twice, but the locals here swear it hit the monastery at least ten times during the worst storm ever recorded in the area. What made you think there was still a monastery here?"

"You say all the monks were killed?" countered Marty, ignoring the man's question.

"Not all of them. Apparently a few of the monks were searching up and down the road for something when the monastery was struck. As far as I know, they were the only survivors."

"As a matter of fact," Grigor continued as he thoughtfully scratched his head, "I think the monastery was destroyed this very same day almost six centuries ago. What a coincidence?"

"Yeah," was all that Marty could say.

# Chapter 18
# The Carpathian Mountains

As the sun reached its highest point in the sky, Marty stood amid the monastery ruins. He anxiously cradled the Grimoire to his chest, while his mind teetered on the brink of insanity.

Had he imagined the entire event? Had he dreamed the whole thing? The modern-day Grigor assured him that the monastery had been gone for centuries. So where had he been last night?

*Maybe I hit my head when I skidded to stop on the road? Maybe I was unconscious in my car the whole time? So where did the book come from?*

That was the one question Marty had trouble answering.

He had no problem imagining that the storm had confused his mind or that perhaps he had some kind of episode in the car, but how could he logically explain the presence of the Grimoire?

He pulled the heavy book from his chest and looked at the unusual cover. The pentagram looked odd balancing on its point, but at the same time he was drawn to the symbol.

*Why don't you just lift the cover? Inside, you will find the answers to all of your questions.*

*No, Viktor said not to.*

*Viktor is a selfish and cruel tyrant who wants everything for himself. All you have to do is open it and all will be revealed to you.*

A warm wind emanating from the west caressed the sides of Marty's face as he struggled to make a decision.

*No, I can't.*

*Yes, you can. Find the strength.*

*No!*

*Do it. Do it now!*

Marty watched from above as his own hand pulled back the leather cover to reveal the first page. On it he saw the same seal that adorned the floor of Viktor's Chamber of Conjuration.

As he looked down, the intricate diagram jumped from the aging parchment and expanded into a three-dimensional hologram.

Marty dropped the book in surprise. The seal didn't move, it remained steady in front of it him, floating in mid-air.

*Quick, pull your eyes from the seal! Don't look at it. Run away or you'll be lost forever!*

The words echoed in Marty's head, but by now he was powerless to heed the warning, for the complicated matrix was already working its magic.

# Chapter 19
# Somewhere in Northern England

The McLain's epitomized British hospitality.

Shortly after clearing customs, Arthur, Analia, and Michael were ushered into Sandy McLain's impeccably clean European station-wagon and then fed elegant sandwiches and mineral water by his thoughtful wife, Margaret.

The McLains then launched into a detailed description of the, "psychic emergency" as they sped through the night toward a mysterious location in Northwestern England. Sandy McLain, who was essentially a walking encyclopedia, began by relaying the history of the area they were all soon to visit.

"The site itself was constructed nearly 4,000 years ago by an ancient Celtic tribe. We aren't certain about the original purpose of the circle, but some historical records indicate that the stones were placed there to mark the convergence of several significant ley-lines."

"Later, during the Middle-ages and even on through the early Renaissance, various cults and sects used the stone circle for a range of purposes, including seasonal rituals and probably sacrifices."

"What is a ley-line?" Analia questioned as she leaned forward in her seat to better hear his response.

"There are several definitions or theories really. Alfred Watkins, an amateur archaeologist, developed the most commonly accepted one around 1920. While looking for areas of interest on several ancient maps, he found a series of unexplained straight lines. Curious, he did some research and discovered that they connected significant ancient archeological sites across great distances. He then had a vision or psychic *flash* of such lines crossing all over the planet, which he recorded in a book titled, *The Old Straight Track*."

"Is there a scientific definition of ley-lines?" Analia re-phrased.

"Not exactly scientific, but there are certainly other ideas, that have been put forth by a variety of groups."

"Some people consider the lines to be simply property markers, trade routes, or even ancient roads connecting important religious sites. Others believe that ley-lines have electrical or magnetic properties and that in areas where they converge, a special vortex is created. Certain groups even believe that these vortices have mystical healing properties."

"Through decades of repeated and deliberate misuse, the healing energy of this particular site has been drained, and it is now a center of disorder. And worse, this vampirizing of its natural properties has opened up several inharmonious gateways."

"Inharmonious in what way?" Michael chimed in.

"Well, the careful balance of energy created by the ley-lines has been shifted through misguided conscious effort and the location is no longer in a state of equilibrium, as it should be naturally."

"How did that happen?" Michael further inquired.

"By ignorant individuals attempting to the use the stone circle for selfish purposes, like material gain or unnatural immortality," Arthur answered.

"Yes, well," Margaret McLain interjected, "most of the mischief created at the site has lain dormant for quite some time, until recently. Apparently a group of college students decided to perform a summoning ritual they discovered in a library at Oxford. The manuscript they used dates to the early 13th century. Normally it remains in a locked room and only a very few recognized scholars are allowed to view it. Somehow this group managed to get their hands on it," Margaret explained with an ironic grin.

"Why would it be locked up?" Analia inquired. "I mean, don't most modern thinkers consider such things to be purely superstition?"

"Actually, education and a belief in the occult or esotericism often go hand in hand. Individuals in all walks of life including those who are working in law, politics, medicine, research, and government believe, at least in part, that there is much more going on in the universe than we are aware. Fortunately, some of these high-ranking individuals see to it that the public is protected from manuscripts like the one this group used."

"Oh." Analia responded with a raise of her eyebrow.

"Generally," Sandy continued, "when self-taught dilettantes venture into the realms of practical ritualism they are protected from their own foolishness by their inability to raise any appreciable amount of power. Except that in this case, the group attempted the rite in the middle of a strong vortex, and they ended up receiving much more than they were looking for."

Continuing his story, Sandy relayed that the negative energy they summoned nearly destroyed everyone in the group. "

"Especially, since the leader realized too late that the pages he was working from did not contain the formula for departure. Luckily for him, his own distress sent a strong surge of adrenaline through his body that enabled him to fall to his side and roll down the hill. His exit broke the spell, but apparently before he could recover, he was almost knocked down again by his fellow ceremonialists as they came rushing past him, robes flapping in the wind and mouths open and screaming."

"Even though Merrick has since destroyed the copied manuscript, and he and his team have promised never to publicly speak of the incident, their actions have tainted the subtle energy network in the area. The impact was so profound that it has even been felt on the inner planes of the collective."

"That's how it first came to our attention. We did a little poking around after that and we were then able to piece the whole event together," Margaret finished.

"And that's the emergency we're here for?" Analia questioned in astonishment as she looked at Dr. Alexander for clarification.

"Look, Agent Arias, this event is significant and very real. If the problem isn't corrected soon, the imbalance of energy will spread like a viral contagion and the global network of ley-lines will become polluted. It could then poison the entire subtle fabric of our planet, which could then have serious repercussions."

"Like what?"

"Well, we could experience global earthquakes or damaging weather patterns."

"You're kidding, right?"

"No, I'm not kidding, Agent Arias. The energy of the ley-lines and inner planes are directly connected to our own world and if they become damaged, we will definitely feel the effects here," Arthur countered.

Open-mouthed, Analia turned toward the window and hoped that it would all be over soon.

# Chapter 20
# Manhattan

Sebastian Howell, CEO of Black Rose Ltd., stood motionless, with his back to the group, while the conversation of the board meeting droned on behind him.

The tall sandy-haired man stared from the 12th-floor conference room window as he looked down at the Manhattan street scene below. To him, the people looked like an army of ants, scurrying around frantically in their imaginary pursuit of happiness. He smiled, thinking about how the slightest whim of those with real power could crush those petty hopes and dreams at any time, just as he used to crush the tiny militant insects in the backfield of his family's upstate farm when he was a child.

Sebastian had learned long ago that true power is the ability to manipulate any crisis to personal advantage. His mentors had taught him this philosophy long ago, and their teachings had been indelibly imprinted on his consciousness.

The industrial revolution had paved the way for venture capitalists like Sebastian and he and his kind now flourished in the free market of the 21st century. Since the late 1800s, the world had experienced a virtual string of crises and wars, ones that smart and heartless businessmen could turn into profit.

In World War I, the arms manufacturers of Europe experienced rapid growth and posted record revenue. But really it was the bankers who made the greatest profit by loaning the money to make the weapons at huge interest rates. And the same deal was given to both sides of the conflict. The idea was that no matter which side won, they were both into the banks for large sums of money.

Over the years, the executives of Sebastian's company had taken that lesson seriously. In line with the doomsday economists, the Black Rose could see the almost inevitability of food shortages on a global scale in the next few decades. Sebastian and his team of advisors had therefore allocated tremendous resources, mostly offset by grants from the government, to develop new hybrid strains of crops. Most of the seeds they grew were highly productive and disease resistant, which immediately drew praise from governments around the world and enhanced the prestige of the company.

What most people failed to grasp right away was that the hybrids could only be used once. Their second-generation seeds were sterile, which guaranteed the frequent return of customers. Sebastian's plan was brilliant. Little by little, the Black Rose Ltd. would control the food source and in turn the policies of entire nations.

And Sebastian was a patient man.

Eventual lack of food would lead to wars fueled by deprivation, which in turn would supply his other business, arms dealing, with a string of high-paying customers. Control the crises, and you had the power to control humanity, which Sebastian felt was the only real commodity worth possessing.

He smiled at the thought.

Feeling satisfied, Sebastian shifted his attention to the reflective glass in front of him and critically assessed his appearance. His hair was combed straight back and locked into place with the gelatin-like hair cocktail his stylist used. He knew it looked a little outdated, but in his world everything had to be neat and straight. Even a stray lock of hair could signal weakness.

Later today he had a meeting with a Washington think tank, and he wanted to make the right impression. Especially since most of its members served as the main advisory body to key members of the Department of Defense.

Continuing his appraisal, Sebastian smiled at his perfectly tanned facial skin and the whisper of wrinkles around his eyes. His personal assistant had suggested Botox therapy to eliminate them, but he knew that the tiny lines gave him both character and the appearance of honesty. He certainly wouldn't want his associates to think him deceitful.

Sebastian then pulled slightly at his tailored blue blazer, smoothing out its imaginary flaws. It hung perfectly over a white, crisp, spun-silk shirt, which met with his personal high standards. At his throat was his school tie, secured in a Windsor knot and affixed to his shirt with a diamond-encrusted clip. He reached down and stroked the accessory possessively as though assuring himself that it was still there. His pants were pressed and cut exactly to his frame, in order to hint at the well-muscled physique beneath. He nodded his approval as he finished his self-review and then turned back toward the group behind him.

While his outward appearance was impeccable, he did have one odd habit, or idiosyncrasy, that seemed a bit incongruous to his otherwise meticulous nature.

Sebastian didn't like to wear socks.

He relished the feel of wiggling his toes inside of his expensive loafers, and even thin socks ruined the effect. He was also very touchy about it. Once, a junior member of the board had joked about it. Two days later, the police received an anonymous tip that photos of nude, underage boys were stored in this unfortunate executive's computer. As a result, the man received a decade long sentence in the state penitentiary. The scandal that ensued demolished his life. His finances left him at the same time as his wife.

Soon after, Howell was reportedly heard to comment, "You would never have thought him to be a pervert, would you?"

Nobody had ventured to comment on the boss' footwear since.

"Sebastian, what do you recommend we do about our Middle Eastern conflict?" asked the Director sitting at the other end of the long glass conference table.

Sebastian insisted that all executive tables and desks at the Black Rose be made of glass. He wanted to know what his staff was doing at all times. Clinching of hands, texting, or caressing of oneself while at work was strictly prohibited. That, and Sebastian was paranoid. He often felt others were plotting against him and so full disclosure was always expected of those in his employ.

"Perhaps you should explain the Middle Eastern crisis, Nigel? All those present may not be as intimately familiar with particulars of the situation as you are," he suggested as he stared at his associate through piercing, tawny-colored eyes.

"Yes, of course," Nigel replied, his dark eyes quick to mask their impatience. "The issue is the rather extensive investments made through our usual and secure channels with the government of Kerukstan. This small country, adjacent to several of the former Soviet-Islamic Republics, has been embroiled in an indecisive civil war for several years. Currently, the rebel forces are concentrated in the southern mountainous region of the country. An exceptionally talented general, Mikal Surrif, who also happens to be a former officer of the old Soviet KGB, is directing them. Until recently, he has had access to military supplies and armament through his old Soviet connections."

As Nigel carried on with his explanation, Sebastian let his mind wander.

*When would his associates ever learn? It doesn't matter which side emerges victorious from this stupid third-rate war. What matters is that both are heavily indebted to the Black Rose for the purchase of weapons and supplies. Whoever wins, we will control the rich petroleum and mineral resources of the ridiculous mud-hole. All we have to do is keep the conflict going long enough, while avoiding international or U.N. interference, to weaken both sides enough to render them unable to resist our control.*

This was where Sebastian's investments in the supposed free press were going to pay off. His majority shares in large corporate media companies provided him with the means to place the occasional phone call and suggest a shifting of the public spotlight away from his enterprises.

"Nigel," Howell interrupted, "it appears we need to rebalance the scales. Call Ibrahim and ask him to contact the president of our favorite country. Let him know that we can supply the government with an adequate shipment of new armament, perhaps some surface-to-surface tactical missiles, in order to subdue the current rebel threat?"

"Then have Ibrahim get in touch with the rebel general. I think perhaps it's time for them to initiate a few civilian bombings with some requisite collateral damage. Tell him we will outfit their team with two new Apache helicopters. That should stoke the fires of freedom, don't you think?"

"Brilliant plan, Sebastian, I'll get right on it. May I suggest we purchase a few more shares of Kerukstan oil stock? It is bound to go down dramatically with the reduction of supply and if we time it right, we can get a bargain."

"Yes, a prudent move," Howell agreed.

"I think we can dispense with the balance of the agenda for now," Sebastian commanded as he gestured for his team to leave the room. "Lillian and Nigel, please join me in my office. I have something to discuss with you."

If anyone was surprised at the abrupt conclusion of the meeting, they were careful to keep it to themselves. Or at least they were while Sebastian was still in the room.

As instructed, his subordinates followed Sebastian through a pair of paneled doors and passed into his private, corner office. It was windowed on two sides, and had its own balcony. Sebastian walked past his well-stocked mini-bar full of mineral water, juices, and healthy sports-drinks, and then asked his lieutenants to take a seat as he reached for the cup of steaming green tea his secretary had just delivered.

Sebastian never consumed alcohol or soda, nor did anyone else in his presence.

Everything in the room, every stick of furniture, was either black or white and not one fingerprint, smudge, or dirt spot was visible.

"I just received some important news," he said as he sipped from the cut-crystal mug. "Apparently a copy of The Book has re-surfaced."

# Chapter 21
# Northern England

They were in the midst of a battle, a battle of wills.

The flames of the fire cast changing patterns of light and shadow on both the tall stones of the hilltop circle and the figures moving between them, while the salamander-like sparks of the central blaze danced with excitement.

To the observers outside of the circle, both the moving forms, and the sounds they made, seemed hazy and muffled.

Several minutes earlier, the robed ritualists had set powerful astral seals at each of the four directions. The result was a "cloaking effect" on their proceedings.

Seals do not change the laws of physics, nor do they bend light or suppress sound. To secure the privacy needed for a successful astral working, they alter individual consciousness and its perceptions. Consequently, any untrained eyes and ears outside of the seals, have difficulty focusing on the activities within. While inside of the circle, energy is confined and concentrated.

"You must understand," Arthur had once explained to a group of students, "we don't actually hear with our ears or see with our eyes. They are simply receptors, or antennae, which, convert the sights and sounds of the environment into a form our brains can interpret. The brain then transmits the images to the true hearer or seer, which is our consciousness. And that consciousness can be altered using a variety of techniques."

Agent Arias stood only a few feet outside of the stone ring, and as far as she could tell, nothing of any real significance was happening. Everything inside the circle was covered in a strange evening fog and all movement was obscured from her vision. Confused, she looked around and noted that everywhere else the night sky was clear.

Any other person in her position might have questioned the seeming contradiction, but Analia had been trained by the Agency and she knew that behind every effect, no matter how unusual, there is always a logical cause. This situation was no different. Her honed reasoning skills quickly found the answer she needed to ease her mind. Analia remembered that fog can crop up in a single spot on moors such as this one, and so without giving it further thought, she shrugged off the coincidence.

Glancing to her side, she saw that Michael was intently focused on the activity inside of the stones.

"What are you doing?"

"I'm watching the ritual."

"What do you mean? They aren't doing anything there except just walking around."

"Oh, there's a lot more going on than that. Try to relax, Agent Arias, open your mind, and let your imagination take over."

With a sigh, Analia turned back toward the robed figures. All she could think about was how cold she was, and how much she wanted to go home. But, after a few minutes she started to feel sleepy and her eyes began to close, for a second or two at a time. Her vision then softened and for a moment she thought she saw....

Startled, Analia's eyes snapped open and she looked over at Michael.

"It's magic."

"It's what?"

Resisting the urge to laugh, Michael tried to explain. He figured he might as well tell her everything since she already thought he was a lunatic.

"Look, magic is not what most people think it is. It's not illusion or trickery. It's the natural consequence of a trained psyche. And that's what is going on in there, *real* magic."

"Real magic?" Analia echoed flatly.

"Yes. Practical magic or ritual isn't even performed here in the material world, but in the astral one Josh spoke of at the Institute. It's also one of those different dimensions we talked about on the plane. Individuals who are trained in perceiving alternate realities are able to alter their own consciousness and attune to particular vibrations."

"So if you can see what's going on in there, why aren't you joining in the ceremony?"

"Because, while some people, like me, are sensitive enough to see the images of the astral world, only a few highly trained individuals are adept enough to manipulate the energy there and channel it into the material world. And that's exactly what Arthur and his senior initiates are doing in there."

# Chapter 22

As always, Arthur had planned ahead.

There is no matter, not at least as most humans understand it, in the world of images. In this dimension, a strong imagination is the only thing that stands between the forces of light and the forces of chaos. Arthur had therefore chosen appropriate *imaginative* forms for his team to use on this unique battlefield.

The four officers were astrally clothed in the attire of pre-dynastic Egyptian priests. On their heads, they each wore a striped headdress, known as a Nemes. On their breasts, over robes of pure white, hung a medallion in the shape of one of the sons of Horus.

For thousands of years, Egyptians used these symbols in their art, religion, and ceremonies to represent protection and equilibrium. For this reason their images remain powerful on the astral plane.

The forms of *this* realm, however, by dint of their very nature, are unstable. Everything here is created by thought. Fear or doubt can degrade images. Unwavering concentration is vital. Chaos is always ready to embrace visitors, and the seductive pull of the shadow is ever-present in this dimension. Every dark or evil thought humankind has ever had is recorded in the fabric of this astral territory, ready to play to just about any nightmare.

*Slowly the group advanced, mentally tightening an electric-blue net made of light around the whirling blackness. As they closed in on the dark mass it was forced to retreat and assume a recognizable form.*

*To survive, the chaotic energy must break the concentration of its attackers. It chose a shape that humankind has used to represent evil, Satan, and the Devil for millennia, The Goat of Mendes.*

*The giant creature stomped at the ground and glared at the initiates. Its powerful jaws opened and closed as it howled wildly in protest of their presence. A fetid odor of decomposition filled the air.*

*The ritualists continued closing, backing the astral demon into an imaginative corner. To defend itself, the angry Devil belched forth a poisonous cloud of yellow gas. The stinging puffs temporarily blinded the teams' astral vision and they halted their attack.*

*The beast shook its massive horned head and roared in triumph. Malevolently, it stared at each initiate until it locked eyes with Arthur. If it could bring down the leader, then it could bring down the entire group, and instinctively the creature knew this man was the one.*

*Its gaze bored deep into Arthur's consciousness, mercilessly searching his mental fortress for weakness. If it could find an image, any image that would generate fear, then Arthur would fall.*

*To counter the mental invasion, the occultist stretched forth the Blasting Rod of Hermes in his right hand and a golden Egyptian Ankh in his left. The beast howled as beams of pure light shot toward it. Red saliva dripped from its mouth. Its huge hoofed feet kicked at the air.*

*Arthur skillfully moved to avoid the attack while his companions visualized astral implements of their own. Streams of light flew in all directions. Working as one voice, the ritualists intoned an ancient word of power known as the Ab Aima, a potent mantra used for re-establishing equilibrium.*

*The beastly Goat wailed as the dull-red pentagram inscribed on its forehead began to rotate.*

*Arthur knew that the ancient symbol acted as both a strength and weakness for the creature. In its current position, the inverted star signified bondage and slavery and the Devil drew its energy from the symbol's strong negative power.*

*But if the initiates could turn the pentagram, then the giant would be rendered helpless.*

*Arthur signaled his team and together they melded the light from their implements into one energized beam. The beast turned its head to avoid their offensive, but no matter which way it moved, the mighty rays followed.*

*As light made contact with the star, it slowly turned clockwise.*

*The Goat tried with all of its might to retard the righting of the pentagram, but its own strength was insufficient. The star soon stood with its single point uppermost, symbolizing perfect balance.*

*A blinding radiance surrounded the beast and a high-pitched sound vibrated through the air. Steadily, light engulfed the beast, ignoring its cries of agony until all trace of its presence disappeared.*

*As the light receded, the holy Archangel Auriel filled the place of darkness, and, with a sweep of her hand, she reenergized the injured network of energy and repaired the damage caused by centuries of misuse.*

# Chapter 23
# Northern England

Analia sat at the breakfast table, nibbling on a piece of buttered toast, while she mentally reviewed the events of the night.

After leaving the stone circle, they drove back to the McLain's home about an hour away. Arthur had insisted on strict silence during the ride home, and so Analia hadn't been able to get the debriefing she had wanted. When they arrived back at the charming British cottage, she succumbed to fatigue and fell asleep in the McLain's guest room.

When she woke, Sandy informed her that Arthur had gone back out to the site just before dawn to make sure that no negative energy remained.

Forced to wait for his return, Analia now contemplated her next move. So far she had only briefly checked in with Banes and she had somehow pacified his inquiries with minimal information. Soon he would expect another message and she would have to give him something of substance.

*What am I going to tell him?*

Analia supposed that her work here was complete, but she had no idea what to put in her report. When she met first Josh Erskine and then Dr. Alexander at the Institute, she thought this ridiculous case might have some underlying merit. Now she had to admit to herself that perhaps her instincts had been wrong. As things stood, it appeared she had flown thousands of miles to stand in a cold moor for hours. And, as far as she could tell, nothing had changed and there were no new leads. No bad guys, no law-breaking. In fact, the more she thought about it, the more frustrated she felt.

After a few more sips of coffee, Analia decided it was time to cut her losses and head home. Following Dr. Alexander had been disappointing and she saw no reason to stick around. Throwing down her toast, she headed out the back door and retrieved her phone from the pocket of her pants.

Assistant Director Banes answered her call on the first ring. Deciding it was pointless to hold back, as he was likely to make her tell all anyway, Analia launched into a narrative of her adventures with Dr. Alexander to date. When she finished, she informed Banes that she was heading home on the next available flight.

"Yes, sir, apparently everything here is wrapped up. I'll call the airport as soon as we hang up."

"I want you to stay with Alexander, Agent Arias."

"Sir, there's nothing left to do here. The so-called, event, has been…" Analia paused unable to find quite the right words, "rectified and I really don't think there's much of a further risk to national security."

"Your assignment included staying with Dr. Alexander."

"What else can I possibly do here? As far as I know, he will be returning to California today as well."

"Do you know that for sure?"

"No, I don't, but he'll be back soon, and I'll ask him."

"Be back soon? You were supposed to remain with Alexander at all times!"

Analia knew she had said the wrong thing as soon as the words slipped from her mouth.

*What the heck is wrong with me? I never make mistakes like this.*

"He should be back any minute. It won't happen again, sir."

"When he returns, you are to stay with him until further notice, do you understand, Agent Arias? The situation is much more serious than you realize, and I need you to behave professionally."

"Yes, sir."

"And you're not to let that blasting rod out of your sight."

"What?"

"The rod he picked up before leaving for the airport. That in itself is a matter of national security. I want to know where it is at all times. Wherever it goes, you go. Do you understand, Agent Arias?"

"Yes, sir, I understand."

"Call me again at 09:00 hours your time. I'll be waiting."

Director Banes then hung up the phone just as Analia was about to slip in another, *yes, sir.*

As she headed dejectedly back toward the house, she realized that something Banes said seemed out of place. *How does he know about the blasting rod?*

Confused, she scrolled through her list of text messages and re-read the one she had sent her boss from LAX. It read:

*Will soon be flying over the Atlantic with Drs. Alexander and Richardson. I will contact you again when we arrive in the UK. We made a brief stop on the way to the airport to pick up some ancient artifact Alexander says he needs. Will make a full report soon. Agent Arias*

There was no mention of the blasting rod in this communication or in any other she had sent.

# Chapter 24
# Northern England

Less than an hour later, Arthur returned from the stones.

"Is everything alright, Arthur?" Sandy McLain questioned as he gestured for Arthur to take a seat. His friend looked tired and Sandy was concerned.

"The site is calm and quiet on all levels. Thank you for your diligence in pursuing the matter and for all the work you and Margaret have done here."

"Anytime, Arthur, whatever we can do to be of service, you know that."

Arthur smiled as he sat down on the padded kitchen chair. He then inhaled deeply several times to revitalize his tired body.

When Michael and Agent Arias entered the kitchen, Arthur noted that Michael seemed completely renewed by a few hours of sleep while Analia seemed strained. Her outward appearance was calm enough, but Arthur could tell that underneath it all, something was bothering her.

"Well, the good doctor has done it again," Michael proclaimed to the group at large. "I guess this is going to be a short trip."

"Not as short as you would expect."

Analia's head snapped up. "What? I thought you said the site is fine."

"It is. But for reasons that would be difficult to explain to you, I feel there is still work to be done."

"What's going on, Arthur?" Margaret asked.

"While we were inside the circle battling the...," he glanced at Analia and decided to leave out the rest. "I had a strange vision. Something dangerous is developing on the astral, something very dangerous."

"Like what?" Analia heard herself asking, even though, she wasn't sure she wanted to hear the answer.

"Like a breach in the space-time continuum of such magnitude that it could destroy most life on Earth."

"I don't understand. How could something like that even be possible, and how could you have had a vision of it?"

"Agent Arias, I know that what we're dealing with here is something with which you are totally unfamiliar. I also understand that you most likely think that I and my colleagues here are complete lunatics. But just because something can't be proven objectively or isn't routinely accepted as truth, doesn't necessarily mean it isn't real or doesn't exist. Modern science has certainly made astounding discoveries in the last century, but you and I both know that we can only quantify that which our current technology has the ability to measure. Anything else is simply speculation."

"You chose to come with us. All I ask is that you try to open your mind to what we are saying, at least as it relates to the internal consistency of the case. Do you think you might be able to do that?"

Analia looked intently at Arthur before responding. "Fine, I will try, for the sake of this case. Now can you please explain what you saw in your vision?"

Arthur took another deep breath before continuing. By nature he was a patient man, but Agent Arias was certainly testing his limits.

"Everything in our material world, and I do mean *everything*, is first created on the astral plane as a mental image. However, not everything on the astral plane corresponds to a physical manifestation. The astral is sort of a realm of all possibilities. But because everything *here*, does have a counterpart *there*, it is possible for someone sensitive enough to predict future events, which can be very useful for certain applications."

"Unfortunately there's a catch. Time does not exist on the astral plane like it does here. Events do not occur in a linear fashion. Ones on the astral may or may not manifest in our world. And, as I have mentioned, many forms there are not stable. It's hard to know for sure what is real and what isn't. Some events though, by virtue of their intrinsic nature, are more possible than others. And all I can say right now is that something is brewing on the astral that has the potential to instigate cataclysms here on Earth. Intuitively, I believe it is connected to this case. I need to visit a friend of mine in order to know for sure."

"Where are you headed, Arthur?" Sandy inquired.

"I need to go see Roget in Paris before we head back to the States."

"Should we come with you?"

"No, it's alright for now. I'll call you and Margaret after I've *flown* with the Parisian group."

"Flown?" Analia imitated.

"I'll tell you all about it on the way, Agent Arias," Arthur answered with a chuckle.

85

# Chapter 25
# Paris

The last thing Marty remembered was getting in his car and driving as fast as he could.

*How could I ever have doubted that book?*

Detailed images of a new show ran through his mind, one right after the next. All reservations about the Grimoire had faded from his consciousness.

While speeding along the treacherous mountain roads, seemingly unconcerned for his safety, Marty decided that he was done playing to small crowds in the tiny nightclubs that Arnie generally booked for him. He was better than that, and he had resented his manager for the meager bookings for a long time.

So Marty chose not to meet Jackie and Arnie in Ostrava as planned, and instead drove straight through the Czech Republic, into Germany, and through to France in record time. After dropping off the rental car, he was now waiting to ride a subway train under the English Channel.

During his uninterrupted drive, Marty had outlined the new performance in his mind. It was almost as if the book was feeding him instructions telepathically, and he quickly became addicted to the sensation.

Along the way, he called Arnie and Jackie and told them to meet him in London for a big surprise. When Arnie pressed him for an explanation, Marty promised that he would fill him in later.

He still had no idea what he was going to tell his wife and manager, so for now being vague was easier. Especially since he had no clue himself what had really happened. All he knew was that he had the book, and it was going to change his life.

As he sat there waiting for the train to arrive, Marty called a man he knew from one of his several prior trips to the UK. Pete, managed a large performance hall near the West End, and Marty decided to call and ask him if, by chance, the venue was available for rent the following night.

Pete informed the magician that ironically the lead singer of the band scheduled to perform for the next week had come down with a severe case of the flu, and had been forced to cancel his shows.

Marty was unsurprised by this information. It was perfect synchronicity. The Grimoire was taking care of everything.

When Pete reminded Marty that the standard auditorium fee was hefty, and that he would have to fill at least two-thirds of the seats just to break even, Marty assured him that the numbers would be no problem.

Pete was skeptical. "Mate, if you don't reach that minimum, you will have to personally make up the difference."

"No problem, I've got it covered."

"No, offense, Marty, but the last I heard, your show wasn't doing very well. Last summer here in London you could barely fill that 100-seat capacity hole-in-the-wall down the street.

"Don't worry about it, man. I've got a whole new show that's going to blow the audience away.  Everything's fine."

"Alright, it's your funeral."

# Chapter 26
# London

Arnie tried to remain calm as he stood near the theatre entrance.

Marty had shared almost nothing about the "big surprise" and Arnie feared that his best friend might be losing it. The magician had been acting bizarre since his arrival in London, and he had so far offered no explanation for his temporary disappearance in the hills of the Czech Republic.

Marty also refused to rehearse in front of Arnie or the crew and even Jackie, his assistant, had no idea what her new role would be. When Arnie had asked Marty for an explanation, his friend had remained silent and behaved as though Arnie's presence irritated him. When Arnie reminded him that they had no time to advertise the show, Marty assured him that he had taken care of everything.

As bodies streamed into the performance hall, Arnie was astonished by the number people who were showing up for this thing. While he stared with an open mouth, he caught fragments of conversations here and there. Nobody seemed to know exactly what the show was all about or who Marty was, but apparently, there were blogs all over the Internet promising that the performance would be like *nothing ever seen before*. Arnie even heard some patrons referring to his client as "Mad Marty the Mystico."

As the last of the latecomers came through the door, Arnie headed to his seat in the balcony and nervously awaited the start of the show.

At 8 o'clock exactly, a green-colored fog poured from beneath the proscenium curtain as it slowly rose to reveal an otherwise-darkened stage. Clouds of emerald smoke rolled across the floor, spilling over into the orchestra pit and the first few rows of seats. The foot lights that rimmed the edge of the stage then started to flicker, illuminating the performance area and creating the illusion of torchlight.

A circle of flame gradually began to burn in center stage. As the blaze flared, a crash of thunder rang through the hall and Marty materialized in the middle of the fiery ring. To Arnie's surprise, nothing covered his entrance. No smoke, no mirrors, no trap door, Marty simply appeared.

He wore a long, black, hooded robe and his face boasted a newly trimmed Mephistophelean beard. He appeared strong and confident, and it seemed to Arnie that Marty looked more handsome than he had in years.

Slowly, music began to play. At first, it sounded like church bells ringing, then it faded into something more like Gregorian chanting, except that to Arnie, it sounded a little strange. The notes seemed discordant rather than harmonious. He looked around the balcony and down into the seats below to see what the audience thought of the music. Everyone appeared rapt and attentive. Apparently the unusual resonance was not disturbing anyone else.

Puzzled, Arnie turned his attention back to Marty who now held a large iron, cross-hilt sword in his hands. The magician lifted it first toward the audience and then high above his head. Another round of thunder pierced through the auditorium as a laser-like beam of light burst forth from the tip of the steely blade.

The audience erupted into applause.

# Chapter 27
# London

A large piece of glass dropped from the stage rafters as Marty began to speak.

"Those who dare to gaze into the depths of the magic mirror will see all they most secretly desire."

The stage lights dimmed and the previously clear piece of glass darkened to become a wall-sized piece of mirror. Collectively, the crowd gasped as their eyes froze in place.

Arnie looked into Marty's new stage prop, and saw the beautiful two-story house in the suburbs of upstate New York that he had dreamed about since he was a teenager. White colonnades, red-brick siding, a circular drive, it was all there. The vision even included the little white gazebo he had imagined at the center of a lush backyard framed by hedges trimmed to look like animals. He himself stood in the middle of the mirror fantasy, surrounded by a loving, attentive family. No traveling, no working nights, just peace. It was unbelievable.

Simultaneously, a plain-looking woman two rows over let loose a series of excited giggles. She had always been much too shy to make the most of her looks, but in the mirror, she saw herself made-up and hot, wearing a sexy red dress and high heels, catching attention wherever she went. Men whistled and stared as she walked by, and for the first time in her life she had the self-confidence she needed to revel in their admiration.

The teenage boy dressed in all black sitting just in front of Arnie saw himself on a light-filled stage, banging away on a guitar while thousands of fans looked on and screamed his name.

An elderly man to Arnie's left saw himself relaxing on a chaise lounge, dressed in a Grecian robe, while gorgeous women fed him grapes and danced before him. Next to him, his wife imagined herself rich, happy, and divorced.

Seconds later, a random arm, groping at some unseen illusion, hit Arnie in the head and jolted him out of the fantasy. As he looked around at the audience, he saw a sea of staring eyes hypnotized by the images in Marty's magic mirror.

Confused, he looked back to see if his own vision remained. He could still see the brick house and the manicured lawns, except this time he didn't have an anonymous blond wife at his side. In her place, Arnie now saw *Jackie* giving him a passionate kiss!

Stunned, Arnie shook his head and tried to clear the image. *Where did that come from?*

For the next hour, Marty amazed the audience with dozens of spectacular effects, and they were quick to verbalize their approval of each. Not only were the stunts remarkable, but everything was so personal. It was as though Marty was playing to each man or woman in the room individually.

As he paced the circle, waved his sword, and recited incantations, he cast a spell of magic and fantasy over the audience, one that they could not seem to get enough of.

"In ancient times, the initiated priests stood high on mountain crests or atop great pyramids. Intently they gazed at the stars, repeating mantras, and seeking knowledge of the essential reality of the universe. We ourselves are not yet prepared for that kind of understanding. We can however, for just a moment, experience the vastness of the celestial universe. Prepare to see the vision of the Cosmos."

There was another clap of thunder as the ceiling of the theater fell away to reveal the starry expanse of a desert night. With a dizzying swoop, the crowd was flying among the stars and planets, swirling through solar systems and galaxies. A large comet flashed in front of their eyes, and they cried out as they averted their heads. In the next moment, they found themselves back in their seats, looking at the stage as Marty smugly bowed to their applause.

"And now, Ladies and Gentlemen, you are about to witness the legend of the Flaming Virgin," the magician proclaimed in a deep almost unnatural voice. "Seekers of the exotic, fantastic, marvelous, and miraculous, behold, I reveal to you one of the greatest secrets of the arcane science of Alchemy and Magic. Since time immemorial, the Ancients have classified the forces of the universe into four primal elements: Earth, Water, Fire, and Air. Each is essential for the creation and maintenance of life, and there must always exist, a perfect equilibrium between all four."

"The secret science further teaches that even a mere mortal, if he or she knows how to manipulate the elements, can perform miracles rivaling God. These elect few can even penetrate to the core of the secret knowledge and create life itself."

"Once, there was a great sorcerer who wished to create a woman who would be more beautiful and more pure than any other in history. His deepest desire was to possess her utterly and enjoy the delights of her body for eternity."

Marty then waved his sword and intoned the name, "Azarelis!"

A ball of flame appeared onstage, and Jackie stepped from the center of the spectacle. She was dressed in a costume of red sequins and she truly appeared to be made of fire.

"From the center of the Earth, he called forth a creature of Fire – a stunning virgin, and sent her out into the Air in order to fan her growing passion."

Marty swept his sword through the air with exaggerated strokes and again intoned the name, "Azarelis!" The audience stared in awe as Jackie's feet lifted off of the stage. Then, slowly, her whole body flew over the heads of the spectators and out across the hall.

Arnie was incredulous. He knew that he had not seen any backstage equipment that could produce this kind of effect.

"But the ancient sorcerer, as powerful as he was, made a terrible and costly mistake. He violated the first rule of equilibrium. He forgot to evoke the element of water during his act of creation, and his challenge to God failed."

As the audience watched with admiration, shade by shade, Jackie slowly dematerialized. Again, nothing covered her exit. For a full minute, the auditorium was silent, while darkness and stillness reigned.

Marty's voice finally cut through the hushed silence.

"Never fear. The gods are ever jealous of men and the divine fire they received as a gift from the courageous Prometheus. The cycle of transformation is like a circle of eternal flame – it is self-fed!"

An explosion rumbled through the hall as the fireball on stage disappeared and in its place stood Jackie.

Arnie held his breath while he waited for the crowd's response.

And then, it came. The audience was on its feet.

# Chapter 28
# London

Arnie picked his way backstage to find Marty and Jackie looking tired, but very happy.

"Marty, your performance was incredible. And all of those effects, tell me, where did you get all those new illusions?"

"It's magic, of course," Marty answered with a huge grin.

"No really, how did you do it?"

"Don't worry about it," he snapped. "I'm the magician, not you. You just earn your percentage, which will grow if you do your job."

"Sure, Marty, I didn't mean to sound bossy. It was, just, well rather unbelievable."

"That's the problem, Arnie, you've never believed in me."

Arnie stared at Marty, unsure what to say.

"By the way," Marty continued obviously unaware of his callousness, "did either of you notice any strange-looking men in the audience?"

"What do you mean, strange," asked Arnie, glad that the tense moment had passed.

"I thought I saw a couple of guys wearing monk robes."

"No, I didn't see anyone like that. Why?"

"No reason. I probably just imagined it," Marty said as he looked toward the floor, lost in thought.

"Listen. We need to celebrate," Arnie suggested, trying to lighten the mood. "Why don't you two change clothes and then we can all go out to dinner. I know a little Italian place just down the street that makes lasagna just like Rigatoli's did when we were growing up."

A half hour later, the trio exited the stage door and walked into the adjacent alley. All previous tension had disappeared as they talked excitedly about the show and avidly made plans for the future. Arnie was still confused about Marty's stunts, and even a little concerned, but he decided to temporarily shelve his many questions. It had been a long time since one of Marty's acts had enjoyed this kind of success, and all three of them needed to revel in the moment.

"Once word gets out, I shouldn't have any trouble booking you anywhere you want to go."

"I think I'd like to play at a big hotel in Vegas, and I won't need tigers to get there, thank God," Marty joked confidently.

As they laughed casually, two dark figures in hooded robes emerged from the shadows and blocked their path.

Marty's response was immediate.

He reached behind his back, grabbed a .38 snub-nosed revolver from his waistband, and then fired wildly at the figures while a low growl issued from his lips.

Jackie screamed. Arnie grabbed her and pressed her against the side of the theatre as he stared at Marty in shocked disbelief.

When Marty lowered his gun, the cloaked figures turned and fled down the alley, apparently unharmed. "How did I miss all six times?" the magician stammered aloud.

"Marty, when did you start carrying a gun," Jackie shrieked. "You might have killed one of those men."

"When you are famous, it pays to be prepared."

"What you talking about? You're not famous! I can't believe you're carrying a gun."

"Really, friend, where did you get that? Guns are illegal here," Arnie concurred.

"Don't worry about it, Arnie. I just did. What's the big deal? Come on, let's get out of here before someone calls the cops and I, we, have to spend the night answering a bunch of questions."

"Marty, don't you think you should report this to Scotland Yard?" asked Jackie, looking very troubled.

"No, they were probably just muggers looking for easy pickings. We'll never see them again. Let's go get that lasagna."

# Chapter 29
# Manhattan

Lillian gasped. Nigel almost drooled.

"How is this possible? Are you sure?"

"Of course I'm sure," Sebastian replied as he narrowed his gaze.

Lillian tensed at his words. "Who has it?"

"Some third-rate stage magician."

"How did he get it?"

"I have no idea. We've had people looking for that particular Grimoire for generations."

"Do you think he knows its value?" Nigel responded, barely able to contain himself. "I mean, do you think he'll sell it?

"I don't plan to ask," Sebastian returned smoothly.

"Lillian, you're leaving for London this afternoon. Your objective is simple. Get your hands on the book, using whatever means you have to. Once you have it, eliminate the conjuror. He already knows too much. Nigel will be there to assist you and to make sure the Grimoire returns safely."

Both Lillian and Nigel nodded in silent reply. Lillian noted though that Sebastian emphasized the safe return of the *book*, not her.

"Oh, and by the way, whatever happens, don't open it. No matter how skilled you think you are in occult arts, trust me, you won't be able to handle it. Only I can activate and control its power. If you disobey this directive, your fate will be both unpleasant and deserved."

Lillian and Nigel nodded again. They both knew better than to question Sebastian's instructions.

"Nigel, on your way out, can you ask Jameson to come in?"

"Certainly," Nigel answered icily.

Sebastian's second-in-command hated his boss' personal bodyguard and chief of security. He thought the man brutish and unintelligent and he had no idea why Sebastian thought so highly of his services. Someday he hoped the red-headed Irishman would slip up and Sebastian would fire him.

Nigel and Lillian exited Sebastian's office just as Jameson made his way in.

As he strode into the room, Sebastian reminded himself why he held the man in such high esteem. Jameson had so many qualities that he admired, street smarts, honed reflexes from years of elite army training, raw physical strength, a perfect photographic memory, and most importantly, loyalty.

Jameson also happened to be completely devoid of compassion. A trait Sebastian found most useful.

# Chapter 30
# London

As Agent Arias and Drs. Alexander and Richardson walked toward the security checkpoint, Analia wondered for the second time that afternoon why Arthur insisted they travel through very public channels.

"Tell me again, Dr. Alexander, why you won't let me lead you through a secured area, or at least, into the private first- class entrance?"

"Why would we do that, Agent Arias?"

"Oh, I don't know? Maybe because, according to you, you're carrying a priceless artifact. One that apparently all kinds of beings would love to get their hands on?"

Michael smirked while Arthur nonchalantly shrugged before he replied. "Agent Arias, why is it that you're suddenly so worried about this?" Arthur questioned as he held up the battered black valise. "You didn't seem so concerned back at LAX. What's changed?"

Analia chose to ignore Arthur's question. She had no intention of telling him that her boss had ordered her to protect it at all times.

"It's just not safe, Alexander."

"I appreciate your concern, Agent Arias, but I'm sure I'll get on that airplane and land in Paris unscathed, rod in hand."

Analia pursed her lips before replying. "Look, ten agents would have trouble securing this airport, and all you have is me."

"I know it may seem hard to understand, but this is the best move for us."

Analia felt her skin burn. She knew she could not control this man no matter how much she wanted to.

And then there was the fact that she herself questioned the validity of her own argument. All Analia cared about now was doing her job and getting back to Los Angeles as soon as possible.

Still, though, she was worried about that phone call with her boss. Why was he so interested in the rod? And if he was, Analia figured that others must be, too.

*Something is wrong here. Stay calm, Arias, don't let this guy get to you.*

Analia often gave herself little internal pep talks. They kept her focused. Today she seemed to need them more than ever. For the moment, she gave up on the rod-is-in-eminent-danger argument.

"Well, at least let me take the rod through security. You know I'll have to go through a special access area, given that I have a gun and all. I think it would be safer if I kept the rod while we are separated."

Arthur politely refused her generous offer.

Analia tried to think of a convincing reply. She knew she would have to leave Arthur alone, even if only for a couple of minutes, and she wasn't happy about it.

When they arrived at the security line, Analia was relieved to see that at least it was short, which was fortunate, given the overall congestion at Heathrow.

Michael followed directly behind Arthur as they queued up and emptied their pockets while Analia flashed her badge and headed into a room just off to the left.

She relaxed a bit when she saw the room was full of monitors. Numerous cameras were shooting down at the outside security line from every possible angle, giving her a full view of the area. While she presented her credentials, checked her gun, and submitted to a routine search, she was able to keep an eye on Dr. Alexander from afar.

She scanned the various displays and spotted Arthur walking alongside his precious case as it made its way by conveyor belt to the receiving area. She tried to see the expression of the x-ray technician while he looked at his screen, but she couldn't quite see his face. Analia wasn't surprised though when Arthur was asked to step aside with his belongings.

As Arthur headed to the indicated table a few feet away, Analia noticed that a very tall pale-skinned man walked to within inches of Arthur, and then sat on a chair just behind him. Curious, Analia looked closer and saw that the man seemed to be paying a little too much attention to Arthur, *and* the black leather case.

*Time to go.*

As Analia reached for her things, the security agent assured her it would only take another second or two. Peeved, she didn't understand what the holdup was. Was this guy lingering intentionally? Or was she just imagining it?

"Is there a problem?"

"No, the computer's just a little slow today. We're almost done."

Analia started tapping her fingers on the counter impatiently while she kept her eyes fixed to the monitor. So far nothing had changed. The pale man was still seated, and Arthur was exchanging words with the British customs agent.

She allowed herself a quick glance back at the security guy to see if he was finished with her credentials yet. Finally, he pronounced her cleared and handed her back her gun and identification.

Analia looked back at the monitor as she holstered her 9mm and was surprised to see Arthur shaking the hand of the customs agent and then walking away. And guess who was right behind him.

"Shit….shit."

Analia sprang to the door. "Let me out. I've got to go now!"

The security agent seemed confused by her manner, but the look in her eyes told him not to question. Silently, he complied by pressing a small red button on his console.

With a buzz, the door unlocked and Analia ran through.

She spotted Michael and Arthur just up ahead. The tall stranger was close at their heels. Moving like a panther she quickly made up the distance. Analia then silently walked behind, while she waited for the pale-faced man to make the first move.

Surprisingly, when Arthur and Michael turned sharply toward the departure gate, her target moved in the opposite direction and then ducked into a nearby restroom.

Analia walked right in behind him.

To her left, she saw two men using urinals. Neither was her guy, but they both eyed her questioningly. She raised her left finger to her lips and placed her right hand on her firearm in response. They quickly got the idea, and promptly kept their mouths shut.

Assuming that the pale man must be in one of the stalls, Agent Arias crept noiselessly down the row, peering into each before she moved on. When she reached the final door, she couldn't believe what she saw.

# Chapter 31
# London

Arthur and Michael walked past a row of duty-free shops, as a varied group of travelers sought bargains among the displays of perfume, liquor, and tobacco.

As Michael angled toward a coffee shop, Arthur headed to the newsstand just across the way. Casually, he picked up a magazine and scanned the pages for an article of interest. While he sorted through the various headlines, he glanced up and saw Michael turning the corner, as the line for coffee twisted toward the register. He then looked back the way he came expecting to see Agent Arias, who was nowhere in sight.

Returning his attention to the magazine, Arthur skimmed an article about wind energy while he wondered just where Agent Arias had gone.

As soon as Arthur turned the page, he knew something was wrong.

He continued to read the story, pretending that nothing changed, while he adjusted the weight of his stance and carefully scanned the crowd out of the corner of his eye. About 20 feet away, and closing fast, walked a very tall, hard-looking man dressed in a dark-colored suit. His animal-like gait and close-cropped hair gave him away in a millisecond. Ex-military, mercenary, or black ops Arthur guessed.

Arthur stood his ground and waited for GI Joe to make the first move.

Once he closed the distance, Arthur's would-be attacker angled his huge shoulder to collide with Arthur's arm.

The occultist didn't flinch. He stood completely still and simply gave with the force, pivoting away from the impact.

His assailant stumbled and glared at Arthur through malevolent eyes as he realized that he had failed to dislodge the case.

"Is this what you want?" Arthur asked him with a smirk.

Snarling, the man threw a lunge-punch at Arthur's jaw. Arthur took a stride back, glided slightly to the side, and grabbed the man's extended arm. He then dropped the case and snaked his hand underneath his opponent's now-trapped arm to deliver a head-snapping upper-cut.

Blood streamed down the man's chin from an open gash on his swelling lip, while Arthur finished the Hapkido move by striking his attacker with his own shoulder. GI Joe dropped to the floor with a moan.

As Arthur bent to recover the case, two men wearing camouflage and carrying automatic weapons approached him at a run.

"Hold it right there," one of them called.

Arthur complied by raising his hands above his head and turning toward the commanding voice.

While the two military policemen held Arthur at gunpoint, a white-haired man dressed in the uniform of a British Senior Custom's Official approached the group.

"Sergeant Bicks," he said authoritatively to one of the camouflaged men. "I saw the whole thing. The man on the floor attacked the Yankee and tried to steal that valise."

"That's the way I saw it, too. I was standing just over there," Michael, who had now joined the growing group, offered as he pointed toward the coffee shop.

Holding her state department credentials and badge as she pressed through the gathering crowd, Analia made her way toward the uniformed soldier. "Sergeant, this man is under diplomatic protection."

Sergeant Bicks, now looking very confused, turned to his partner.

"Corporal Weeks, take the bloke on the floor into custody. Be careful with his arm.   It looks like his shoulder may be dislocated," he commanded while he looked at Arthur with a mixture of awe and skepticism.

"And, sir," he continued while turning to the customs officer, "would you please call upstairs and have them run down a copy of the security tape for this station to interrogation room 3A? The rest of us will meet you there," Bicks finished while he handcuffed Arthur and led the party away.

# Chapter 32
# London


Arthur sat alone in the interrogation room, his case on the table in front of him.

On the other side of the two-way glass, Analia, Sergeant Bicks, the custom's officer, and a handful of airport security agents stood hunched over the playback of Arthur's encounter at the magazine stand. While everyone watched the recording for the second time, Analia looked over at Arthur through the darkened window.

It was incredible to her how still he sat. Most people fidgeted, shifted their position, crossed and uncrossed their legs when sitting alone, especially in an interrogation room. But not Arthur, he sat motionless.

*It's like he's asleep with his eyes open.*

"That's it then. Let's go talk to him," Sergeant Bicks instructed as he led everyone into the next room.

"Well, Dr. Alexander, it's obvious that it all happened just the way the witnesses say it did. You were clearly defending yourself."

Arthur nodded toward the Sergeant.

"Just one more thing, I need to look inside that case of yours before you leave."

Arthur seemed surprised by the request.

"It's standard procedure. We need to make sure you're not some kind of smuggler or something," Bicks returned.

Analia looked at Arthur, her face full of apprehension.

Arthur simply smiled and pushed the case toward the soldier. "Certainly, Sergeant, go right ahead."

Bicks reached down and opened the case.

Analia took a deep breath. Obviously Arthur was no criminal, but a priceless artifact was certainly liable to raise a few questions, ones that she would rather not have to answer.

Bicks threw open the lid and looked inside.

All he saw was a case filled with threadbare velvet.

---

As the custom's officer escorted them back toward their departure gate, Analia whispered anxiously to Arthur, "Where is the rod, Alexander?"

Arthur turned toward the custom's officer.

The white-whiskered gentlemen responded by reaching into his coat, and gingerly removing the blasting rod. "Perhaps, Frater, I should be giving this back to you now," he said with a twinkle in his eye. "It's always a pleasure to assist a fellow traveler."

# Chapter 33
# Burbank, CA

Josh Erskine winced when he heard Stone's footsteps in the hallway.

The agent's eminent return signaled the end of his short time alone, and the IIRPP chief felt unprepared for another encounter with the inquisitive bulldog.

Agent Stone had practically become a fixture at the Institute since Arthur's departure, and Josh was feeling less and less able to deal with the growing pressure of his job. Between answering Stone's endless questions, dealing with his increasingly agitated assistant Stan Myer, and reassuring the Institute's psychics, Josh had been stuck in the office for the last two days. Meals had been rushed, and the only sleep he got was the occasional quick nap on the little orange couch in his office.

Agent Stone had been there through it all. A couple of times the G-Man actually stepped out for food or something, but always when Stone returned, he demanded updates on the *operation* in Europe. His inquiries were then usually followed by a whole new list of questions about the Institute. Feeling frustrated, Josh had recently taken to making stuff up just to keep him quiet.

What he found most frustrating was that while Stone demanded detailed frequent reports, he also seemed indifferent to Josh's answers. Outwardly, Stone appeared exactly as he should whenever they spoke. He sat straight in his chair with his head up and eyes focused on Josh's face. Even his gestures screamed attentiveness. But at the same time, Josh felt certain that Stone essentially ignored much of what was said and at times he seemed to already know the answers to his own questions.

If Josh's instincts were right, and Agent Stone was actually uninterested in the whole situation, why then was he there? Why did he make repeated queries into Arthur's whereabouts? And, while Stone seemed ambivalent to the whole "psychic-breach" thing, he simultaneously seemed very interested in the day-to-day operations of the IIRPP. He wanted to know all about the Institute and the responsibilities of its various employees, which was sounding warning bells in Josh's head.

The IIRPP chief had really become suspicious when he told Agent Stone about the Heathrow incident. Before Josh relayed any specific details of the event, the agent had jokingly said, "What? Did someone try to steal the rod from Alexander?"

After Josh explained, Stone acted like his guess was just an innocent coincidence, but Josh felt sure that something else entirely was going on.

# Chapter 34
# Somewhere Over
# The English Channel

Lost in thought, it was now Analia's turn to be quiet while they flew over the English Channel toward Paris.

As she starred sightlessly down the aisle, she ruminated poignantly on the humiliating events of the day.

*How did I lose that guy? I know he went into that bathroom.*

She played the entire scene again in her head, trying to figure out what had gone wrong. She saw herself walking down the row of stalls, the two men to her left, and the final door.

*How could the last stall be empty? Where did he go?*

Analia knew there were no windows or alternate exits. She also knew that the pale-faced man did not come back toward the entrance. It appeared as though he had vanished without explanation, and right about now she was feeling like a total idiot.

On cue, Arthur, who was sitting in the seat next to her, interrupted her session of self-recrimination. "So tell me, Agent Arias, where were you during all of the rod-stealing activity?"

Michael, who was sitting in the seat just in front of Analia, turned around and eyed her curiously.

Analia looked embarrassed as she answered.

"I got sort of side tracked. There was something important I needed to look into."

"Something more important than protecting this rod you seem so concerned about?" Arthur countered, playfully teasing her.

"Actually, that's what I thought I was doing."

He looked at her quizzically.

"Look, I'm sorry. I know I should have been there. Don't you know how stupid I feel? Thankfully, you took that guy down yourself. Where did you learn to fight like that anyway?"

"For what I do it's important to keep in shape."

A variety of colorful replies formed in Analia's mind before she responded.

"I told you we should have taken a separate entrance. You just got lucky. Anything could have happened."

"If we had done what you wanted, that guy would still be following us. He would probably be on this plane right now. Plus, now you know there really are people trying to get a hold of this case."

"And I suppose that you somehow knew all that was going to happen?"

"Well, not exactly. I wasn't sure how it would all play out. I only knew that I needed to be on my guard and ready for possible interference. For a moment I even considered taking your advice and giving you the rod. In the end, I decided to give it to Frater John just to make sure it was safe while the whole drama unfolded."

"You chose to give it to some guy you knew at the airport rather than give it to me?"

"I was even a little concerned myself for a while," Arthur continued, momentarily disregarding her comment. "But I believe that giving into fear is failure. And, I knew that following the original plan would set up future events that in the end would aid us."

"How can you possibly have known all that? What you did was reckless. You put yourself and the rod at risk just on a hunch. You're fortunate to be alive."

"I'm sorry, Agent Arias, I just don't see the world as you do. I believe that the rational mind can get you only so far. It's great at getting us through the day and making intellectual observations. But when it comes to everything else in life, it's rather limited. I've spent years developing senses that most people pay little or no attention to. And I've learned to trust them implicitly."

"You talk in riddles, Dr. Alexander."

"Actually, it's simple."

"Then why don't you try explaining it to me, especially since it looks like we've got an hour here with nothing better to do," Analia challenged.

"Look Analia, you were listening to Josh Erskine at the Institute. You heard him speak of telepathy, telekinesis, and other forms of popular psychism. When someone uses words like "extrasensory perception," these are the things most people think of. While fundamentally I agree with Dr. Erskine's work, I also believe that there is much abuse in the field. No matter how scientific they try to be at the Institute, and no matter what new technology they use, it's difficult to measure the inner workings of another person's consciousness. Results are always open to a variety of interpretations."

Agent Arias nodded in agreement.

"We can however know what we personally are thinking. What if it's only possible to prove to *ourselves* that we do in fact possess senses other than the five external ones? Ones that don't break down with time as our outer senses have the tendency to do."

"Exactly how would that be done?"

"The best way is to start paying attention to those little intuitions we get almost daily."

"For instance?"

"I think my colleague here might be able to provide some constructive examples."

"I often explain this to my students," answered Michael, obviously happy to be included in the discussion.

Analia looked over at Dr. Richardson as he pumped up like a Cheshire cat and slipped her a wink. She felt simultaneously repelled and attracted to his boyish antics. They were somewhat annoying but she also felt drawn to his charm.

"OK. I'm still listening."

"Let's say you lose your keys and while you're looking for them you get a feeling where they might be. You go to the place indicated by your intuition and *bam*, that's exactly where they are."

Analia pursed her lips.

"So you don't like that one. Here's another. Let's say you're a student and your grade is riding on the final exam. You take the test but you're not sure how you did. You start running the questions and answers again in your head over and over trying to figure out what grade you got. You worry and get stressed out and no matter how much you think about it, you just can't decide how you did. Or at least your rational mind can't. Frustrated you go to bed, have trouble sleeping, and then finally you doze off. When you wake up in the morning, the answer is totally clear. Either you know you passed, or you know you didn't. Later, your *feeling* is confirmed when you actually receive your test score."

Analia didn't need to reply. Her eyes said it all. She thought Michael was full of it.

"Let's try another one. Something we've all experienced. You're having a normal day. Everything seems fine. You're going about your business at home, work, whatever. And then, you get this feeling that you're going to get sick. You don't really feel bad. Nothing hurts. You just, *know*. And then, the next day, or the day after that you wake up and your nose is running, your throat is sore, and you feel miserable. And you say to yourself, 'I knew I was going to get sick.' But you don't pay any attention to the internal connection."

"That all sounds great, Dr. Richardson. Too bad it's easy to explain each of your examples rationally. In the first case, that person knew where the keys were. They were just having trouble accessing the right file in the brain. He or she might have been flustered or frustrated. Once the person relaxed, the brain found the needed information and the keys were located.   As for the school test, that's a no brainer. Anybody who has ever taken a test knows that you either know the answer to a question or you don't. My guess is that your mythical person did some mental tallying in her sleep and arrived at the logical conclusion in the morning. And as for the sick person, no doubt his body was giving off some subtle cues all day, a little less energy, a very slight ache, or something like that."

Analia turned back to Dr. Alexander. "I work for the Agency. I know how people think.   Just as you have, I have spent my life developing keen senses of observation and I have learned one thing. Every occurrence has a logical, rational explanation if you take the time to look for it. I don't believe in superstition, and I don't let my mind carry me away to explain simple phenomena with elaborate conjurations. That's just ignorant."

Arthur smiled. "How's that been working out for you so far?"

"Quite well, thank you, Dr. Alexander," Analia replied. "I graduated at the top of my class, I was recruited by the Agency immediately afterward, and I have been moving up the ladder ever since."

"Very impressive, Agent Arias, but what I really meant was, how is that working in your life overall? You know, happiness, fulfillment, interpersonal relationships, inner peace?"

Analia sat mutely while she chose a reply.

"Look, while you think about Arthur's question, let me share a few more examples, ones that might be a little more convincing," Michael offered.

"Suppose during the day a friend you haven't seen in years keeps popping into your mind and you feel the urge to talk to that person. This keeps happening throughout the day until that evening, much to your surprise, that person calls. Or maybe you run into him somewhere like the grocery store or the post office or someplace like that."

"Again, most people rack the experience up to coincidence. But really, what are the odds that you would think of that person on the very same day that he or she made contact?"

109

"Or perhaps you are in your car, stopped at a light, and for some reason when the light turns green, you decide not to accelerate. You can't see anything wrong. Traffic is moving as it normally does. You can't see or hear any signs of danger, but still you get a bad feeling. So you idle the car for an extra second or two. Just then a car speeds through the intersection from a place or view you couldn't have seen in your peripheral vision. Or maybe, a pedestrian, steps into the street from out of nowhere and you miss hitting the person by literally a split second."

"How often has this happened to all of us? How many times have we been near disaster when we avert catastrophe by inches? Did you ever stop to wonder why that is?"

"Better still, haven't you met someone new before, as I'm sure you do in your profession, and for some reason you feel immediately repelled? Later you learn that the person is a liar, a cheat, or a thief?"

"Yeah, I run into that a lot in my profession, Dr. Richardson. We're trained to follow our instincts. I couldn't do my job without it."

"Then have you ever stopped to think about what your instincts are, and why you should rely on them? I mean, where do you think that "gut feeling" originates? Is it a function of the brain?"

Analia sat quietly, puzzling it out.

"I could go on, Agent Arias, but these are the common experiences that most everyone I have ever interviewed has encountered at one time or another. I believe, as does Arthur, that these events are far too common to be written off as chance."

"If these events are so commonplace, then why aren't we all living our lives according to our inner feelings and promptings? And, more importantly, why are most people ignorant of these inner senses you speak of?"

Arthur decided it was time to rejoin the conversation.

"The answer to that is simple. Our society doesn't emphasize their cultivation. At best, most of us get a few hunches here and there and occasionally we even act on them. Unfortunately, we don't credit the source nor encourage it to continue, so its performance is spotty at best. Young children are taught to read, write, and follow the dictates of social convention, and yet almost no one trains their children to heed the inclinations of their intuition."

"Alright, I'll bite. So what happens when someone decides to cultivate these amazing inner senses?"

"Imagine for a moment that the internal perceptions most people fail to recognize, honor, or believe in, could be honed meticulously. The process might begin by simply acknowledging that inner voice that guides. Later, through hard work and dedication, the aspirant might be able to fine-tune the senses to the point where inner consciousness opens itself to powers beyond imagination."

"What if your whole being became an instrument perfectly sensitive to all universal forces, both seen and unseen? What if our consciousness could access the multiple dimensions outlined in M-Theory? Imagine still, the possibility that the strings themselves might vibrate not only under the direction of some universal intelligence, but also under the impulsion of your own thoughts?"

"That sounds like one of those cheesy you-are-what-you-think manuals," Analia commented with a giggle.

"No, not quite, those books tend to oversimplify the whole process," Arthur returned in all seriousness. "If all our thoughts manifested, we would annihilate ourselves. Fortunately, for most of us, ignorance is bliss. We tend to think a fairly equal amount of positive and negative thoughts, which generally cancel each other out. Plus, there's a lot more to the process than just *thinking*. Other factors such as our emotions, our internal belief systems, and our cultural values combine to lend power to our thoughts. To really develop our inner senses, we have to clear away everything that distracts us."

"Like what?"

"Oh, little things like fear and insecurity," Arthur answered with a smile. "Learning to get in touch with your inner faculties isn't easy. It's kind of like training to become an Olympic athlete. It takes the four 'D's, desire, drive, dedication, and discipline. "

"I'm beginning to regret that I even started this conversation," Analia whispered. "And just how would someone go about all this hard work?"

"The information is out there if someone sincerely looks for it. There are many published methods of meditation and visualization that assist in the process. Most have limited applications or are only starting points. Usually the serious seeker attracts a personal teacher or school of training through his or her own desire. If an individual genuinely looks for guidance, it will come."

"So are you telling me that you used some advanced inner sensory work back there at the airport?"

"Well, yes, I did actually. As I've said, I wasn't sure what was going to happen, but I did know that someone was going to try to steal the rod."

"So why didn't you give it to me when I asked?"

Arthur looked at Analia thoughtfully. He understood that his actions had bruised her ego, so he chose his words carefully.

"I didn't give it to you, Agent Arias, only because it didn't feel right. I knew that another opportunity would present itself, which of course it did, when I ran into Frater John at the security checkpoint."

"Why do you call him Frater John? I thought only college fraternities use that word. Judging by the ages of your members, it doesn't seem like that applies here. That, and apparently women are part of it too."

"Many groups refer to their members as fraters and sorors. In English, it means brothers or sisters and we use the terms to signify a spiritual bond."

"No matter what title you give him, it seems to me that it was just a coincidence that you ran into Frater John."

"You call it a coincidence, we call it a synchronicity. The more a person develops their inner senses, the more they experience these little *accidental* happenings. Eventually one who has trained long enough can move through life encountering them all day long."

Analia needed time to digest all they had discussed. Whether she believed anything these two men said or not, it was obvious to her that they believed it, and their convictions were proving to be an increasingly important part of this case.

"Why are you telling me all of this? Do you guys go around doing some kind of road show trying to sell people the secrets of the universe?"

Arthur looked at Michael, waiting for him to respond to Analia's inquiry.

"Actually, I've known Dr. Alexander here for a while and I've never known him to share so much with someone he just met."

Analia paused. She had no idea what to think of this enigmatic man. "So why me, Alexander?"

"That's a question you'll have to answer for yourself," he answered simply.

"Let's just say for the moment that I believe you. Not that I do, let's just say. What if someone with less-than-altruistic intentions were to get in touch with his or her inner senses? What if someone had the power to impel those strings to vibrate disharmoniously?"

Arthur leaned a little closer before answering. "Well, that person might be able to do a lot of damage."

# Chapter 35
# London

Marty sat in his backstage dressing room while he waited for the start of his second show.

As he reached for his costume, his hand shook slightly, reminding him how out of control he felt.

Ever since he opened the book back in the Czech hills, Marty felt like two different people. One was confident, self-assured, a star destined for great things. The other was impatient, paranoid, and cruel.

*Why am I acting like this?*

*It's the book. You have to get rid of it!*

*I can't. It's the reason my show is a success. It's already a huge hit and the house will be packed tonight. I'm only a stupid stage hack without it. If I let it go, I'll lose everything.*

Reluctantly, Marty slid the black monk robe over his head. Why had he chosen this hooded get-up? He couldn't remember, but it seemed to suit him. It said to the world, *here is the Master of the secrets of the Universe.* And Marty liked that. But it also reminded him of Viktor, and the monks, and an experience he was trying hard to forget. He looked at the hood in the mirror, and his mind wandered back to the monastery.

He saw himself walking into the deserted chapel, creeping down the darkened passageways, and making his way to the Chamber of Conjuration. There, in his mind's eye, he saw Viktor summoning his minions.

As Marty looked down at the evil monks he felt disoriented and the room swirled around him, just as it had before. Only this time, when he opened his eyes, he didn't see Grigor standing over him. Where the tall monk should have been, he saw a young helpless woman tied to the altar. And he was seeing her through Viktor's malevolent eyes! Marty watched helplessly as his own hand reached down and grabbed the iron sword. He, *they*, then lifted it and in one swift stroke…

"Marty?"

Jackie, who had been watching her husband unobserved, interrupted his reverie.

"What do you want?" he snapped almost unconsciously, still feeling confused by his vision.

"Marty, I want to talk to you about the part in the act where I disappear."

"Yeah, what about it?"

"It scares me. Last night it felt like I really disappeared."

"What are you talking about?"

"Until you called me back, I was in a dark place, and something there was snatching and grabbing at me."

"It was just your imagination."

"No, Marty, it wasn't. I'm really afraid to go out there again," she persisted.

"Why didn't you say something last night after the show? You seemed fine then. I think you're just making this up to ruin my night."

"No, Marty, I'm not. I didn't say anything before because you seemed so happy, and the show was such a success, and I didn't want to screw things up."

"Look, if you're that scared, I'll get someone else to assist me. You're getting too old to be cast as a virgin anyway," he laughed. "I probably ought to think about replacing Arnie, too. You guys are just going to hold me back," Marty finished as he picked up his sword and stalked out the door.

Jackie stared after Marty in shocked silence. As she walked behind him, she wondered where the thoughtful and loving man she married had gone.

# Chapter 36
# Paris

Analia sat crammed in between Michael and Arthur in the back seat of a taxi as they headed to Frater Roget's Chateau on the Rue LaSalle. While her "partners" looked silently out at the Parisian cityscape, Analia reflected on Arthur's recent communication.

Twenty minutes ago, he received a text message from Josh at the Institute. Apparently Stone was behaving suspiciously and Erskine thought the Agent knew more than he should, something she herself had experienced with her own new boss.

*Could the events be related? Was there more going on here than she realized?*

She still did not believe in all this psychic power, astral workings nonsense, even if she had promised Arthur that she would try. But she was starting to wonder if maybe there was some kind of mundane conspiracy surrounding the case.

Analia was still thinking about the possibilities as the taxi pulled into a long driveway.

When they entered the old, well-maintained residence, a member of Roget's staff informed them that the "messier" was currently conducting a private class in his study and that he would be unavailable for another hour or so.

"Please, come in and I can bring you a glass of wine while you wait," he suggested.

"Arthur, you've got to be kidding me," an incensed Analia was quick to retort. "We're not going to sip a glass of wine and sit around again, are we? I feel like all we've done on this trip is travel, eat, and wait. I'm tired of wasting time. Why don't you go tell this friend of yours how important it is that you speak to him?"

"I have a better idea. Let's go join the class. I'm sure someone with your highly trained powers of observation will find this most entertaining."

Analia rolled her eyes in resignation. At least their presence might move the Frater's session along a little faster.

As they crossed the threshold and followed their escort to the study, Analia tried again. "Perhaps you could tell him that the fate of the world is hanging in the balance? Maybe then he might decide to cut the class a bit short?" she said with her signature sarcasm.

"Or maybe this class holds the key to saving the world? One really never knows, do they, Agent Arias?"

Analia followed behind him, shaking her head the whole way.

Roget, a cheerful-looking man, enthusiastically embraced them with a tight hug and an affectionate kiss and then introduced them to his admiring pupils, tactfully omitting Analia's title and credentials.

As Roget spoke Arthur's name, an excited murmur spread through the class.

Roget smiled while he skillfully reigned in his students. "Dr. Alexander and his guests are here to observe our class. Let's make sure they feel comfortable and see us at our best."

He then ushered Analia, Michael, and Arthur to the only available seats in the room. Once again, Analia found herself sitting in-between Michael and Arthur as she adjusted her weight on the small sofa.

"I didn't realize you were such a big star, Dr. Alexander," Analia whispered once they had settled in.

"He's kind of a big fish in a little pond," Michael explained.

They three giggled while Roget eyed them dubiously.

"Dr. Alexander, we were just about to play a game that I believe is one of your favorites."

Arthur grinned and then whispered in Analia's ear. "I think you might like this one."

Analia smiled politely while wondering why a group of adults were playing some kind of game.

"This technique," Roget continued, "was used originally in the temples of ancient Khem, as a way to train new seekers. Since then, several forms of the exercise have been created and utilized for training purposes. Many well-known organizations, such as the British Secret Service and the Central Intelligence Agency, use some form of it."

Roget looked over at Analia as he finished his last sentence.

Analia returned his attention with a hesitant tilt of her head. She had no idea what he was talking about, but her curiosity was peaked nonetheless.

"The method itself," Roget continued, "is invaluable for developing certain essential skills needed for inner work. And, whatever its original name, it was popularized by Rudyard Kipling in the 19th century in one of his many novels. These days it is referred to as 'Kim's Game.' Some of you may have read the book and will recall this exercise?"

He looked from one face to another and found that a few students were nodding.

Roget then turned his attention to a small table situated in the corner of the room. On it, several objects were covered by a linen tablecloth. With the help of a frater and soror in the front row, Roget moved the table to the front of the class without disturbing any of the veiled articles.

"Concealed from your view are a number of objects of various types and sizes. Your task, once I have removed the cloth, will be to observe each and commit them to memory in as much detail as you can. You will have only the time allowed by this minute-glass," Roget explained as he held the timer high.

"Once the sand runs out, I will replace the linen and you will record your observations on the pad of paper you were given when you arrived."

"I wouldn't want you two to feel left out," Roget said as he handed a pad and pencil to both Michael and Analia.

With a grand gesture, Roget then removed the cream-colored fabric and dramatically turned over the timer. The students gathered around excitedly, jockeying for a favorable position to view the objects, as the grains of sand relentlessly passed through the small opening in the top chamber of the minute-glass.

Rather than joining the huddled group, Analia hung back and peered at the table through a fortuitous opening between two slender sorors.

She first noted some of the ordinary everyday articles, mentally ticking off a watch, teaspoon, fork, penny, and a baby shoe before she moved on to some of the more elaborate items, which included an Egyptian scarab, a winged bull, and several crosses of differing shapes and sizes.

As she finished her scan, she noted that Michael looked intense as he fervently viewed the selection, while Arthur seemed to be paying more attention to the students than he did to the small table.

As the last grain of sand made its way through the etched glass chambers, Roget promptly announced, "time's up," and he quickly replaced the veil.

"Please start your list now and be as thorough as you can."

The students furiously listed as many items as possible, racing against the invisible cloud of fog that threatened to obscure their short-term memory.

As Roget surveyed the class, his eyes paused for a moment on each student. Arthur looked only at Analia.

"Aren't you going to join in, Agent Arias? You haven't even picked up your pencil."

Various replies ran through Analia's mind, including telling Dr. Alexander just where he could stick that untouched pencil. In the end, she decided to simply smile and cross her arms.

After a few minutes, Roget asked the class to put down their writing implements while he called for volunteers to share their results.

Virtually every student in the room raised his or her hand, eager for the opportunity to show off in front of Dr. Alexander. But rather than selecting from the sea of outstretched limbs, Roget walked closer to Analia.

"Ms. Arias, I'm sure that I saw you looking at the pieces on display, and yet you have not listed them."

"That's because I didn't need to. There were only 20 items."

She figured it was time she put these so-called initiates in their place. Their alleged "unseen" powers were no match for the skills she had acquired through her years of training in the real world.

"Please, do share with us then."

Analia nodded before enumerating every article for the class without hesitation. Her plan had been to catalog the most common first, and then to move on to the more elaborate pieces. But for some reason one of the golden crosses kept popping into her mind and she blurted that one out first.

Then, getting a hold of herself, she continued according to plan by reciting the ordinary articles and then completing her list with the scarab, bull, and remaining crosses.

When she finished, Analia glanced around the room and noted that while the students looked impressed, Roget and Arthur's expressions remained cool.

"That's excellent, Ms. Arias," Roget finally pronounced. You didn't miss anything."

Analia was silently pleased with herself.

"However, I think perhaps we should let Dr. Alexander explain the purpose of Khem's game in its entirety before we review your response."

"While your ability to memorize is most impressive, Analia, the secondary function of the game is to observe what types of articles the student lists first. In this way, the personal choices made by the student provide the instructor with a glimpse into the psyche of the participant. And your choices are most interesting."

Analia felt her confidence drain away. *How is he going to twist this?*

Before we look more closely at your choices, maybe we should ask some of the other students to share their observations with us.

Arthur then asked several members of the class to read from their own lists. Without exception, the most eye-catching pieces were mentioned first, while the everyday articles were recorded last or omitted altogether.

"You see, Analia, you started with the simple, smaller items, which is the exact opposite of everyone else here. It tells me as an instructor, that you think in a linear, structured fashion."

"You say that as if it's a bad thing, Dr. Alexander."

"No, it isn't, it's just different from the way we think."

"All except for the cross with a rose," Michael interjected.

"Yes, Ms. Arias, that was very curious. Why did you list that one first?" Roget agreed.

"I don't know. It just caught my attention. Is that important?"

"Only you can provide the answer to that question," Arthur answered.

Noting that Analia looked ready to throttle Arthur, Roget swiftly changed the subject.

"As time is short, let's move onto the final exercise. Tonight we will experiment with a technique generally considered a bit more glamorous than Kim's game."

Roget reached into his briefcase and pulled out a packet of maps and a long, small, clear crystal suspended at the end of a silver chain.

"This is a pendulum and its power is used for a variety of specific tasks. This evening, one of you will work with it to locate a missing item."

He held up the crystal and let it dangle for a few moments. "Can anyone summarize for us the Esoteric Law of Contagion?"

A young man in the front row raised his hand. "Basically it asserts that any two objects that have been in intimate contact will maintain a psychic connection after they are separated."

"Excellent. And are all objects created equal?"

"No, some items have properties that hold a connection, or charge, longer than others such as metals, minerals, or crystals."

"Wait a minute, isn't that just superstition?" a student in the back of the room suggested.

"Exactly what I was thinking," Analia echoed in a whispered tone as she leaned a little closer to Michael. *Maybe at least one person here isn't crazy.*

119

"Is that your impression?" queried Roget as he gazed inquisitively at each pupil.

The class remained quiet, obviously somewhat intimated by their instructor.

"I see that most of you are undecided. That being the case, I propose a little experiment. One for which the piece of quartz crystal is perfectly suited."

Roget spread a map of Paris and the surrounding area on the now-cleared card table and then held up a small red velvet jewelry bag. "In preparation for this session, I concealed a consecrated talisman somewhere in the greater Parisian area. Tonight this bag will serve as a link between the talisman and the pendulum. We will use the city map as a symbolic representation of the actual physical terrain of the area, one that our consciousness is already comfortable using for associative purposes."

"Please join me again around the table."

Analia remained in her seat. She had no intention of participating in this farce.

"Please join us, Analia. I promise you will find the experiment worthwhile," Arthur cajoled.

Reluctantly, Analia slid from her seat and positioned herself next to Roget.

"Emily," Roget gestured to a very quiet, shy soror who was standing a little back from the others, "would you please serve as our operator in this experiment?"

Emily blushed as she nodded her acceptance and stepped forward.

"What do I do?" she asked.

"Come closer and hold the pendulum in your power hand," Roget instructed as he handed her the chain.

Emily reached out with her right hand and waited.

"Now hold the velvet bag in your left hand and take a moment to relax and center yourself."

Roget paused as the woman performed a technique designed to activate her inner sensorium.

"When you feel the energy moving through you, hold the pendulum's chain between your thumb and forefinger and let it hang freely over the center of the map, but try not to move it yourself. Then, concentrate on this question, "Where is the talisman located?""

Emily performed the exercise as instructed. After a few moments, the crystal moved vertically to a part of the map designated as Montmartre.

Roget reached out and steadied the crystal. "Now we must switch maps to one that more closely details the indicated neighborhood."

He then cleared the original map from the table and replaced it with a street map of the area.

"Now we will repeat the procedure."

Once again, Emily suspended the pendulum over the map and this time it moved toward the right-hand corner of the paper.

"Now, very slowly, move your hand in the direction you feel the pull. Not too fast. Good. Now when you feel a strong pulse of energy, sort of a tingling, stop and let the pendulum stabilize."

As Emily completed the exercise, the crystal began to oscillate as it moved in a small circle above the intersection of two streets.

Jean, the student who first suggested that pendulum energy is superstition, looked at the indicated street names. "Hey, that's where Fernando's restaurant is."

Roget grinned and answered, "That is correct.  As Fernando will testify, he and I placed my sun talisman in a small box that rests on the fireplace mantel in the banquet room. Well done, Emily," Roget praised.

While the students excitedly discussed the experiment, Analia sat back down on the sofa and reflected.

*They don't pay me enough for this job.*

# Chapter 37
# Paris

After the last class hanger-on had left, Arthur, Roget, Analia, and Michael sat around the dwindling fire in Roget's study to discuss the purpose for the visit.

"It is good to see you again, Roget. It's been much too long," Arthur began.

"Indeed, mon ami. Tell me, how can we of the Paris temple be of service to you?"

Arthur launched into an abbreviated, but thorough account of the events at the IIRPP, and then his astral encounter when cleansing the stones in northern England.

"Roget, I need to fly tonight to get some answers. Will you and Marie stand vigil for me?"

"Of course, it will be our pleasure. Marie should be home any moment," Roget assured him.

"Is there anything else we should know about?"

"No, just that I have a strong feeling I need to be available on the inner planes tonight."

"You will want to meditate and rest. Would you like to lie down for a while?"

"Let me arrange the furniture in the temple first. Agent Arias, you will have to wait here for now."

Analia nodded. Waiting never thrilled her, but Banes had ordered her to stay with Alexander and that's what she was going to do.

Roget pulled a key from his pocket as he led Arthur across the study to a locked door on the northern wall. Once on the other side, they walked down a small hallway and through another door until finally they arrived at a concealed inner chamber.

In the center of the room was a three-foot-by-one-foot double cube. On top, a candle burned inside of a red-glass lamp. The small flame lit the dim room.

"I will require a bier so that I may work in full trance tonight.  And, Roget, we will need the incense of Geburah."

"It will all be arranged for you," he answered without hesitation.

# Chapter 38
# London

The auditorium was filled to capacity.

Halfway into Marty's second performance, the crazed crowd began chanting, "*Mad Marty...Mad Marty...Mad Marty.*"

When the magician reached the point in the act where the ancient sorcerer violates the first rule of creation, Jackie dematerialized over the heads of the spectators.

The response was huge, just as it had been the previous night.

But while the audience was astounded and Marty was steeped in self-admiration, Jackie was surrounded by darkness in a dimension that defied description.

# Chapter 39
# Paris

Arthur was lying on the requested low couch in the center of the temple, his feet pointing due west. Roget sat in a throne-like chair in the east while Marie sat in a similar chair in the west. In her hand, she held a silver sword embossed with golden pentagrams, the same one she had used moments ago to set the wards of protection.

While Arthur's body lay silently, his consciousness roamed the concourses of the astral plane.

*Clothed in a simple white robe, Arthur materialized in the middle of an ancient city square, a place known as the Court of Seekers. It served as an entry portal for the inner-plane headquarters of his Fraternity, and intently, he crossed the square and made his way to the sacred precincts through an obscured iron gateway.*

*Once inside, rather than walking up the Avenue of the Sphinxes to the great Temple of the Sun, as he normally did, Arthur turned and walked over a small hill to the Hall of the Records. An impressive-looking man with jet-black hair and a neatly trimmed beard greeted him.*

*"My Frater, it is good to see you. I have an important mission for you. Tonight, we need you to defend an innocent who has wandered unknowingly into a place of shadows."*

*Arthur nodded and stepped through the Hall of Images and into a corridor filled with fog. Many visitors found the hall disorienting, especially the inexperienced, but Arthur had made this journey many times and he knew what to expect. This was a place without time, without boundaries, where all possibilities exist at once. In this space, the past persists and the future reveals, to those who know their way, of course. To others...*

*Careful to control his thoughts, Arthur strode into the mist and disappeared.*

*It took him several earthly minutes to reorient his consciousness until in the distance he could see the flickering light of a soul in danger.*

*There, a woman dressed in red knelt in horror as a large lizard-like being menaced at her relentlessly. Fervently, she prayed to God for help as it moved steadily toward her. Behind the astral beast, a swarm of grotesque insect-like creatures clicked their mouths open and shut, emitting an unnerving high-pitched sound, while their misshapen pinchers snapped in the darkness.*

*Usually a natural shield of protection defends misguided souls who wander by accident into this realm. But in this instance, it was easy for Arthur to see that this woman had entered the inner territory through a polluted gateway, one which had immediately attracted the dark. Arthur also guessed that she had been led here against her will, which was probably, the only thing saving her.*

*Long trained in the ways of the unseen, Arthur understood that on this plane of existence, symbols are reality and what you think is what you are, literally.*

*Arthur began his visualization by seeing himself covered in gleaming armor. He then imaged a powerful sword of light in his left hand and a golden shield in his right. On his head he "saw" a crown of silver stars.*

*Next, he imagined at his side a mighty war chariot, drawn by two ferocious sphinxes, one white and one black.*

*The mighty steeds sprang to life and pawed at the ground, anxiously ready to serve their master. Arthur slid into the driver's seat and snapped the astral reigns. As they flew through the air he bellowed a fierce battle cry.*

*"Hekas! Hekas! Este Bebeloi!"*

*The sphinxes responded immediately and both the chariot and sword-wielding warrior materialized in the middle of the circling creatures of shadow.*

*Frantically, the lizard and insect creatures tried to flee, stumbling and scrambling over one another in alarm. Arthur's sword and the jaws and paws of the sphinxes relentlessly sliced through the panicking denizens. With each stroke, their grotesque astral bodies dissolved into a sizzling cloud of smoke, until finally none remained.*

*When the task was complete, Arthur dismissed the astral forms with a single thought and then assisted the woman to rise.*

*"You court great danger in coming to the planes of imagination in this way."*

*He then turned and sketched the outline of a portal. "Return now to your own world of time and space, and do not use this gate again."*

*Gently he pushed Jackie through, and then sealed the portal behind her.*

126

# Chapter 40
# London

Jackie materialized on stage before Marty was finished with his Sorcerer monologue. Her face was white and her legs were unsteady. Marty looked over at his wife, and noting her panic-filled expression, smoothly altered his speech.

Once they were backstage, Jackie expected Marty to confront her about the early re-materialization, so she readied her explanation. She felt certain that if Marty understood what was really happening, he would rethink that part of the act. To her surprise, Marty ignored her and instead played to the crowd of reporters and stage door groupies who showered him with congratulations and requests for interviews.

While Jackie stood alone in silent disappointment, Arnie pushed his way through the throng, and walked straight over to her. Without hesitation he reached out his arms and gave her a protective, reassuring hug.

"Are you alright?"

Jackie nodded.

"I saw the way you looked out there. Everything is not alright."

"Let's talk about it later, Arnie," Jackie suggested.

Reluctantly, Arnie let go and walked over to Marty.

"That was quite a show friend, but I have to talk to you about some parts of the act."

"I think I'm going to stay here a little longer" Marty replied as he eyed an attractive blond who was patiently waiting for an autograph. "Could you run Jackie back to the flat? I'm sure she's tired. We'll talk later."

"I guess," Arnie answered with mixed feelings.

As he walked back toward Jackie, he noted that she looked on the verge of collapse. He had never seen her so unhappy and he truly felt sorry for her.

———————

As the crowd thinned, Marty noticed that the woman he had eyed earlier was still backstage flashing him looks full of promise. He smiled back as she lifted two glasses of champagne in unspoken invitation.

Marty nodded and moved toward her, taking the glass from her outstretched hand.

"You should celebrate. Your show was amazing."

Marty smiled as he sipped the bubbling liquid.

"Your assistant seemed a bit frazzled, though. You know, with the potential your act has for expansion, you might want to consider adding another cast member to the show."

He nodded but said nothing.

"I realize your wife, she is your wife, isn't she, well, she's pretty enough, but maybe the audience would enjoy seeing someone with a bit more flash?"

"Sounds interesting, do you have someone in mind Miss..?" Marty questioned.

"Please, call me Lillian."

"Lillian, do you have any other ideas for me?"

"My hotel room is only a few blocks away. We can talk all night if you want."

# Chapter 41
# London

Marty followed Lillian up to her top-floor hotel suite and tried to kiss her as she opened the door. With a playful smile, she pulled away, slipped her card-key into the lock, and sauntered inside.

After tossing her wrap and purse on a small table, she headed toward the bathroom. "There's more champagne in the refrigerator, help yourself. I'll be back in a minute."

Marty walked to the bar and placed his briefcase on the floor with a *clunk*. Inside was Viktor's heavy book. He now carried with him at all times.

As Marty loosened his tie, his eyes scanned the room. The large suite was immaculate and beautifully appointed. He guessed that Lillian must be paying over a thousand pounds a night for a hotel room like this, and it put his shabby rented flat to shame. He had no idea what this woman did for a living, but she was obviously successful at whatever it was.

The balcony door was open and a soft breeze floated through the air. Every few seconds, a strong rush of wind filtered through the opening and the white gauze curtain floated off the hotel room floor. While watching the hypnotic motion, Marty mulled over his new-found success and reached for another bottle of champagne.

As the magician opened the small refrigerator, he smiled at own his reflection in the mirrored wall behind the bar. "Yes, Marty," he thought to himself as he poured the drinks, "your fortune has certainly changed."

His thoughts then turned to Lillian and her unbelievable body. But the more he fantasized about the sultry blonde, the more Jackie popped into his mind.

*Am I really going to do this?*

*Satisfy yourself, you deserve this. Everyone else does it. It's time for you to get your fair share. Play by your own rules, Marty.*

Marty's internal dialog was cut short as Lillian returned from the bathroom wearing a long, sheer nightgown that clung to her body like a second skin. Unabashedly, she walked straight up to Marty and kissed him deeply.

"Now that I have your attention, let's continue our little discussion."

"What discussion?" Marty stuttered as he tried to reorient himself.

"Mr. King. I represent some individuals who recognize talent when they see it, when I see it. I believe together we could have a long and productive relationship that would be profitable to all," Lillian explained as she leaned over and revealed her cleavage to the best advantage.

"I'm certainly willing to explore the possibilities," Marty agreed as he eyed the display in front of him. "What type of arrangements do you have in mind?"

"Mr. King, I'm no novice. I've studied magic for years. Real magic, that is. I had a chance to look around a bit back stage tonight after your show. I know that your effects are not the result of mechanical devices."

"What do you mean?" Marty questioned suspiciously.

"Relax. There's no reason to be uncomfortable. I just wanted to let you know that we admire your showmanship. We also understand how you do what you do."

"I don't know what you're talking about."

"We know about the book," she answered, the smile now fading from her face. "We also know more about its potential than you, and we know exactly how to harness its power. We can help you. We want to work *with* you. We know that your talent has not brought you the success you seek, and we can change all of that for you. The mere fact that you have the book in your possession," she said as she gestured toward the briefcase at his feet, "shows that you have extraordinary courage and resourcefulness. Just the qualities needed to be a great leader. Besides, I believe we could mix a little pleasure with business and produce a most rewarding relationship."

"How do you know about the book?" Marty demanded.

"I represent a special organization, and we have made an intense historical study of it."

"I don't need you or anyone else. The book chose me as its avatar."

Marty had no idea why he called himself an *avatar*, and he had no idea what the word really meant.

"There are other ways of accessing the Grimoire, Mr. King," Lillian threatened as her eyes narrowed.

Marty reached for the briefcase protectively. As he bent down, he heard something whistle past his head and the mirrored wall behind the bar shattered. Looking up, Marty saw a bullet hole and spider-like impact lines in the broken glass.

Lillian stood perfectly still, staring scornfully out the open window.

Not waiting for an invitation, Marty bolted for the door and ran down the stairs. As he left, he could hear Lillian cursing behind him.

130

---

"You pig," fumed Lillian. "He was just about to give us the book when you shot out the mirror!"

Nigel was drinking his third scotch.

"I was following orders, Lillian. Sebastian's instructions were clear. What is your problem?"

"I told you to take photos from the other building, not to take a shot at him. What do you think Sebastian will do when he hears how you screwed this up?"

"What makes you think Sebastian will do anything to me? You're the one that wasn't following orders."

"What are you saying?"

"Yeah, I was impatient and make a stupid mistake, but you were trying to make an unauthorized alliance with that guy. All you were supposed to do was get the Grimoire."

"How do you know what we were talking about?"

"I was using a directional microphone. I heard every word you said."

"Oh my God, Nigel, you have to believe me. I fully intended to carry out our plan. And then, I don't know, something went wrong. As soon as I got near that book it was like everything I know to be true went fuzzy, and all I could think about was taking it for my own. The Grimoire is incredibly powerful Nigel. Please forgive me. You're not going to tell Sebastian, are you?" Lillian pleaded, her voice laced with fear.

"Well, that depends on how willing you are to convince me that I shouldn't," Nigel answered as he reached over and squeezed her exposed breast, *hard*.

131

# Chapter 42
# Paris

Arthur was thoughtful as he walked ahead of his companions down the Rue de Regina Montmartre. Just a few steps behind, he could hear Roget talking animatedly to Analia. He smiled to himself as he heard his friend boasting to her about his recent trip to Egypt. The story was interesting, but it was obvious to Arthur that Roget was trying his best to impress her. Michael noticed it, too, and he didn't seem too pleased as he brought up the rear.

While Arthur strolled down the ancient Parisian street, he replayed in his mind everything he had seen during his inter-dimensional trip in Roget's temple. After years of highly specialized and intense training, Arthur was usually able to recall even small details of his excursions, and he was now able to effortlessly playback the entire encounter as though he were watching an uninterrupted movie. One by one, he reflected on each image from start to finish. Again he saw the astral temple, the young woman in distress, and the defining characteristics of each threatening creature.

But, the more he thought about it, Arthur realized the astral battle had been fairly straight forward, in occult terms. Either an individual or a group of people had stumbled onto the means to tamper with unseen worlds, which in this case they were totally unprepared to handle. Arthur had then remedied the situation and sent the bewildered girl home. It seemed simple enough. And yet, he knew there had to be more to it than that.

This particular astral journey must have been related to the dreams of the psychics at the IIRPP, as that had been his very clear intention when he set out on his out-of-body errand at Roget's temple. The first rule of any successful ritual or astral travel is to be clear of your *intention*, and Arthur had been specific. The two events had to be related. But no matter how much he thought about it, he couldn't make the connection, and it was bothering him.

*The pieces just don't fit together.    How can a simple astral tampering be related to a possible space-time continuum breach of such magnitude that it could threaten the well-being of the planet?*

The more Arthur thought about it, the more annoyed he became, which was an unusual occurrence for the typically calm and centered occultist.

*I'm thinking too much. I've got to get out of my head.*

The realization alerted him that it was time to take a mental break, so he shifted his attention to the familiar Parisian sites. Ahead he could see the Eiffel Tower illumined by a few stray rays of sunlight that fought their way through the lingering morning fog. To his left was a charming gothic church, resplendent with high arches and hand-crafted stained-glass windows.

As its cheerful bells heralded the break of day, Arthur glanced to the other side of the street and focused on a picture-perfect community park. Meditatively, he looked at the lush green trees, the rows of multi-colored pansies and gladiolas, and then finally the park's main attraction, a double-decked carousel. With a sense of nostalgia, Arthur watched as the painted ponies galloped in circles to prepare for another day of patronage.

But no matter how much he tried to distract himself, his mind continued to wander back to the events of the prior evening. And with them, came the familiar feeling of frustration.

To center himself, Arthur closed his eyes, took a deep breath of the sweet autumn air, and then exhaled with a barely audible sigh. The morning was uncharacteristically warm for this time of year, and his body relished the infusion of energy. As the air rushed in and out of his eager lungs, he blanked his mind and then concentrated on the image of an elaborately robed priestess sitting on a throne with an ancient scroll in her hand.

Almost instantly, a sense of quiet purpose flooded his being. As he opened his eyes, his mind presented him with the information he needed to take the next step.

Slowly his attention drifted back to the present and as he and his companions arrived at their intended destination.

# Chapter 43
# Paris

The intimate café held a special place in Arthur's heart, and he visited the landmark whenever he came to town. The eatery itself was rich with history, and Arthur always felt it provided subtle inspiration for their informal meetings.

In the early days of the 20th-century several esoteric writers had visited this same establishment and often used it as a meeting place to discuss various occult topics. Each time Arthur entered the famed bistro, he felt as though the walls welcomed him with a faint record of these long-ago gatherings.

Fulcanelli was one of the most famous individuals to frequent the café in years past. Over several decades in the early 1900s, he wrote a series of books and papers, detailing the elements of lost ancient esoteric arts. In one of his early manuscripts, he postulated that the famous statues and carvings of the Notre Dame de Paris contain a hidden sequence of symbolic keys, which if read correctly, unlock the mystery of the philosopher's stone. Indeed, Arthur learned through his readings that most of Fulcanelli's writings were based on the formulaic process known as alchemy. Many esoteric scholars of the day even insisted that Fulcanelli discovered the exact combination needed to create the "elixir of life" sometime around World War I. Arthur liked to think that perhaps the alchemist had written some of his best material while sipping cappuccino in this very location.

As the group entered the small historical establishment, also previously patronized by the controversial turn-of-the- century British occultist Aliester Crowley, Arthur quickly made his way to a small corner table tucked away behind a lively screen of greenery. Roget, Analia, and Michael followed behind him.

There, three men sat in hushed conversation. Two appeared to be about the same age as Arthur, and the third looked to be in his early thirties. As Arthur approached their table, they shouted exclamations of pleasure and stood as one to give their friend a hearty embrace and kisses on both cheeks.

They eagerly motioned for Arthur and Michael to join them, but then hesitated when they saw Analia.

"I know what you're thinking, gentlemen, but I assure you it's alright. I've invited Agent Arias to join us and I'm asking you to accept her into the discussions."

"Arthur, she's not one of us," one of the men commented in a whispered tone.

Arthur turned thoughtfully to his long-time friend. "First of all, Jean, in the purest sense, we are all one.  And secondly it's easy to see that Agent Arias is special, if one bothers to look."

With these words, Jean's expression changed and he transferred his questioning gaze from Arthur to Analia. He narrowed his eyes and stared into space just above and around Analia's flame-colored coif.

Analia looked around the table confused, wondering just what the guy was up to, when she realized that his two friends were looking at her the same way.

"What's going on, Arthur? Your friends here are being kind of rude."

"It's alright, Agent Arias, rudeness is not their intent. I'm sure we should be able to get started now."

His fellow fraters nodded their heads affirmatively, and Analia sat down in her seat.

"Well, gentlemen, I see that you have ordered us a delightful petit dejeuner," Arthur exclaimed as his eyes roamed the selection of baguette, croissants, and pain au chocolate.  He also noted that his French hosts had ordered American-style coffee to augment their typical café au lait. Analia wasted no time in reaching for the warm carafe and filling her cup.

"First off, I want to thank you all for taking the time to meet us here so early on a Saturday morning."

"Not a problem, Arthur. Roget said that there was a free breakfast in it if we came," joked Franz, in a slight Germanic accent.

Arthur smiled and then asked Roget to fill everyone in on the essentials of their recent astral projection work.

When he finished, Christian, the youngest frater, was quick to offer a suggestion. "It sounds like a case of someone forcing a medium out on the astral to recover some hidden knowledge, or some such. My guess is that she couldn't handle the job and the darker forces of the realm reacted exponentially to her own fear.  Probably nothing to worry about now that you have rectified the situation."

The others nodded.

"Generally, I would agree. But in this case, I think it was much more serious than a simple astral poaching. There was something unusual about the incident that I haven't mentioned yet to Roget."

Roget feigned insult with a smile as Arthur continued.

"You see, more than her astral body was involved. It was almost as if, how should I put this? It almost seemed as though her *physical* body was part of the projection."

"Why is that unusual?" Analia asked.

"Because, Agent Arias, astral projections involve human *consciousness,* not the physical body. Only the astral body travels to other dimensions. The physical body is not part of this process, at least normally it isn't. I can't imagine this happening unless someone or something is pretty serious about opening a portal into our physical world."

The fraters looked thoughtful as they processed Arthur's revelation.

"Have any of you ever heard of such a thing?"

"I read once about something similar being performed by an Order of the Left-hand Path in the Middle East during the time of the Crusades. If I remember correctly, this organization made use of a specific Black Grimoire," Pierre offered.

At the name of the book, Arthur looked up from his plate with a start. "The Book of the Gates?"

"Yes," continued Pierre, "only a few copies, if any, exist today. Most are reported to have been wiped out during the Inquisition. Allegedly one is housed in the Vatican. Some scholars believe there may be a few others scattered around the globe. No one really knows for sure. The book apparently details how to channel the Princes of the Qlippoth and open the Gates of Chaos."

"This particular group in the Middle East was supposedly wiped out by the Saracen ruler Saladin, during the time of the Third Crusade. And it's a good thing Saladin took care of them because apparently the group's black magicians were quite close to permanently breaching the time-space continuum."

Arthur's expression narrowed.

"There is also a legend that an off-shoot group of this Left-Hand Lodge may have migrated to the mountains west of Russia and taken one or more of the books with them."

"Franz, you know more about occult history than anyone I've ever met. Do you have any ideas how this Middle Eastern group may have come into possession of one of these Grimoires?"

"No, not exactly, but if it made its way off the continent," he stressed while looking over at Analia, "then it could have been sent to any one of the other black cults working at that time. Given that it may have been used by a group in the Middle East, I would guess, based on proximity, that they may have received it from one of the larger Dark Schools that ruled in Egypt before the time of Christ."

"This is all very interesting," Analia interjected, "only, how exactly does any of it relate to what Arthur experienced in Roget's temple?"

"It's possible that someone has gotten a hold of a copy of the Grimoire, or at least part of it, and they are trying to finish the work that was started centuries ago. Or, maybe they are trying something totally new, but just as dark," Arthur answered frankly.

"Why would someone do that?"

"Oh, for the usual reasons, like lust, greed, or power. You see, much of man's desire in the physical world is present in the non-physical world as well. It seems there is never a shortage of such want in any dominion of human consciousness. As I explained to you before, the astral world is a place where all human thoughts and images reside, good and bad alike, and some of them are very dark indeed. Fortunately, we are protected here by a natural barrier between our worlds that few people, corporeal or otherwise, have the power to breach. If, however, a less-than-honorable occult operator *is* able to open the threshold between that world and ours, well then, trouble will definitely ensue."

"Do you think this is what the psychics at the Institute warned about?" Michael questioned, just before he popped another piece of buttered croissant into his hungry mouth.

"Most likely," Arthur answered. "Actually, we don't really know anything for sure yet. Someone is probably using an ancient device, such as the book you describe, Pierre, to stir up some mischief. In this case though, I think there's more involved."

"So what happens next?" Roget asked.

"I was giving that question a lot of thought on the way over here this morning, when I realized that the answer to that lies in the events of the astral projection itself."

"How so?"

"I was able to catch a glimpse of the point of origin when I returned the young woman through the portal."

"Really, where did she come from?" Roget inquired.

"Oddly, it appeared to be a darkened theater. I think perhaps she was performing in some kind of show if you can imagine. I guess that would explain her red sequined costume. Fortunately, for us, I recognized the

137

venue by the signature white columns that framed the stage proscenium. I have seen them before."

For the first time in days, Agent Arias perked up. At last, it seemed like they might be on to something she could actually participate in, *real* people at a corporeal locale. Finally, she might get the chance to do her thing.

"So where do we go, Alexander? Tell me we are leaving soon."

"Yes, we'll leave soon, but you're going to have to wait a little longer."

"Why?" Analia asked, almost scared to hear the answer.

"Because, the theatre is back where we started."

"You're joking, right? We're not going back to L.A."

"No, not that far back Agent Arias. The hall in question is in London."

"So why wait? We can be there in less than two hours."

"We wait because we're not going anywhere near that auditorium until the next show starts."

# Chapter 44
# New York

"Jameson, have you ever heard of an object known as the blasting rod of Hermes?"

"Well, Mr. Howell, you know that I'm not nearly as educated as Nigel and Lillian, but it seems to me that I have read something about it," Jameson replied without the slightest hint of the disdain he felt for his two rivals.

"Do you remember where?"

"I believe it's mentioned both in the *Grand Grimoire* and the *Grimoire of Pope Honorius*. The best description I think, though, is detailed by Eliphas Levi, in *Transcendental Magic*."

"Good, I'm glad that you have kept up your research. You must be both skilled and knowledgeable to work as my chief of security."

Jameson nodded, "Why the interest in the rod, sir?"

"The blasting rod is one of the only occult weapons ever created that can control energies of a particular influence. If used in conjunction with certain seals or matrices, ones detailed in a unique Grimorie, the operator of the rod is able to control and command an incredible amount of power."

"I have personally had a team of people looking for it for years and we recently tracked it to a location on the West Coast. Now, after some rather ingenious maneuvering, the rod is out in the open. And more importantly, a copy of the exact Grimoire we need is now within our reach as well. We've been waiting for this for a long time, Jameson. This is a special time in the history our organization."

"And I'm glad to be a small part of that history, sir. What can I do to assist?

"I need you to help me retrieve both the rod and the book."

"Don't you usually use Nigel and Lillian for such errands?" Jameson asked, immediately regretting his words when he saw Sebastian's face darken in response.

"Lillian and Nigel have been overseas attempting to obtain the Grimoire for the last two days. They have, however, completely screwed it up and so you and I will have to clean up their mess."

"Yes sir, absolutely. If you don't mind me asking, why not bring along a few extra members of my team? I have trained them well and this sounds important."

"I'd love to, Jameson, but these objects are special. They are very powerful and can bend undefended minds. I can't trust anyone. I tried sending my two senior-most lieutenants and even they couldn't handle it. I have to do this myself and you are going to help me. I will, of course, deal with Nigel and Lillian later."

Suddenly, Jameson seemed more interested in the conversation. Nigel was his main competitor for Sebastian's trust and attention, and Jameson couldn't wait to see what the boss had planned for him.

"You should also know that there are some other parties who are actively looking for the book."

"Who?"

"An old sect of medieval monks who think they need the book to solve all of their problems."

"Sir?" Jameson responded confusedly.

"I know, Jameson, it sounds unbelievable, but it's true. This is not something of which I speak often, given that it's a bit of an embarrassment to our prestigious organization."

"Centuries ago, one of our older groups got themselves stuck in an astral loop when they tried to open the Gates of Chaos and usher in the Qlippothic Prince, Azarelis. Their leader, a monk named Viktor, was not properly trained and he didn't really know what he was doing. He did manage after repeated attempts to partially open a portal into our world, until something interrupted his ritual. We don't know what it was, but Viktor and several of his chief monks were sucked back through the portal along with whatever part of Azarelis had managed to form."

"Since then, they have been stuck in a realm that exists in a place between ours and that of Chaos. And they will remain there forever if they don't find a way out. Viktor is trying to use the magician who currently has the Grimoire to redeem himself and his followers."

"Wow, that's quite a story."

"Yes, it is. And I don't ever want to hear it repeated, is that clear?" Jameson nodded.

"You and I will have to get to the book before Viktor does, which I don't think will be too difficult. How Lillian and Nigel let it get away I'll never know. As for the blasting rod, I rather doubt that its present self-righteous protector will relish parting with it, so we will just have to convince him.  My usual occult means of persuasion aren't likely to work, as its current guardian is rather well-versed in that science himself," Sebastian explained with irritation.

"Your skills and talents, on the other hand," he continued while closely examining his manicure, "being more, shall we say, centered in the physical world will be essential.  Do you understand?"

"I understand perfectly, sir," Jameson answered as he flashed a mirthless grin.

"Good.  Get your passport and pack some clothes. We're flying to the UK tonight. Everything else we will need for our job will be waiting for us there.  Meet me at our private hanger at midnight."

Jameson agreed and headed for the door while he wondered about the monks trapped in another dimension. *Where does Sebastian get all of his information?*

As soon as Jameson left, Sebastian reached for his phone and answered the call that had been buzzing in the lapel of his jacket for the last few seconds.

"Don't worry.  I'll have both the book and the rod within 24 hours."

After hanging up, Sebastian walked over to the cabinet opposite his desk and punched a series of numbers onto a shiny black keypad. The doors swung open to reveal a hidden panel.  Sebastian then unlocked a second inner set of doors, which opened to a private altar of worship.

Methodically, the CEO lit two slender black candles that illumined both the dark cabinet and an iron plaque that hung just above the tapers. Inscribed on the plaque was a bronze equal-armed Teutonic cross. In the center, was a black rose superimposed over a silver inverted pentagram. Reverently, Sebastian bowed to the image, and then slowly he began to chant.

As his words echoed through his office, they vibrated through the walls, out into the dark night, and finally right through to a dimension where space and time do not exist.

# Chapter 45
# The Carpathian Mountains
# 1429

The skeletal figure hunched over the small wood table as his long ink-stained fingers clutched the small silver dagger. Passionately, he caressed the cold steel blade while his mind drifted back to the day he arrived at the monastery. Grigor had been born into a small noble family living in the remote hills of Czechoslovakia. Unfortunately for him, he was the third son, which meant that his options were limited. His older brother stood to inherit his father's farm, manor, and holdings while the second eldest went to London for schooling. Grigor had been educated at home by his mother and the occasional tutor.

As a child, he showed tremendous academic ability, but by the time he was a young man, there was simply no money to send him abroad. His family decided his life would be most productive spent as a scribe, and they signed over his small inheritance to Viktor and the monastery. Thus, the life of a monk had been chosen for Grigor. A life he hated.

He was so bitter when he arrived that he had fallen easily under Viktor's spell and his promises of eternal power. From then on, darkness filled his thoughts and he lived only to satiate his desire for control. Hatred fed on his soul, and with time, he had been able to close his heart and mind to the blood that poured through the monastery. Year after year, Viktor sacrificed innocent strangers while Grigor stood faithfully at his side.

Until today.

For tonight's ritual, Viktor had demanded the monks bring him a young girl to sacrifice. All day she had awaited her fate in Viktor's private quarters.

Viktor had insisted that Grigor watch her himself, as he could trust no other monk to leave the girl inviolate. She was unusually beautiful, and Viktor suspected that some of the other monks might be tempted to break their vow of chastity.

Virgin blood was much more powerful than any other, and Viktor needed its purity for a special ceremony. For years, Viktor had been trying to harness the strength needed to open the Gates of Chaos, but to date, none of his attempts had been successful.

After years of failure, some of the other monks had started to doubt Viktor's ability to deliver his promise of power, and he had been forced to hypnotize them more frequently to maintain control. Grigor had come to suspect that he was missing some important part of the ritual, something that his mentor had never had the chance to pass on to him before his death. That, or his teacher simply never had enough faith in Viktor to give it to him. In any case, Viktor's time was running short, and he was starting to get desperate. Recently, his sacrifices had become more frequent, and tonight he vowed to all that he would finally open the Gates.

Earlier in the day, when Grigor had entered Viktor's lair, and seen the girl's sleeping form, something inside of him snapped. He knew her. She was the daughter of Stefan, one of the local farmers and one of the few friends Grigor had known growing up. Generally, his family had kept him close to home, but occasionally as a young boy he was able to sneak away and play in the village. Stefan had always been nice to him, even while others shrunk from his strange looks. The pair had roamed the local hills for hours at a time in those days.

When Grigor entered the monastery, his friendship with Stefan ended.

Since then, he had only glimpsed his childhood friend from time to time when Viktor sent him to the village on some errand. And he'd seen this girl with him. Once, Stefan had even approached Grigor, and Marie had looked up at him with her shining angelic eyes, completely unafraid of his odd appearance.

When he saw her today, lying on Viktor's altar, just hours away from slaughter, the fog that had descended over his senses ever since his arrival at the monastery, lifted just long enough for Grigor to see with clear eyes what Viktor really was, and what he himself had become.

As he sat at his table now and stroked the carved hexagonal hilt of the small dagger, he thought of that beautiful young face, and he knew what he had to do. Stefan's daughter had to be saved. Viktor had to die.

With a long sigh, Grigor slid from his seat and turned toward the battered crucifix that hung from his cell wall. Silently he said a prayer and asked God for help, something he hadn't done since his family condemned him to an unhappy life of servitude more than two decades ago. He knew that he himself was beyond redemption so he did not bother to beg God for mercy. He had been party to too many deaths over the years. Nothing he could do now would redeem his past wrong doings. The best he could hope for was to stop the evil reign of Brother Viktor, and he made an inner vow to accomplish that task at any cost to self.

Grasping the dagger again, he headed toward the door. He stopped when he heard a hushed voice outside his window. In this place, his senses were always on high alert. They had to be. Still, Grigor was surprised. Nobody ever visited the monastery, especially at night. The local peasants knew better.

He flew to the window and strained his eyes. As they adjusted to the darkness, he waited, until finally he saw several shadowy figures move stealthily across the frozen ground just across from the front entrance of the monastery. Each of them carried some kind of a weapon, a knife, a pitch fork, a sharpened staff, whatever these poor men could find he supposed. Viktor had finally pushed the villagers too far. They must be here for the girl.

"Unbelievable," Grigor murmured. "This may be easier than I thought."

Filled with renewed confidence, he again headed for the door, but as he stepped into the hallway, his fellow cleric, Morgan, halted his progress.

A look of distaste crossed Grigor's face. He hated the man. Morgan's entire purpose for living was to serve his twisted master Viktor. Grigor suspected that he hoped to be Viktor's successor and he used all of his natural talent toward that aim. Morgan was smart, efficient, and heartless, the perfect combination for service in this monastery. Grigor considered him a mortal enemy.

"Oh, Grigor, I'm glad I found you, we must hurry. Viktor and the others are in danger. I just saw several armed men enter the monastery from the northern gate. We must warn him quickly."

Hiding his elation, Grigor nodded as Morgan turned to continue down the corridor toward the Chamber of Conjuration. Grigor then moved behind him and slowly reached for the weapon inside his right sleeve.

Sensing something out of place, Morgan turned around and stared intently into Grigor's eyes. As they locked, Grigor felt his mind under attack. The monk was actually probing his thoughts. Morgan was clever, very clever, and he was renowned in the monastery for having strong psychic powers. At any other time, Grigor might have panicked, but not now. He had made a commitment and nothing was going to stop him.

144

He willed his mind to think of Viktor's safety and after a few moments, Morgan loosed his mental grip.

With a final glare, the wicked monk then turned back around and continued down the hallway.

This time, Grigor didn't hesitate.

In one swift motion, he grabbed Morgan from behind, locked his right arm around his neck, slid the dagger from his sleeve, and thrust the silver blade through the shorter monk's robes.

As though guided by some higher force, it pierced Morgan's ribs and landed right in the center of his rancid heart.

Morgan cried out, but all he could manage was a gurgling sound as blood spewed from his mouth and the life-force drained from his body.

# Chapter 46
# London

Jackie seemed to be somewhere else as she listlessly swallowed the bitter liquid Arnie insisted she drink. Slowly, a warm sensation spread through her limbs and torso, numbing the pain she felt both inside and out. She stared silently at Arnie while he cooked the only meal he knew how to make.

"You know I'm not going to eat those eggs, Arnie."

"Come on, Jackie, have you seen yourself lately? Your face is pale, and you look like a light wind could blow you over. You need my pepper and cheese omelet."

"What I need is to know what is wrong with my husband."

Arnie didn't immediately reply. Marty had been acting like a different person since he had driven alone through the Czech Republic, and Arnie was at a loss to explain the change. Marty was grouchy, on edge, and utterly obsessed with the new show. Arnie barely recognized his childhood friend, and it was obvious that Jackie had serious concerns about the new routine.

But, at the same time, Arnie felt torn. He had been waiting for a hit just as long as Marty had, and this ancient monk-like sorcerer routine was certainly showing promise.

"Well, the audience seems to like his act. And the next five shows have already sold out."

"Oh, come on, Arnie. Have you paid attention to anything that's going on?"

"What do you mean?" Arnie returned, feigning ignorance.

"What do I *mean*? So I suppose that you haven't noticed that there's absolutely no equipment backstage? How do you think Marty is performing all of those amazing new tricks? When I start to fly, I can see the audience 30 or 40 feet below me, Arnie, and even I don't know how I'm doing it. There's absolutely no support!"

Arnie looked thoughtful and started to reply, until he realized that Jackie was just getting started.

"And when I dematerialize," she continued, her voice a mixture of sarcasm and fear, "I start to lose consciousness and fall into a deep sleep. One minute I'm in the auditorium totally alert, flying through the air, and the next I'm alone in what seems like a dark cave and I can't seem to think or move with any amount of control."

"And then these creature things surround me. They claw at me with sharp talons and they chomp at the air in front of me with decaying jagged teeth that stink! They taunt me, Arnie, and there's nothing I can do to drive them away. And what's worse, the longer I'm there, the more *they* seem real while the show and the stage feel like the distant fantasy."

"The first time Marty called me back before they got too close. Then, last night, it was as if Marty and the audience had vanished. And the more afraid I became, the closer the creatures moved. It was if they could sense my weakness, Arnie, and they fed on it. Thank God that man appeared just before they reached me."

Jackie looked toward the floor, her voice now almost a whisper.

"If he hadn't, I don't think Marty would have been able to bring me back. I think I may have disappeared for real."

Arnie gawked at Jackie, his mind unwilling to accept what she was saying.

"Then, when I come back into the burning circle, I feel like I am actually part of the flames, and they are fueled by my own energy."

"Jackie, what are you saying?" Arnie pleaded.

"It's like I'm part of the fire Arnie, living and breathing with it, and yet, I don't get burned."

Marty stared at Jackie, words temporarily eluding him.

"How can this be happening? How is Marty doing it? Are any ideas coming to mind, Arnie?" Jackie challenged.

"Not immediately," he responded with a shrug.

Frustrated, Jackie shook her head and sprang from her seat. "I need you to take this seriously, Arnie. Something is very wrong here, and we need to do something about it."

"OK, sit down."

Arnie looked around the room as though an answer might be embedded in the beige-colored walls while Jackie returned to her place.

"Have you asked Marty about it?"

"He told me that I was imagining it all and that if I couldn't handle it, he could easily replace me."

Arnie couldn't believe what he was hearing. Marty had always been devoted to Jackie. He felt a surge of sympathy and an overwhelming desire to hold Jackie close. He didn't know what was going on with

Marty or the show, but he knew that he wanted to be there for her. Deftly, he slid across the couch and put his arm around her shoulders.

"I'm sorry. We'll figure this out."

Feeling momentarily weak and needy, Jackie welcomed his warm, reassuring arms and she laid her head on his shoulder. It was obvious to Arnie that Jackie was genuinely frightened and he had no doubt that she believed every word she said.

As Arnie's gaze roamed Jackie's slender body, his mind wandered back to the fantasy that Marty's magic mirror had shown him the night before. Again, he saw himself holding Jackie in front of a beautiful suburban home, his lips passionately kissing hers. At that moment, Arnie wanted Jackie like he never had consciously wanted her before, and just for a quick second he even allowed himself to believe that maybe someday it could happen.

"What a touching sight," a hate-filled voice interjected from behind.

Jackie and Arnie snapped their heads around and saw a red-face Marty standing in the open doorway.

"Marty, I.."

"Don't even try to explain this, Arnie. How long has this relationship of yours been going on?" Marty accused as he glared at Jackie.

Jackie jumped off the couch and flew to Marty's side.

"There's nothing going on, Marty, and I wish I could say the same about you," she returned with fire in her eyes. "I saw you eyeing that woman backstage tonight. Where have you been for the last four hours?"

Marty was stunned. He hadn't realized that Jackie had noticed Lillian, and he was embarrassed by his own behavior.

"Well, Marty? I'm waiting for an answer."

Humiliation quickly turned to anger, and Marty seemed to lose whatever hold he still had on reality. He stormed across the room, reached into his jacket pocket, and leveled the .38 at their heads.

"Get out, both of you. Don't come back here. And don't come back to the show. You're fired. I never want to see either of you again."

Jackie and Arnie exchanged unbelieving glances. Either Marty was on drugs, drunk, or experiencing a psychotic break. They paused, unsure what to do, until Marty made up their minds for them.

"I'm serious. Get out now or I will kill you both."

# Chapter 47
# London

Analia walked rapidly down Regent Street, still fuming from her latest argument with Arthur.

Banes had given her a single directive, *stay with Alexander and the rod,* and she was about to mess even that up.

After arriving at Heathrow just after noon today, Analia suggested a quick visit to the theatre to do some preliminary recon work. Arthur had a different idea. He insisted they remain in their hotel and wait for the evening show. The only explanation he offered was that he needed to watch the entire act before he could determine for sure what was going on.

And the worst part of it all was that Arthur had also insisted on leaving the rod with hotel security. When they checked in, he wrapped the black case in brown parchment and then deposited it in the hotel safe.

Analia had vehemently objected, while Arthur refused to listen, or explain his outrageous behavior.

So here she was without a rod to protect, or an occultist to guard. She had no idea what Arthur was even doing at this moment, although she figured he was probably meditating or something like that.

Following orders had gotten her exactly nowhere so far, and she decided it was time to start following her *own* inner guidance. Especially since she had been on this case for days and had, up to this point, accomplished nothing.

Well, almost nothing.

At least she had managed to get some personal information on Dr. Alexander. When they first began their journey, Analia sent a message to her old assistant back at the Agency and asked her to do a background check on Alexander. When they landed at Heathrow today, and Analia was able to turn her phone on again, she saw that the information she wanted had arrived while they flew over the English Channel.

For the second time now, Analia reviewed Arthur's curious personal profile.

He had no criminal record, but he did own several pieces of expensive property. He also had a diverse financial portfolio, including a majority interest in several corporations. The data in itself was not unusual, but Analia was suspicious given that all she knew about Arthur professionally was that he was a college professor.

As she considered the possibilities, several ideas came to mind. None of them were satisfying. She assumed he must be a trust fund recipient or otherwise have inherited the money, except for some reason, that seemed wrong. She made a mental note to delve a little deeper into Arthur's mysterious background when she had the chance.

Other than that, Analia had zilch, and she decided it was time to turn things around. As she walked down the crowded sidewalk, she used her phone to search the Internet for local theatres. Arthur, being a practical man, had most likely chosen a hotel near the auditorium they were to visit that evening.

Instantly, the search engine presented a long list of shows currently playing in the area, and Analia avidly scrolled down the list of titles. Most were either big-name Broadway musicals, or small dramatic re-interpretations of old classic plays. Analia thought it unlikely that there would be any kind of occult shenanigans going on in any mainstream production, so she decided to look for other types of performances. On impulse, she typed in the word *magic* just to see what would come up.

Immediately, a picture of Marty the Magnifico floated across her screen, his red lips and glowing eyes promising her a *personally* unparalleled magical experience.

Intrigued, she read the show description and scanned the attached map of the city. The venue was only a mile away, and she knew without hesitation that she had a winner.

———————

As she neared the theatre, Analia reviewed the mental plan she had formulated during her brief walk. All she would do was look around as unobtrusively as possible just to see if she could find anything that looked like this book Arthur described. That, and maybe ask a few basic questions.    When she arrived, it quickly became apparent that her plan would need to be altered. All of the entrance doors were bolted shut, and the theatre appeared completely empty.

"Don't they need to rehearse or something?" she asked herself as she continued to bang on the glass doors.

What she didn't know was that Marty had fired half of his crew the night before in a crazed frenzy, and the rest were not scheduled to arrive until just before the performance.

She walked around the building to see if she could find another entrance. As she turned the corner, Analia saw two strange-looking men wearing long brown robes, hovering around a door at the other end. She moved closer and saw that they were attempting, quite unsuccessfully, to break and enter.

"Hey, what are you guys doing there," she called out as she sped up to intercept them.

At the sound of her voice, they stopped what they were doing and sprinted down the alley in the opposite direction.

Analia broke into a run.

As they rounded the backside of the building, the taller of the two men turned to the side and Analia recognized his profile at once. He was the same man she had chased down, *and lost*, at the airport.

"Déjà vu," she thought to herself as she followed more insistently. She pumped her arms and legs as fast as she could, until she turned the corner herself.

What she saw there stopped her in her tracks.

The two robe clad men had disappeared, *again, a*nd in their place, stood two well-dressed men in suits. One was smoking a pungent cigar and the other was leaning against a long black limousine.

She recognized Sebastian Howell immediately.

# Chapter 48
# London

"I wish you would get some sleep, Jackie. We can always talk about it more in the morning," Arnie suggested as he made up a pallet for himself on the floor.

After Marty's meltdown, Jackie and Arnie had streaked through the midnight rain to Arnie's small hotel, several blocks away.

After an hour or so of sobbing, Jackie recovered a bit and starting asking Arnie questions. Ones he felt ill-equipped to answer. Simple queries like, "what are we going to do, Arnie?" left him feeling utterly helpless.

At one point, Jackie reached for the phone to call the police. She was worried that Marty might hurt himself or someone else with that gun of his, and she couldn't think of anything else to do.

Arnie stopped her before she finished dialing the number. Unlicensed gun possession in the UK was a major offense, and Arnie feared that his best friend could end up in a foreign jail for years.

Arnie then suggested psychiatric help, until Jackie pointed out that if she told a doctor the whole story, she herself would probably be the one they would commit. Moreover, the whole *gun* thing would undoubtedly come out, and they would be right back to that possible prison sentence.

Feeling desperate and inadequate, Arnie suggested again that Jackie lie down and get some rest.

"Arnie, I'm not going to be able to sleep until we do something. I think it's time that we started talking about what's really going on, no matter how uncomfortable it is or how crazy it seems."

"Alright, you first."

Jackie shook her head. "Look, we know something extra-ordinary is going on here. Stunts without contrivances, Marty acting like he is possessed by demons, and me visiting alternate dimensions. I think we should seriously consider the possibility that something supernatural is going on."

No matter what had happened during the show, Arnie was not ready to go there yet. He had worked professionally in the magic business for a long time and he knew that all tricks, no matter how convincing, could always be explained. Experience had taught him that lesson. At the same time, he did have to admit that Marty's new routine certainly had him baffled. "Jackie, do you realize what you're saying? Do you really think that Marty is possessed?"

"All I know is that whatever is going on must be related to that book that Marty's been carrying around since he returned from his so-called road trip. He never lets it out of his sight, Arnie. He even sleeps with the damn thing. Last night I saw him put it under his pillow! How weird is that?" Jackie finished.

"Let's suppose just for now that you're on to something. That this is more than a nervous breakdown or early mid-life crisis on Marty's part, and that you aren't imagining being part of the fire. What then do you think we're talking about?

"I don't know, Arnie. Maybe Marty's mixed up in some kind of black magic."

Arnie gawked at her.

"You know, sorcery or something."

Arnie rolled his eyes.

"Heck, I don't know, maybe Marty was abducted by aliens in hills of the Czech Republic. Or maybe he met Count Dracula on the road to Ostrava. I don't know, Arnie, stop looking at me like that. All I know is that something or someone has warped Marty, and we need to find out what."

Arnie stared across the room while a pained silence hung in the air.

"Jackie, I don't know anything about stuff like this, but it so happens that I have a cousin here in London who does."

"Don't tease me, Arnie. I'm not in the mood."

"I'm not kidding, Jackie. He works here for one of those whacked-out tabloids that chase space-ship sightings and such. He used to visit the family back in Toronto when I was a kid. I haven't seen him in years, but I know where he lives and maybe he can help us."

"Are you serious, Arnie?"

"Yes, his name is Moshe, and he used to give me the creeps when I was a kid. His grandfather was a Jewish mystic and he trained Moshe in a lot of ancient mysteries and the like. He loves research and has a degree from Oxford, if you can imagine, even though now most of his work centers around crop circle theory. He might know something about that book Marty's carrying around, or at least he might know where to find some information about it."

"Do you think he would be willing to help us?"

"Well, we can ask."

# Chapter 49
# London

"I'll tell you, cousin, I know you have never have taken my interest in mysticism seriously and, to be honest, I haven't always been a diligent student," Moshe Roth said with a smile, "but since I started working for the paper, oy vey, I've seen some strange things."

"I know that about you, Moshe. That's why we came to see you. We thought you might be able to help us."

"Sure, if I can."

Not quite sure where to start, Arnie suggested that perhaps Jackie should begin.

"Chicken," Jackie thought to herself as she narrowed her eyes at Arnie.

Nervously, Jackie recounted the events of the last few days, explaining in as much detail as possible her strange experiences during the show, Marty's hostile and erratic behavior, and then finally how her husband had been carrying around an odd black book.

Moshe was quiet and attentive while Jackie spoke, seemingly taking in each of her words thoughtfully. His expression remained neutral until Jackie spoke of the book, at which point he sat straight in his chair and looked at her inquisitively. When Jackie finished, Moshe sat silently while he processed the details of her story. For a moment, Arnie was worried that Moshe might throw them both out.

"Tell me more about this book Marty is carrying around."

A little surprised that Moshe was still talking to her, Jackie described it as best she could.

"Well, it's large, black, and I think the cover is made of leather. Marty won't let me or anyone else get near it, so I don't know much more than that."

"Did you ever see the cover? Maybe a word or two of the title, or a design?"

"Well, I did sort of get a quick peek once. It was only for a second or so. I didn't see a name or title. I don't even think there were any words on the cover."

Jackie bit her upper lip while she dredged her memory for answers. "There may have been some kind of picture on the cover. It seemed like there was a lot of overlapping lines, maybe some kind of flower?" Jackie relayed more as a question than a definitive answer.

"What kind of flower."

"I have no idea."

"Come on, if you had to guess."

"I'm not sure. It could have been a rose."

"And there was no title?"

"Not that I saw, but during the show Marty keeps referring to some guy named Azarelis. Does that help?"

"It might," Moshe replied as he got up from his chair. "That name sounds familiar."

While Moshe headed to a large bookcase at the far side of the room, Jackie decided it was time to find out if he believed anything about her story.

"So what do you think, Mr. Roth? Does any of this sound real, or do you think that Arnie and I are crazy?"

Moshe replied quickly and honestly. "I believe you. What would be the point of making up such a story?"

Jackie smiled with relief while Arnie looked incredulous.

"I have heard of these strange books on magic called Grimoires. Judging by the way you describe Marty's recent change in behavior and the magical elements of his new show, I would say that it sounds like the work of one of these ancient books."

"What about the name Azarelis? You seemed to think that might be important," asked Arnie.

Moshe turned his head toward his cousin and continued. "Yes, it sounds familiar. So does a picture of a rose. Wait a minute."

Carefully, he reached toward the uppermost shelf of the built-in bookcase and looked through the titles. After a few moments, he pulled down a small, well-worn book titled, *The Sixth and Seventh Books of Moses.* Moshe then headed back to his seat and set the book down on the table for Jackie and Arnie to see.

"I thought there were only five books of Moses?" Jackie asked.

"There are. They comprise the Pentateuch, what we Jews call the Torah or Law. They are also the first five books of the Old Christian Testament, Genesis, Exodus, Leviticus, Numbers, and Deuteronomy.

The Sixth and Seventh books are compilations from the Faustian schools of magic in old Germany.  While they are unknown by most, they are quite famous among the Pennsylvania Dutch communities in America."

Moshe flipped nimbly through the yellowing pages looking for something in particular.

"Let me see, yes, here it is.  According to this, Azarelis is the name of one of the four great Princes of the Qlippoth."

Moshe sat back in his chair.  "Wow.  That's a rather nasty energy."

"What do you mean?   What's a Qlippoth?"  Arnie and Jackie questioned in unison.

"Basically, a Qlippoth is just plain old ancient evil."

Arnie and Jackie exchanged confused glances.

"Let me try to explain.  In Hebrew, the word Qlippoth means, *husks* or *shells*, something that is left over after the life force is gone. Jewish mystics, or Qabalists, believe that our world is only one in a long succession of worlds and universes that have existed and will exist into infinity, each one shaped uniquely by its own Divine Plan.   Each universal plan in turn is defined by its own laws, principles, and operating procedures."

Jackie and Arnie looked completely confused.

"You know, basic scientific formulas and natural laws."

Jackie and Arnie were still lost.

"Like gravity or motion or evolution. Anyway, the theory states that each new universe carries with it a part of each prior one, referred to as 'husks.' These husks are types of living energy that remain in our present world. In relationship to us, some are higher, divine, and guiding entities, while others are quite the opposite. These Qlippothic husks are leftover demonic beings from a prior Cosmic Order who have managed to survive in our present-day universe. Some Qabalists believe that they preside in a realm of unbalanced force and that they are in fact," Moshe was now directly reading from the book, "the furthest thing from God that has enough power to remain in existence."

Jackie and Arnie looked at each other again.  "I'm sorry, Moshe, all of this is all new to us and we just don't understand.   Are you talking about real demons that can reach into our world and commit evil acts?"

"Yes, I am.  The Qabalists explain their influence on our world using what they call the Tree of Life."

"Do I want to know what that is?" questioned Arnie, resistance resonating in his words.

Moshe looked to Jackie who nodded for him to continue.

157

"Any thorough explanation could take days to relay, so let me just try to give you the basics. The Tree of Life is a schematic of the universe and God's creation. The tree itself depicts 10 sephiroth or attributions of God and 22 interconnecting paths."

"Here, let me show you a picture."

Moshe reached for an old book on his coffee table and turned to a page displaying the desired diagram.

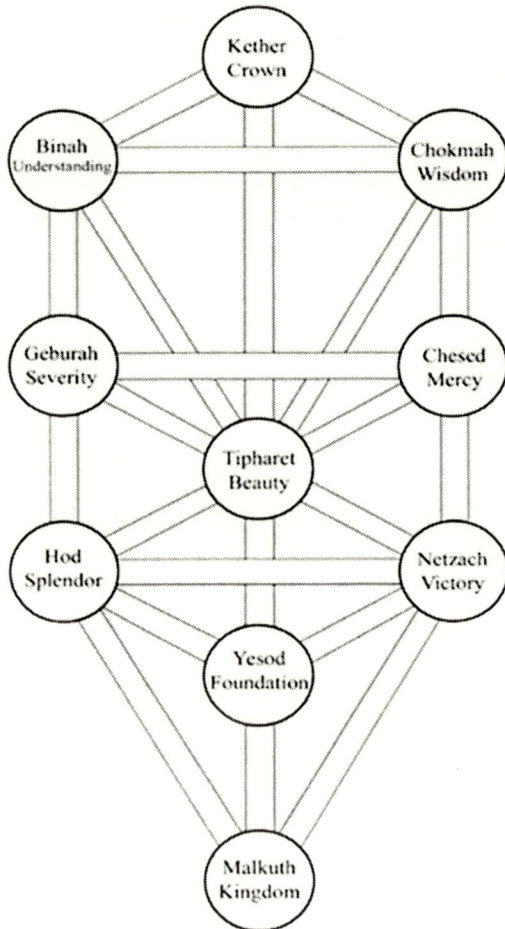

Arnie and Jackie perused the illustration with interest, noting both the English names, and Hebrew transliterations of each Sephiroth.

"In a nutshell, God created the universe beginning with Kether and then stepping down His energy though the next eight sephiroth, finally creating Malkuth, the physical world we live in. Notice that every circle on the tree is in balance. Kether complements Malkuth, Binah does the same with Chokmah, and then down the line in pairs, Chesed to Geburah, and finally Hod to Netzach. The sixth Sephiroth in the middle, Tipharet, is then the central balancing point or place of equilibrium."

"All except number nine, Yesod," Jackie noted. "It's all alone."

"You're very observant. Yesod represents the astral world or place of imagination, and it is balanced by an 11th Sephiroth that is not drawn on this diagram. If you're interested, I can tell you more about it at another time."

"What is important for our purpose is to understand *how* the Qlippoth manifests in our universe. And to do that, all we need to do is turn our attention to Sephiroth four and five, Chesed (Mercy) and Geburah (Severity)."

"Some Qabalists believe that our world today is out of balance at the juncture of these two important attributions of God. That, as a race of humans, we have become too *Geburian* with our severe judgments and treatment of one another, and that we have for the most part turned away from *Mercy* or Chesed where God loves all equally. This unbalance has created a co-existing dimension to ours where evil entities are fueled by our own negativity. Our thoughts and actions actually provide them with the environment they need to thrive."

"Are you saying," Jackie questioned, "that humans are responsible for creating Qlippothic demons?"

"Creating, no, only God can do that. We only sustain and nurture them. That's the theory anyway."

For a moment, everyone in the room was silent.

"So how does this Grimoire Marty is carrying around relate to this?" Arnie questioned in an attempt to bring the conversation back to reality.

"Grimoires are the keys to this dimension of malevolence. Normally our world is protected by four Cosmic Gates that corral these entities and keep them in their own pen of chaos. Some Grimoires, though, detail instructions for unlocking the gates and unleashing these Qlippothic energies into our own world."

"Why would anyone want to do that?" asked a wide-eyed Jackie.

"Who knows? In Marty's case it looks like he's using their power in order to perform his show. I have no idea how he's doing it or what the consequences will be, but it can't be good."

"So what can we do?"

Moshe looked pensive before he replied. "I have no idea. This is way beyond me. I only know some of the theory, not the practical application stuff."

"Great. So we're right back where we started," muttered Arnie in frustration.

"Maybe not, I said that I don't have the knowledge you need. It so happens I may know someone who does. He's an American actually, and I'll send him a message immediately. Until we get some answers, I think you two should stay away from Marty and that show. And you'll need some protection, too, in case he decides to come looking for you."

"We'll be fine," returned Arnie.

"Mate, this Azarelis your friend is summoning is quite literally the Prince of Darkness. You need some sort of defense."

"So what do we do?" Jackie asked.

"Well, regardless of the source of negative energy or its point of origin, there are generic ways to insulate oneself from their influence. It's simply a matter of belief and conviction."

"What do you suggest, Mr. Roth?"

"I think I will make an amulet for you both. I'll put a special talisman inside, which should give you at least a little protection against other-worldly beings."

Again Arnie and Jackie exchanged looks of doubt.

"I know it sounds kind of ridiculous. Let me tell you a story and then you can decide for yourself. Remember our great uncle Abraham, Arnie?"

Arnie nodded as though unsure if he *wanted* to remember.

"Now there was a Qabalist. He's the reason I first started studying the subject. Years ago, when you were just a child, he and Great Aunt Ruth lived in a large apartment in the then newer part of Prague. One evening, several of us gathered for a sort of family reunion, about 12 of us, I think. I remember because Aunt Ruth was so proud of her new full-length mahogany dining table that she invited the same number of guests as seats so that the table would be perfectly balanced."

Arnie put his hand over his face and shook his head slightly. Moshe had a tendency to get wordy, and he was praying that his story wouldn't be too long.

"Anyway, during the course of the dinner, we started to hear sirens and alarms. Apparently, a fire had broken out in one of the other apartments, although we didn't know how close it was to us at the time. Unbelievably, when we tried to leave the table, Uncle Abraham insisted that we stay seated and continue our celebration.  He said that he had everything under control."

"That sounds like Uncle Abraham."

Jackie smiled.

"After that, the old Qabalist went over to his desk and pulled out a square piece of parchment paper and a book named, *The Sepher Ratziel*. He then wrote out several characters from an alphabet he called Malakhim, and taped the parchment to the southern wall of the room."

"Reluctantly, we continued eating and toasting, trying, you understand, to ignore all the commotion outside while simultaneously we were ready to run from of the apartment if we needed to.  Really, I don't know how the old man kept us in our seats.  It was like we were hypnotized or something."

"After a while, the noise died down and we never saw any smoke or flames, so we assumed it was either a false alarm or that the fire had been isolated and dealt with quickly."

"Imagine how surprised we were when hours later as we were leaving, we saw that the fire had almost gutted the two apartments next door to Abraham and Ruth's. In fact, on the neighbor's side, the wall was charred, while on our side, the wall wasn't even warm!"

Jackie and Arnie waited for him to finish the story until after a while they realized he already had.

"Moshe always was a little unusual," Arnie thought to himself. "So you plan to do something similar with us."

"Yes, give me an hour, and I'll transcribe a pair of protection seals on parchment and you can both carry them as an amulet. It may sound foolish, but if you believe it works, it will.  Faith is the strongest protection there is.  Most people have no idea how powerful their own thoughts and convictions are."

And then Moshe added, "Well, at least it can't hurt," he said with a shrug of his shoulders.

As Moshe withdrew into his study to begin his task, he suggested that Arnie and Jackie visit a nearby esoteric bookstore to see what else they could learn about Azarelis. He also promised to contact his friend in the States and to do some research online.

Jackie and Arnie agreed and then made a date to meet Moshe back at his apartment in the late afternoon.

161

# Chapter 50
# Burbank, California

"I'm telling you, Stan, something here isn't right. Agent Stone is definitely not what he appears to be."

For the last few minutes, Stan Myer had sat in Josh's office listening to his boss' concerns about Agent Stone. Apparently the G-man was snooping around the Institute, looking into files he should have no interest in and interviewing employees who had nothing to do with the visions of their psychics. Josh had even been informed that Stone was now interrogating the custodial staff.

Stan became more nervous with each word Josh spoke. *Does Stone know? Has he figured out that I'm involved?*

While Josh droned on, Stan did his best to hide his growing fear.

"And you know what, I think he's even listening in on my phone calls and hacking into my text messages."

"Come on, Josh, how could he be doing that? Wouldn't he need a search warrant or something? Surely, this case, especially given its incredibly non-mainstream nature, wouldn't justify that kind of intelligence gathering to a judge."

"I don't know, Stan. He's said some things that make me think so."

"Like what exactly?" Stan asked, hoping that he didn't sound overly eager to hear the answer.

"Like how he knew that someone tried to steal Alexander's rod before I told him."

"That could have been a lucky guess," he countered, hoping to allay some of Josh's concerns. The last thing Stan wanted was for Josh to know that Stone might just turn up some information that could put the Institute in a compromising position.

"Maybe, but what about the fact that Arthur described his attacker as military? It's occurred to me more than once that Stone might be involved somehow."

"Is that all you're worried about?"

"No, yesterday I sent Arthur an email explaining my concerns, and today Stone makes an offhand comment about how some people around here don't trust him. What was *that* supposed to mean?"

"Josh, I think maybe you haven't got enough sleep and you're reading too much into his words."

"Well, you know what I think. I think Stone knows exactly how I feel about him and he's screwing with me."

"Maybe, but don't let him get to you. Soon Arthur will solve this case and Stone will be a distant memory."

"I hope so, Stan, I really do," Josh replied dismally as his associate stood up and headed back to his own office.

After Stan left, Josh received a text from a friend in London. As soon as he read the words, "possessions, magic, and a strange book" Josh knew that he needed to pass the information on to Arthur immediately, which posed a problem.

Josh really did believe that Stone was monitoring his communications, and the last thing he wanted now was for him to be privy to any more personal information he sent Arthur.

Josh sat frustrated at his desk while he considered the alternatives.

Finally, he had an idea.

# Chapter 51
# London

Armed with a city map, Arnie and Jackie found the Phoenix Bookstore located just off the major thoroughfare in central London.

The Phoenix had a large selection of books, crystals, and incense, and they quickly busied themselves browsing the various selections. Interestingly, Jackie was immediately drawn to a group of books marked *spells and protection.* As she sifted through the diverse collection, avoiding those that promised love, sex, or money, a young woman with purple hair and a nose-ring, approached her and reached for a book two shelves down.

"Here, I think you might like this one," she said with a grin and then walked away.

Surprised, Jackie looked down at the book titled *Psychic Self-Defense.* She turned to the first page and noted that it was written by an early 20th-century British Occultist by the name of Dion Fortune. As she flipped through the pages, she reflected on how strange it seemed that the odd-looking girl should know exactly what she was looking for.

"Hey, Arnie, come over here."

Arnie walked to Jackie's side. "I can't find anything about Azarelis or a Grimoire."

"I haven't seen anything about the Qlippothic Prince either, but I did find this book about psychic protection, or rather that young woman there did."

Arnie looked across the room to the girl Jackie indicated, and then shook his head. "I don't know, Jackie. This is all just a little too strange for me."

Ignoring his skepticism, Jackie continued. "This writer claims there is a special spiritual organization called the Occult Police. Let's see, she says, 'they are advanced, sincere esotericists who are pledged to help innocent people combat the forces of the Left-hand Path.'"

"What is the Left-hand Path?" Arnie asked as he rolled his eyes.

"By the context I would say it means the forces of evil. I think we're on the right track here."

"Oh sure, Jackie, and just where do you think we can find these advanced sincere esotericists that combat occult evil? I don't suppose Dion gives an address?"

"You're such a smart ass, Arnie," Jackie retorted, "Fortune says there is something called a contact symbol we can use to get in touch with them."

"What is a contact symbol?"

"Dion says we look at it, visualize it in our minds and then, mentally, place a call for help."

"Jackie, please. I think I've been fairly level-headed with all of this crazy superstition stuff up until now, but really, you must be joking."

"Come on, Arnie. It's no stranger than anything else we've seen or heard in the last two days. What could it hurt?"

"Whatever, Jackie, fine, let's give it a try. So what's the symbol we're supposed to use?"

"The book says we should draw a black Calvary cross on a circular crimson field."

# Chapter 52
# London

After making a side trip to an arts and crafts store to pick-up
supplies, Jackie and Arnie sat down on Arnie's hotel room couch,
propped up their newly constructed contact symbol, and lit a little
incense they picked up at the bookstore.

"Now, Arnie, remember that Dion says we are supposed to look at
the symbol for a few minutes, visualize it in our mind, and then make a
mental plea for help."

"I'll try," Arnie answered listlessly.

They soon learned that gazing at the symbol was easy enough, but
when it came time to hold the image mentally, they had trouble keeping
their minds from wandering. After several attempts, they almost gave up,
until Jackie pleaded with Arnie to try one last time.

Determinedly, Jackie first stared at the symbol, then shut her eyes
and imagined a giant black cross superimposed over a red background.
Her breathing became even and rhythmic and gradually she felt herself
slipping into a state somewhere between waking and sleep.

*Slowly the contact symbol grew in size until Jackie felt she had
become a living, breathing part of the design. As she looked around, the
cross took on a three-dimensional quality, and then faded until it was
replaced by an ordinary-looking office building. The outer walls
dissolved away and Jackie found herself walking down a long hallway.*

*Identical doors lined both sides, and she looked curiously at the
placard on each. Most announced mundane services such as legal
assistance, accounting expertise, or medical care.*

*When she reached the end of the row, she knew she was in the right
place. The final door had no name plate, but a black Calvary cross shone
brightly in the middle of a crimson circle. Jackie hesitated for a moment,
and then opened the door.*

*What she saw inside took her breath away. Mirrors ran the length of
the room, covering each of the four walls from top to bottom. Their
gleaming surfaces refracted the light of a large crystal chandelier*

*hanging from the ceiling. The effect was surreal as they reflected each other's image back and forth into infinity.*

*At the center of this extraordinary room, seated around a boardroom conference table, were 12 of the most remarkable looking men and women Jackie had ever seen.*

*It wasn't their physical appearance that was so special, although most of them were very attractive. It was the fact that each person seemed to embody perfect health, wisdom, and love. How they conveyed that impression to Jackie without a single word, she couldn't explain.*

*As they looked back at her, Jackie felt strongly she should say something.*

*Before she did, a 13th man with snow-white hair and pale-blue eyes approached her. "Good evening, Jackie. We were expecting you."*

*"What? How could you expect me?"*

*"We know what is happening. You have asked for help in all sincerity and you will receive it. But also be warned. You and your friends are treading very treacherous waters. One wrong move and you will be sucked into a whirlpool of chaos."*

*"What can we do?"*

*A red-haired woman seated at the end of the table answered Jackie's question. "Expect someone to visit you soon." And then with a smile, she repeated herself. "Expect someone to visit you soon."*

Just as Jackie was about to ask who would be coming to visit her, Arnie's cell phone starting ringing.

Instantly, Jackie was jolted out of the vision and her eyes flew open. For a moment, she felt disoriented, as though she had woken from a long sleep.

While Arnie conversed with the caller, Jackie returned to normal consciousness.

"That was Moshe. He says he sent a message to his friend in America, and he's waiting to hear back from him. He also said that he found the name of a guy online who is supposed to be an extremely impressive trance medium. He thinks that maybe a session with him will help us better understand exactly what we are dealing with. Moshe wants us to meet him over there in half an hour."

*Perhaps this would be the expected visitor.*

# Chapter 53
# Westminster

Arnie, Jackie, and Moshe met in front of a small apartment building, located on a cul-de-sac in a southern section of Westminster.

As they walked up to the basement flat, Moshe handed them both a small leather pouch tied together with a long thick string.

"Here, put these on."

Arnie looked hesitantly at his cousin.

"Come on. It took me a long time to make these."

Arnie looked over at Jackie and then reluctantly placed the amulet around his neck.

Moshe knocked on the door and after a few seconds a very thin, very young man answered.

"Hello, are you Dr. Malowski?" Moshe ventured.

"Oh no, my beloved awaits you in the oratory," he said in hushed tones as he pulled aside a heavy curtain and ushered them into the next room.

Inside, identical dark curtains covered the walls. In front of each was a polished concave mirror. In the center of the oratory was a black eight-sided pedestal table. On top was a medium-sized box made of opaque glass.

As strange as the room was, it seemed relatively mundane compared to the individual who sat at the table looking up at them. The large, corpulent man was wearing a sort of pajama-like suit made completely of black satin. His hair and beard were long and thick, but for some reason he had shaved his eyebrows completely off.

"Beloved," the smaller man announced, "some humble seekers wish to behold your light."

The man nodded in the direction of his guests.

"Madame, gentlemen," the smaller man continued. "May I present the most beloved of the spirits, Dr. Steven Malowski."

"Welcome to our Adytum," Malowski greeted in a low baritone voice. "Please, everyone be seated," he said as he motioned to the empty chairs on the other side of the octagonal table.

"The moon is nearly full tonight. The energies will be powerful. Do you seek one who has recently passed over to the summerlands? One who can now see without the restrictions of our mortal, material vessel of clay?"

The trio looked confusedly back at Dr. Malowski.

"No matter," he continued. "My guide, the fully awakened entity, Ra-Aural of ancient Atlantis can see all. Is it hidden knowledge that you seek?"

"We seek those individuals known as the Occult Police," Jackie responded. "I was told to expect someone."

"Both myself and my guide, the mighty Ra Aural, are this planet's special envoys of all the masters of the Great Brotherhood. Rest assured, my dear," he leaned forward and patted Jackie's hand, "you have been guided to the right place to find the forces of light."

"My chela will collect the usual offerings. I must not touch the money, you know. It would reduce my capacity to channel higher, spiritual vibrations."

Arnie leaned over to Moshe and whispered to his cousin. "If the cash is so bad, I wonder why he doesn't dispense with it altogether. And what's a chela?"

"A chela is someone who is devoted to a sort of guru," Moshe whispered in return. "I think maybe this guy is a fake. Something here just doesn't seem right. Maybe we should go."

"No, it's alright. Let's wait and see what happens."

"Let us open the portals unto the inner realities," Malowski commanded.

The lights in the room dimmed while the box on the table pulsed with light. The cube then sent a beam of light out to each of the concave mirrors as the rest of the room went completely dark.

"Nice effect," murmured Arnie under his breath. "This gig must pay pretty well, effects like that don't come cheap."

Jackie elbowed him in the ribs.

After a few moments, a faint green light shone on Malowski's face. The effect was eerie. His head seemed to float like a bearded, longhaired Jack-o-lantern above his seat as he recited a prayer. "May the central effulgence of the Cosmic Lavender Flame enlighten us with the secret knowledge of the Inner."

Malowski then began to moan and groan, his deep voice rising and falling through an impressive range of notes. "I am here," he finally announced in a quiet voice.

"Greetings, oh mighty Ra Aural," responded the chela. "We are so honored by your presence."

"I have journeyed far through the corridors of space and time, from the misty halls of the ancient city of Atlantis, from the drowned kingdom of light that existed in the midst of the great ocean. From this echo in the Akashic memory have I come to be of service to all true seekers."

"What is it you seek?" Ra Aural now questioned Jackie.

"My husband has been taken by Azarelis. We seek the protection of the Occult Police for both ourselves and for him."

"Your quest is worthy. I shall find the information you need in the lavender flame. You must have faith. Your husband is like a bird that has flown. Keep the cage open and he will... he will..."

Before Ra Aural could finish his sentence, Malowski's head jerked back and forth rapidly.

"Noooo!" He yelled as his eyes opened wide. The veins in his forehead pulsed and throbbed in the ghostly glowing light as spittle foamed at the corner of his lips.

"That's kind of impressive," Arnie whispered. "Don't you think that hurts?"

Clearly distressed, Malowski's chela turned on the lights and rushed to his master.

"Beloved! Beloved!"

The medium's head fell to the table, his long hair drenched in perspiration. "Oh, God, it's so horrible. The blackness, the void," he wailed as he sobbed uncontrollably, his body racking and shuddering with each breath.

Malowski's assistant then looked accusingly at the three of them. "How dare you do this to my beloved? Get out and take your evil money with you," he spat as he flung their cash on the table.

# Chapter 54
# London


Marty gazed at his reflection in the mirror as he sat at the make-up stand in his backstage dressing room.

He knew he should be enjoying his new-found fame, but all he could think about was how he had fired his wife and best friend.

*What have I done?*

*It's the book. I told you not to open it. Now it controls your thoughts and actions and soon it will take you over entirely.*

*How can that be? It's just a book.*

*It's not just a book. It's a Grimoire. This is what it does.*

*What's happening to me?*

*"There are more things in heaven and earth than are dreamt of in your philosophy."*

*What's that supposed to mean?*

*It's Shakespeare.*

*I don't like Shakespeare. Why am I thinking about him?*

*You're not Marty, I am.*

As Marty stared in the mirror, he caught sight of something moving behind him. He shifted his attention to the shadows, and there beside an exposed water pipe, Marty saw the smiling, burned visage of Viktor forming in the darkness.

With a startled cry, he jumped from his seat, sending makeup jars and brushes crashing to the floor. When he turned around, the image of Viktor had vanished. He tilted the shade of the table lamp toward the corner of the room, but nothing was there.

Marty pounded the table with his fist.

*What is happening to me? Shadows are pacing me in the alley. Somebody tried to shoot at me through a window. And robed monks are taunting me in every corner!*

He reached for the flask of whiskey in his pocket and took several long swigs.

*When did I start drinking again? I haven't had any alcohol since that drunken biker killed my father.*

*Don't burden yourself with guilt. It's time to set yourself free, to rule, to revel and take pleasure. Let yourself go Marty, all is well.*

But it wasn't his own voice that Marty heard in his head now. It was Viktor's.

He felt a cold hand rest on his shoulder. As he looked up, he saw the burned monk standing at his side.

The last thing Marty saw before he faded into blessed oblivion was the light from the small lamp shining right through Viktor's shadowy form.

# Chapter 55
# London

Michael, Analia, and Arthur sat in the tenth row of the theatre balcony, waiting for Marty's show to begin.

"Wow Agent Arias, you look great tonight. I thought you were all about the conservative suits," Michael complimented with obvious appreciation.

"I'm wearing the same old pants and shirt I have for the last three days," Analia replied coolly as she re-settled herself in her seat.

"No way Agent Arias. You look amazing," he countered as his eyes roamed her hip-hugging slacks and low cut satin blouse. Her hair was loose and streaming down her back, and the heels she wore were a little higher than the utilitarian ones she had adorned thus far on their trip.

Analia would never admit it to Michael, but she had chosen her outfit carefully. After seeing two more men disappear this afternoon, followed by the unexplained appearance of international arms dealer Sebastian Howell, she felt it she should be prepared for anything. She had no idea what the connection was between the Black Rose executive and this Marty the Magnifico, but it was too much of a coincidence that Sebastian had been at the theatre today. Howell must be involved in all of this somehow and she had the feeling he would turn up again this evening.

That was why she was dressed as she was. Her clothes were simple enough that she could still move, run, or even fight hand-to-hand if she had to, yet they were also feminine and alluring and she was not above using whatever weapon she could to disarm opponents.

So when Michael commented on her appearance she felt validated. What bothered her was that she felt flattered by his words. Analia did not want to have any personal feelings for Michael or for Arthur, and in general she was anxious for this case to end.

But if Analia were honest with herself, she would have to admit that she was getting used to their company. Except when Arthur drove her crazy, just like he was doing now.

"I can't believe you left the rod at the hotel, Alexander."

"We're not going to go through this again are we?"

"I'm just saying that I think it was a bad move. No safe can be *that* safe."

"It would have been conspicuous here, you know that, but I have other reasons as well. If this Marty person does have a Grimoire, then it's just not a good idea to have both items in the same place. Trust me on this one."

"Alright, fine, the rod isn't safe here. So why are we sitting so far away from the action? If I had known this was the best *you* could do, I would called in a favor to get us tickets a little closer to the stage."

"I *wanted* to sit this far back Agent Arias. I need to see absolutely everything that happens during the show. This seat is perfect for observation. Besides, apparently this performance is sold out."

Sold out or not, she knew from her background check on Alexander that he had enough money to buy any seat he wanted.

"At least we're sitting near an exit," Analia thought with a certain amount of comfort.

Analia shrugged. She knew she'd never win this argument with Arthur and she wasn't in the mood to try. So again she began surveying everyone around her, just as she had been doing since they arrived. So far nothing looked out of place, and no one looked suspicious.

Inwardly she prayed that tonight would not be a bust. She felt like they had waited forever for something to happen and she was more than ready for a fight.

With fifteen minutes to go until curtain rise, Analia decided to dig a little deeper into Arthur's mysterious background. Aside from the financial questions, she still didn't understand what this organization he belonged to was all about. And Banes had sent another message only an hour ago.

*Continue staying with the rod and find out more about Alexander.*

# Chapter 56
# London

"Tell me more about this secret Fraternity of yours, Dr. Alexander."

"What do you want to know, Agent Arias?"

"Well, what do you do there, exactly? And how is it that you are involved in cases like this one?"

"We train our members to open the portals of their inner awareness, just like Josh explained at the Institute."

"Yes, well, how exactly do you do that?"

"There are many ways, Analia, most of which I am unable to share with you. Not at this time anyway. But I can tell you that we often meditate on certain symbols."

"Symbols?"

"Yes. In order to tap into extrasensory perceptions, a person needs to speak the correct language. It is kind of like programming a computer. To make changes you need to be able to speak the language of the system. Humans work exactly the same way. Our conscious mind interprets the incoming sights and sounds of our environment using our five senses. Our brain then combines that information with all of our acquired knowledge and experience."

"Our subconscious mind works a little differently. It not only maintains all of the body's autonomic functions, but it also acts an as intermediary between our conscious objective mind and other deeper levels of awareness. To access the information available at these levels, we have to speak the language of the *subconscious mind*. And that's where symbols come in. The subconsciousness doesn't relate well to words or verbal communication. It deals in pictures, just like when you dream."

"Excuse me?"

"Think about it, when you dream you rarely see printed words, if ever. Almost all communication in our dreams is visual. That's why my organization uses a variety of symbolic systems. We do it to communicate with our subconscious mind and ultimately with other forms of intelligence."

"What kind of symbols?"

"Some are simple drawings or pictures. Others are complex geometric designs."

"What about the robes, candles, and incense you all use every time you travel astrally or whatever you call it?"

"We use them for the same reason we meditate on symbols. Everything is designed to unlock the powers of the subconscious mind, which responds favorably to drama and imagination."

"What do you do with all of this information you get from higher sources? I mean, why bother?"

"We encourage individuals to discover what they really are and what their purpose for existence is. We are also dedicated to serving humanity."

"Lots of people serve humanity without using ritual or symbols. People fundraise for the poor, work in shelters, make donations to those in need, or have jobs that help people, what do you guys do that's so special?"

"Analia, most people think they are purely separate individuals, and that their thoughts, wishes are desires and all completely their own. In reality, even though 'yes' we are individuals, that is only part of our nature. Humans are really individual parts of the same whole and at a deep unconscious level we are all tied together. Our thoughts and emotions actually affect everyone around us, or humanity as a whole."

"Think it of it like cells in a body. They all work together to keep the body healthy and functioning normally. If just a few cells mutate, the body's defenses generally take care of it. But if enough cells mutate then you have cancer, which can infect the entire body and possibly destroy the organism."

"The consciousness of humanity works in a similar fashion. When people understand that their thoughts and actions affect others they can alter their own behavior to transmute the errors of others, just like white blood cells can annihilate aberrant cells."

Analia looked inquisitively at Arthur.

"Look, I'm not the first person to ever postulate such an idea. I'm sure you've heard of a man named Carl Gustav Jung? He wrote extensively about the collective unconsciousness, although he approached it somewhat differently."

"What most people don't realize is that we are all connected. We are all part of the same universe and the same cosmos. There is no separation. That is an illusion. Humanity is one, and how we treat each other *matters*."

"OK Alexander. This is where I get off, too much information."
Michael laughed.

"That's enough out of you, Richardson," Arthur returned.

"Oh, come on. It's all in good fun. Look Analia, I can prove to you what Arthur is saying, that humans are connected."

"Of course you can Dr. Richardson," she answered with her usual veiled cynicism.

"No, really, how about we try a little experiment?"

Analia remained quiet and Michael interpreted her silence as a "yes."

"Have you ever stared at someone when you thought they weren't paying attention?"

"What?"

"You know. Have you ever been caught looking?"

"Yes. And I've caught other people looking at *me*," she said with emphasis.

Michael blushed before continuing. "It happens to everyone. You're driving along the road, or sitting in a restaurant or in some other social place and you feel like someone is looking at you, so you turn in the person's direction. This happens in all kinds of public places, especially in singles bars."

Analia took a deep breath.

"Most of the time, we catch people looking at us in our peripheral vision."

"Yes."

"Well, what if you stare at someone from *behind*, where they can't possibly see you. What happens then?"

"Nothing happens then."

"Really, are you sure about that? Should we give it a try? You see that man two rows down with the brown hair and blue suit."

Analia nodded.

"Let's look directly at him for a while."

"Are you serious?"

"Are you afraid this might just work Agent Arias?"

"No," Analia responded, taking Michael's bait.

"And don't forget that you also need to make a mental request for him to turn around," Michael explained.

Analia did as instructed just to get it over with.

After two minutes of staring at the man's back and sending him mental messages, the man was still facing forward, and his posture hadn't changed.

"I'm so impressed, Michael. Thank you for sharing that."

177

"Wait a minute. We're not done yet. Now you pick someone."

"Fine, how about that woman in the blue dress, three rows down on the end, the one with the 'big' hair?"

Michael agreed and they repeated the procedure. This time, the woman started squirming in her seat. She shifted her position, crossed her legs, and even started swatting at her ears as though a fly were buzzing around.

"Coincidence, Richardson. Don't get all excited."

"We'll see. Let's have Arthur pick someone."

"Don't get me involved in your childish games. I'm here strictly to observe."

"Come on, Arthur. Just one," Michael begged with enthusiasm.

Reluctantly Arthur nodded his head toward a young man with dark skin and curly hair sitting nine rows down.

"Now again, Agent Arias, if you will."

"This is the last time, Michael."

Again they stared intently from behind at the chosen young man. At first, his position remained unaltered. Then, after a half a minute or so, he turned around and scanned the crowd behind him as if he was looking for someone in particular.

"There you go, Agent Arias. Explain that."

"Pure luck. If we tried the same procedure again, it would never come out the same."

"No, and that's why telepathic communication cannot be proven empirically. But two of those people *felt* our stares."

"Are you forgetting that the first guy didn't move?" Analia questioned.

"He was probably preoccupied with something else and he either ignored the inner prompt, or he's so far out of touch with his inner voice that he doesn't even hear it anymore. Besides, it doesn't work the same with everyone, and it's much more powerful among people who are close to one another. Have you ever noticed how siblings, married couples, or close working associates often seem to know what the other is thinking without exchanging a word?"

"That has nothing to do..."

The lights in the auditorium flickered on and then off to signal that the performance would start momentarily.

"Hold that thought, Agent. I need to make a pit stop before the show begins," Michael said as he quickly headed to the exit.

"He certainly has excellent timing," Analia commented to Arthur as she turned back toward her other companion. Although he seemed so lost in thought that Analia doubted he even heard her.

*These guys are the strangest people I have ever met.*

Realizing she had become too relaxed while playing along with Michael, Analia quickly resumed her earlier inspection of the theatre. As the auditorium grew dark, she spied a man on the ground floor walking down the aisle toward the stage door. He was very tall and walked with self-assuredness.

"Give me your binoculars, Arthur."

"I don't have any, Agent Arias."

"You're useless sometimes, Alexander."

Looking around, Analia noticed that the woman in front of her had a pair.

"Excuse me miss, would mind if I borrowed those for a moment."

"Certainly," the lady replied flatly as she handed them to Analia.

Agent Arias quickly centered the man in her sites and then waited anxiously for him to reveal his face.

One, two, three more steps.

He opened the door and for a minute Analia was sure the man wouldn't turn around. And then, he did. Just as he walked through the doorway, he looked to the side, and Analia was able to see enough to know who he was.

It was him. It was Howell.

"Damn."

As she turned to leap from her seat, Michael returned and bumped her arm, nearly knocking the binoculars from her grip.

"Hey, what are..."

Except that it wasn't Michael who blocked her exit.

Analia stopped in mid-sentence as the unfamiliar man slipped a very hard, very cold semi-automatic pistol into the space between her blouse and the back of the chair.

"Don't be in such as rush. Just return those binoculars very casually and very quietly and then we will be on our way."

By now, Arthur knew exactly what was happening. And he couldn't believe that he'd allowed this man to sneak up on them.

Analia turned and glared at her assailant.

"Do you know who I am?"

"Yes, I do, Agent Arias. And I'm the man who's going to kill both you and your friend Michael, who now happens to be in the custody of

179

an associate of mine, if you and Dr. Alexander over there don't do exactly as I tell you to. Do you understand?"

Analia nodded.

"And you, Dr. Alexander, I assume you have heard everything I have said."

"Perfectly."

"Good. Then here's what we're going to do. The three of us are going to quietly walk out the door, down the stairs, and into a blue van waiting for us just outside."

"And don't bother yourself with this, Agent Arias. I'm more than happy to assistant you," he offered as he slid her 9mm from her waistband.

# Chapter 57
# The Carpathians
# 1429

The small group of men, mostly farmers, moved surreptitiously along the rough mountain track. Their faces were determined, but their eyes were filled with apprehension.

The wind cut razor-like around the rocks and boulders while clouds rolled over the peaks and periodically obscured the path they walked. These men had been born and raised on this mountain and they knew its ways and dangers. The terrible weather had little impact on their progress.

When they neared the monastery, the leader, Stefan, gestured a long calloused finger in the direction of a shrub-covered overhang. His ancestors had lived in these hills for centuries, long before its current inhabitants had seized it for their unholy purposes. His own great-great grandfather had built the monastery alongside his fellow villagers. When Stefan was a child his father had showed him a secret underground tunnel that led right into the monastery. It was the same tunnel they would use tonight.

The cords in Stefan's neck betrayed his tension, but his body, used to long hours of work in the fields, showed no signs of weakness as he stepped into the hidden entrance.

Behind him, Yuri, a small, compact man, darted his ferret-like eyes around the darkened space. As he searched each shadow of the dank passageway for movement, he turned to the villager at his side. "That pistol of yours *does* work, doesn't it?" he questioned with concern as he looked down at the rusty firearm.

Peter answered while nodding his weather-worn face for emphasis. "Yes, Yuri, it works. Try to relax. We have God on our side."

Despite the forbidding darkness of the tunnel, their leader moved quickly down the passageway. Not because they were armed, or because they had the element of surprise on their side, but because he knew Marie would not survive if they failed.

His youngest daughter was missing. Her kidnappers had snatched her from her small room during the night. Stefan had found her bed empty in the morning, the imprint of her head still on her pillow. He and his wife knew without a doubt what had happened to her. *They* had taken her.

Their village and the surrounding area had lain under the shadow of a dark curse for decades, one which bled them of their life's blood as surely as if their necks had been cut beneath the sacrificial knife of the monks themselves.

It was a well-established pattern.

At least once a year, and sometimes more, the village would find that one of their neighbors had simply disappeared. Usually it was someone young, but not always. And now, it had happened again. Rumors and myths surrounded each disappearance, but everyone knew the truth. The villagers were just too afraid to think it, let alone speak it, as they feared retribution from Viktor and his evil brothers.

This time the outrage of the mountain village had finally been awakened. Marie was loved by all. Even a cruelly beaten dog will cower for only so long before it springs at its tormenter. These farmers, used to facing starvation at the hands of nature almost daily, had courage and faith, and they would face hell itself to prevent another sacrifice of one of their innocent.

They moved down the tunnel, feeling their way along the damp, uneven walls. The only audible sound in the darkness was that of their anxiety-filled breath.

When they finally emerged from the long tunnel, the five men found themselves standing in the middle of a long torch-lit hallway. The sounds of chanting filled the corridor.

For a moment, they hesitated. Their respect for the music they associated with worship was strong. But soon their resolve resurfaced, and they continued moving forward. As the chanting grew louder, the realization that these blasphemers were perverting their holy rites fueled their indignation and anger.

Using the monks' intonations as their compass, the villagers made their way to Viktor's Chamber of Conjuration.

Stefan and his companions flattened themselves against the wall as they soundlessly crept into the adjacent gallery. When they arrived, the men stared down at a scene below that both sickened and enraged them.

# Chapter 58
# London

The drive from the theatre to Arthur's hotel was both uncomfortable and uneventful.

Forced to lie on their stomachs with their hands tied behind their back and their faces pressed firmly to the van floor, Arthur and Analia rode in silence as their red-haired captor held his pistol steady at their heads.

"If either one of you moves or looks up, I will kill you both."

*You've already threatened us with that, you moron. Don't you know any other intimidating phrases?* With each passing moment, Analia's impatience was growing, and she couldn't wait for the chance to show this guy just how mad she was.

Arthur's thoughts were running along the same line, except that he was also trying to figure out who these men were and why they wanted the rod.

Two blocks before they reached the hotel, the driver pulled over and switched places with the gunman.

"Listen closely, you two. The three of us will enter the lobby posing as good friends, while my associate here watches us from the door. Dr. Alexander, you will walk directly to the front desk and ask for the rod. You are not to make any stops or talk to anyone else. If either of you tries to run, Michael will die. Once you have the rod, we will all take the elevator up to your suite."

The kidnappers then switched places again and the van pulled into the parking lot. As the two men scurried around and prepared to enter the hotel, Arthur strained to hear the words they whispered to one another.

Once they were ready, the Irishman reached down and cut the ropes from their wrists.

As Analia stood up, she wasn't surprised to see that the driver, who up to this point had not showed his face, was Sebastian Howell.

*How could I be so stupid? I knew Sebastian might be at that theatre. I should never have let Michael talk me into playing that ridiculous game with him.*

Analia felt as though she had done nothing but make mistakes on this case and she knew it was time to turn things around. Right then she made a personal vow to pull it together and take these two men *down*, no matter what she had to do.

As they entered the lobby, Sebastian spoke to Arthur in a low voice, "And no secret signs either, Dr. Alexander. Remember who is waiting for you to get this right. His life depends on it."

Arthur nodded as he headed to the reception desk. The clerk there greeted him with a professional, even-tooth smile.

"Hello, sir, how can I help you tonight?"

"I have a package in the hotel safe that I would like to pick-up."

"Certainly, sir. Please fill out this form and I'll call the manager." The clerk then passed a preprinted slip across the desk.

Arthur looked over at their kidnapper, who was standing just a few feet away. The man glared back at Arthur, clearing indicating that he was watching his every move. Arthur turned back and completed the short questionnaire.

"How long will this take?"

"Just a minute or two. Mr. Atkinson has to get the key. We don't keep it here in case of theft," the clerk answered with a chuckle.

"Right," Arthur replied, while he felt those cat-like tawny eyes crawling all over him.

Moments later, Mr. Atkinson arrived at the front desk with a brown paper package in his hand. "Good evening, Dr. Alexander, if I could just see your passport for verification?"

Arthur reached into his pocket and retrieved the requested document.

"Thank you. And now, would you please sign this slip of transfer? Good. Here's your package, sir."

Arthur nodded his thanks and then turned back to rejoin his companions. The three then headed for the elevators and stepped in.

As the doors closed, Arthur turned to face his adversary. He noted that the man held his gun close to his body with his jacket casually draped over his arm to conceal the weapon from observers. It was obvious to Arthur that the man knew what he was doing, and he decided this was not the time to make a move. As one of his Hapkido masters had once told him, "Movies excluded, there is no effective martial arts technique for defense against a gun."

Arthur then looked over at Agent Arias who stared back at him blankly. He knew that she was having similar thoughts and for a moment, Arthur was concerned that she might behave rashly. But, as they arrived unscathed at the sixth floor, Arthur knew that he had underestimated her level of patience.

"Now open the door very slowly. Don't make any sudden moves or give me any reason to blow Agent Arias' pretty little head off."

Without saying a word Arthur took out his card key and followed instructions.

# Chapter 59
# London

The light-haired man was quick to get to business. He threw Agent Arias down onto a nearby couch and then motioned for Arthur to take a seat across the room. His red-haired associate then wandered in from the hall and shut the hotel room door with a brisk push.

The leader instructed his second-in-command to level his pistol at Analia's head, while he and Arthur completed their transaction.

"Let's see what we have hidden underneath all that brown paper, shall we?" he directed.

Reluctantly, Arthur peeled the wrapping away to expose the black embossed case.

"Please now, very slowly open it and let me see the blasting rod," the man coached as his yellow eyes hardened.

Dutifully, Arthur opened the valise and then tilted the contents in his captor's direction.

"Good. Now, carry it over to the bar and place it on the top of the counter."

Arthur complied, but rather than bringing the entire case to the bar, he opened it, took out the rod, and then dropped the case to the floor.

Neither man seemed to notice or think Arthur's behavior abnormal, but Analia knew he was up to something.

Arthur then walked to the counter, set the wrapped rod down, quietly walked back to his seat, and remained standing.

Analia carefully watched Sebastian's every move as he glided across the room and then placed the rod in his jacket pocket. "I can feel the pulse of its power," he said with a look of awe on his face. "Thank you for your cooperation, Dr. Alexander and Agent Arias. I am most appreciative."

"I hope you're not planning to use that thing, Sebastian. I don't think that you can handle it," Arthur returned.

Both men turned their heads in Arthur's direction.

"How do you know my name?" Sebastian hissed.

"I heard your friend over there whisper it when we were in the van. You really should choose your companions a little more carefully. This guy makes mistakes."

Sebastian shot an angry look in Jameson's direction and then walked over to Arthur. His lips curled into a sneer.

"What do you know about it, occultist? I know all about you and your ridiculous Fraternity. Dedication to humanity, what a joke! Humanity isn't worth saving. All you have to do is look around you to know that. You're fighting a battle you can't win, Alexander. You and I both know that men and women inevitably give in to their darker side."

"Every time someone commits violence or acts out of fear, *we* grow stronger. Fear that they are un-loved, fear that they aren't good-looking enough, or rich enough, or strong enough, or successful enough. All of their negative emotions feed the dark. Every day people choose money over love. Every day they lie, or think jealous thoughts of their friends or family. Every time a person behaves selfishly or thoughtlessly, the dark edges closer to dominion. Every time hurried, self-interested individuals ignore someone in need on the street or at work, or at home, we grow stronger. Every time a boardroom member makes the decision to fire thousands of employees while drafting his own golden parachute, our cause is strengthened."

"Most of humanity is stupid and ignorant. You know that. They curse each other, they ignore one another's plight, they judge each other by standards they themselves could never hope to live up to. They self-centeredly wrap themselves in concern only for what goes on in their own life as though what happens to other people doesn't affect them. They don't even understand what or who they are, and they are blind to the fact that their own crazy, vehemently anti-humanity thoughts actually increase the darkness that envelops their lives."

"And the more they try to justify their own self-serving behaviors, the more entrenched in evil their lives become. You'll never stop it, Alexander. You can't. Countries invade each other. Governments make shady profitable deals. Genocide reins, people suffer. We rape our own planet to the point of global destruction. Pain is everywhere. People break each other's hearts, they ignore their own children. What can you do? You're outnumbered. You're a dying breed, Alexander. You're losing the fight, just like you're losing here tonight. Society is headed for oblivion, and I'm going to make sure that I'm in charge of the new world order."

187

Sebastian then spat in Arthur's face and motioned for Jameson to join them.

Arthur could feel the red-haired man's eyes bore into his skull as he came to stand at a place just behind his back. Arthur could even feel the Irishman's warm breath on his neck as he whispered words only Arthur could hear. "You shouldn't have lied like that. I know I never used Sebastian's name in the van. My name, however, is Jameson and I want that to be the last word you hear before you pay for that error with your life. Ja..me..son."

In the next second, everything went black.

# Chapter 60

The Master of Will commands Arthur to follow.

He and several other initiates walk through a rocky, sun-baked wilderness as they obediently follow a white-bearded hermit, one of their beloved and respected teachers.

The old man veers to the left, walks quickly over a small rise, and comes to stand on the edge of a high cliff. Arthur and the others watch as he jumps up and down in place. Delight colors his features as the ledge crumbles beneath his sandaled feet. The Hermit turns and waves his staff at Arthur, almost losing his balance in the act.

Startled, Arthur feels his old fear of heights returning.

"Come, come and see, Arthur," he calls.

"No, Master, I cannot," Arthur replies, his apprehension building.

"Arthur, come! Come to the edge and see the glorious vision."

Arthur watches as the rim of the abyss continues to collapse beneath the old man's dancing feet. The Hermit seems either unaware, or unconcerned.

"No, Master. It isn't safe and I am afraid I will fall."

A distant memory struggles to resurface in Arthur's mind. Once, long before, and mostly forgotten, Arthur remembers a feeling of horror as he watches somebody fall. He doesn't know who, but he is sure it is someone he cares about, longs for, or loves?

The Master's face darkens as his voice thunders, "Come to the edge!"

Arthur reluctantly complies, his dread growing with each step.

"Fear is failure," shouts a voice inside his head.

Arthur wrestles to control the dark emotion he knows is an illusion. He stands beside his teacher and gazes at the expansive vista before them. The sun reflects off the walls of the canyon and catches fire in Arthur's breath.

The Hermit turns and laughs like a madman as he pushes Arthur over the edge.

Arthur hangs in space as screams pour from his mouth.

He opens his eyes and finds that he is standing in the middle of a vast featureless stone plateau.

*In the distance, three figures approach him like dots of a trailed-off sentence. As they move closer, Arthur sees a blue road forming beneath their feet. Each of the men is wearing a majestic white robe beneath capes of different colors. The figure on the left is garbed in crimson, while the one at the other end is draped in bright azure. The center form is vested in brilliant gold.*

*They walk to within inches of Arthur. He feels the heat of their gaze, cutting like a laser, through to the depths of his soul. The Master in the center speaks straight to Arthur's heart.*

*"You must take the leap of faith," he says while stepping closer and grasping Arthur's arms. "Are you willing to trust us?"*

*Unable to move his mouth, Arthur is powerless to reply.*

*"Arthur, do you trust us?"*

*He tries harder, but still he cannot answer the Master.*

*"Arthur. You must answer!"*

*"I..."*

*"Fear is failure, Arthur. Find the strength within."*

*"Arthur! Arthur!"*

# Chapter 61
# London

"Arthur, Arthur, wake up. Can you hear me? You can't die Alexander, I need you," Analia pleaded as she used her emergency medical skills to try to revive him.

"I didn't know you felt this way about me, Agent Arias," Arthur whispered faintly, his eyes still closed.

"Thank God. I thought you were dead. How do you feel? Can you move? I'm going to call an ambulance."

"No," Arthur commanded as he slowly sat up and opened his eyes. "There's no time. Sebastian has the rod and probably Marty's book, too. He also still has Michael and he won't hesitate to kill him, I'm sure. And as soon as he uses his newly acquired *power* tools, we're all going to be in trouble."

Without argument, Analia walked to the bathroom and quickly returned with a wet towel. As she bent over, she placed the cool rag on Arthur's swelling head injury. He seemed different as he looked into her eyes.

"Thank you, Analia."

"You're welcome," she replied as she intently returned his gaze.

"So you need me?"

Analia paused. She was feeling many things at that moment, most of which were far too personal to share. "You know what I mean. I can't exactly chase after astral bad boys without you," she said with a hesitant smile.

"Of course," Arthur answered.

"Damn," he said aloud as he changed the subject. "I should have seen this coming. How could I just be sitting there meditating on the upcoming show while Michael was being abducted?"

Analia assumed that his question was a rhetorical one and didn't answer.

*I practically invited Jameson to sneak up on us. What was I thinking? And what was that dream I just had all about? I know it was important and I can't remember a thing.*

Arthur knew that his subconscious mind had been trying fervently to get a message to him after Jameson had hit him over the head, but he just couldn't seem to bring it through to his conscious mind.

Analia interrupted Arthur's thoughts before he could make sense of any of it.

"Alexander, we have to go after Howell."

"I know. Give me a minute," he responded as he slowly stood up. "What happened after Jameson hit me on the head? Why didn't they kill you?"

"I'm not sure. Right after Jameson knocked you out with his gun, he walked over to me to finish the job. Sebastian stopped him. I have no idea why. Then they left and told me that if I followed them, they would kill Michael."

"I almost did follow them, but I was worried about you. I knew that Jameson hit you hard enough to kill you and I'm sure that was his intention. I really can't believe you're alive," she finished as she looked over at Arthur with awe.

"I'm guess I'm just lucky," he said unconvincingly as he very carefully and very slowly walked across the room, picked up the case Sebastian had left behind, and handed it to Analia.

"Why are you giving this to me, Arthur? I think maybe that head wound is worse than it looks."

"Very funny, this is how we're going to find Howell."

"What?"

"Didn't you notice how I purposely took the rod out of the case before I handed it over to him?"

"Yeah, I thought that was kind of peculiar. Why did you do that?"

"You saw the experiment last night in Frater Roget's study. We'll use a pendulum to locate Howell and hopefully Michael as well."

"Are you serious?"

"Absolutely, that rod has been in this case for the better part of 200 years. The two objects are intimately linked now, and the process should be simple. I'm surprised Sebastian didn't think of it himself. I guess his black magic isn't quite as strong as he thinks," Arthur said with a wink.

"Black magic? What are you talking about, Sebastian is an arms dealer."

"An arms dealer?" Arthur questioned.

"Yes, I recognized him immediately when I saw him this afternoon. I used to track the movements of international arms smugglers before I started chasing crazy occultists. Sebastian is only a semi-legit businessman. He's a very powerful and very evil man."

"Why didn't you tell me that you'd seen him today?"

"At that time I wasn't sure if he was involved. And besides, I was mad at you for leaving the rod in the safe."

"Well, arms-dealing isn't all he does."

"How do you know that?"

"First of all, because he wanted the rod."

"And?"

"And secondly, malevolence permeates every fiber of his being. You can't get *that* from just some shady business practices. Didn't you feel it?"

"I'm not sure what I felt. How did you know his name if you didn't know who he was?

"Because, you were practically shouting it."

"No I wasn't. I never said anything."

"No, not out loud you weren't."

Analia gaped at Arthur.

"Look. Let's not get into it now. I don't know how much time we have."

"Oh, so now all of a sudden you're all about hurrying?"

Arthur set the case on a small table near the center of the room.

"We need a street map of London. Do you have one?"

"Oh, right," Analia answered with her hands on her hips. "I just happen to have one stuck down my blouse."

Arthur looked toward the indicated area of her anatomy, but said nothing.

"Get serious, Alexander. No one but your friend Roget uses maps anymore. I have it all right here on my phone. Can you use that?"

"Never mind," Arthur retorted with a shake of his head. "I'll call down to the lobby and see if they can send some up."

While they waited for the maps to arrive, Arthur set out everything else they would need to find Sebastian, including the pendulum and some other key items he retrieved from his luggage. As Arthur busied himself around the room, Analia noted that he seemed to be moving a little slower than usual.

"It pays to be prepared," Arthur offered as he pulled out some interesting items from his larger suitcase. One was a small silk-wrapped ring. The other was a red-handled dagger with a wavy blade. As he set them on the table, the needed maps arrived.

Once everything was in place, Arthur picked up his ceremonial dagger and methodically traced seals around the room to guard against any intrusion from the darkness. When the ritual was complete, he roused the centers within his subtle body, and then picked up the pendulum in his right hand and the case in the other. Arthur then formed a clear, vivid mental picture of the blasting rod.

But as he hung the pendulum out over the map nothing happened. He took several deep breaths, re-centered himself and then tried for the second time. Again, the pendulum didn't move.

"Come on, Arthur. This is a waste of time. I'm going after Sebastian," Analia pronounced as she headed to the door.

"No, please wait, Analia. The problem is me. That bang on the head has temporarily scrambled my internal wiring. I'm sure that's the problem. You're going to have to do it."

"Me! I have no idea how to do this crazy magic stuff. I don't even believe in it. Count me out."

"Come on, Analia. It's the only way. Sebastian could be anywhere by now. How do you think you're going to find him?"

Analia knew Arthur was right. The odds of finding Howell now were slim.

"Fine, give me that thing," she blurted out as she walked back across the room.

Gently Arthur passed the pendulum to Analia's outstretched hand. "Now relax. This won't work if you resist the process."

"OK," Analia responded as she first relaxed the muscles in her head and face and then those down her body until gradually she released her pent-up tension. When she finished, she then let out a long, deep sigh.

"How did you know to do what you just did?" Arthur asked with curiosity.

"I don't know. I always do that when I'm frustrated. It helps calm me down. Why?"

"No reason," Arthur answered.

"What do I do next?"

"Just try to stand perfectly still and hold the pendulum out over the center of the map. Breathe slowly in and out and try to keep your hand steady. Don't intentionally move the pendulum, but at the same time, don't resist any motion. Just let the pendulum guide your hand."

"Alright," she said in an even tone.

As instructed, Analia held the pendulum out over the map. After a very long minute passed, nothing happened, the pendulum didn't move at all.

But, Analia didn't get frustrated or give up, determinedly she kept at it. In fact, the longer she waited, the more focused she became, until finally she could no longer perceive any separation between her finger and the chain of the pendulum.

As her concentration intensified, the energy in the room changed, and for a moment Analia could swear she felt a tingling sensation running up and down her body. Slowly, the pendulum began to shift its position. Gradually it pulled her hand and arm to the north-west corner of the map until it settled in one place and moved in a circular pattern over a spot near Wiltshire on the road toward Bath and Avebury.

"Don't move, Analia," Arthur directed. "I'm going to switch to a more detailed map of the area."

Carefully, Arthur slid the greater city map from the table and replaced it with a detailed street map of the indicated British neighborhood. Soon the pendulum moved and then settled once again.

Arthur leaned over the table. "That's an old chapel just outside of Bath. I don't know if Howell is there, but the rod certainly is. Hopefully Michael will be too."

"Are you sure, Arthur?"

"Yes, I know the operation worked. I can sense it."

Analia set down the pendulum and reached for her things, until she realized that Sebastian had taken her gun and her purse. As she headed to the door she reflected on how naked she felt without her *own* power tools.

# Chapter 62
# Somewhere near Bath

The stone floor was freezing, and Michael hurt all over. As he opened his eyes and tried to move, the tightly tied ropes around his wrists and knees abruptly halted his progress. He wriggled his arms and feet but the bindings wouldn't budge.

Michael had always been claustrophobic and physical restraint of any kind generally tested his sanity. He was just about to scream when he heard voices exchanging animated conversation in the next room. Slowly, he remembered what had happened to him, and he realized he was in serious danger.

While Michael had been in the theatre bathroom washing his hands, a well-dressed man with red hair had introduced himself just before slipping a gun under his coat and pressing it firmly into his back. His assailant had then made it clear while he escorted Michael to a van parked outside, that unless he followed all of his instructions perfectly, he would put a bullet in his liver. When they arrived at the van, someone else, a woman Michael suspected, placed a rag smelling of chemicals over his mouth. That was the last thing he remembered.

*These guys aren't messing around. If I don't calm down, and figure this out, I'm surely a dead man.*

The unpleasant thought forced him to slow his breathing and he commanded his flailing limbs to stop moving. Michael then closed his eyes and visualized himself standing in the middle of a rose garden, surrounded by calming fountains and singing birds. He then imagined a soothing breeze caressing the sides of his face, and his whole being relaxed.

When Michael re-opened his eyes, he felt centered and renewed. He looked carefully around the small room, hoping to see something he could use to free himself. Quickly his eyes took in each of the four walls and even the floor beneath him. Regrettably, the room was bare and he could see nothing that could be of any assistance.

"So for now I stay tied," he told himself, willing his mind to stay focused.

Turning to his other senses for help, Michael decided to listen more carefully to the voices in the next room. As he strained his ears, he smelled incense, much like the kind that burned at the church his father used to take him to when he was a child. Wistfully he wondered if he was inside a chapel.

In the next room of the old abandoned Anglican Church, recently commandeered by the Black Rose Ltd. as a perfect out-of-way location, Michael's captors were discussing current events.

And, the glare from Sebastian's eyes told all that their leader was not pleased.

---

"Sebastian," Lillian explained, "yes, it's true we didn't complete our mission, but we..."

"Meaning," Howell cut her off, "that you don't have the book. A stupid stage magician outwitted you. You, who have the resources of the Order of the Dark Rose at your command, you, who I have invested so much time and effort in training, you who couldn't evoke a minor elemental without screwing up, you let Marty the Mystico slip through your hands!"

"There was an unforeseen complication," Nigel spoke up as Lillian shrunk back in her seat.

Sebastian leered at Nigel. Generally he and Lillian were close, but very competitive friends. He wondered now why Nigel was coming to her defense.

"I suppose you are going to enlighten me on the nature of that complication."

"Evidently," Nigel continued, glancing at Lillian, "there are other people interested in the book. Just when Lillian was about to get Mr. King under her control, a sniper shot at them from a building across the street. If his aim had been better, the magician would now be dead and we would have the book. Unfortunately, that's not how it happened. The guy missed, and Marty ran out the door with the Grimoire in hand," Nigel finished while he silently prayed that Sebastian would believe his story. If his boss found out what really happened, he knew he and Lillian were likely to end up in the next room with the Richardson guy.

Unconvinced, Sebastian stared coldly back at them. "And now that damn monk Viktor has managed to take off with both Mr. King and the Grimoire."

Nigel wondered what Sebastian was talking about, but said nothing. He was just thankful that the spotlight was off him for the moment.

"What is our next move?" Jameson boldly inquired, hoping to refocus his boss's tirade.

"We get the book from Viktor of course. It shouldn't be too hard. There is only one place anywhere near here that has a strong enough vortex to open the Gates of Chaos. Our Order has kept detailed records of such sites around the Earth for millennia and it has been passed down from one group to the next for centuries. Viktor must know exactly where these powerful ley-line convergences are, and no doubt he's headed there right now. What he doesn't know, is that he's never been successful in ushering in Azarelis because he doesn't have the blasting rod. And I do. Getting the book from him with this in my hand will be child's play," Sebastian explained while lightly tapping his coat pocket to indicate that he kept the rod safely on his body at all times.

"Where do we go?" Nigel blurted out before he could stop himself.

Sebastian walked across the room and stood within inches of his Nigel's forehead.

"Up the coast to a cave. Not that it should matter to you, since you and Lillian have done absolutely nothing to contribute to this endeavor," Sebastian answered with a sneer.

"Are we all ready to go, Jameson?" Howell commanded as he stepped from Nigel's side.

"Not quite, sir. We just need to finish loading the ritualistic instruments into the van."

"Nigel, Lillian, start packing up the van," Sebastian barked in response. "Jameson, go take care of that Richardson character. I'm tired of carting him around, and we don't need him anymore. It's time we started eliminating the dead weight around here," he said as he stared vehemently at everyone in the room.

Without hesitation, they all sprang into action while in the next room, Michael braced himself for what was about to come.

# Chapter 63
# Somewhere Near Bath

"Are you sure this is the right place, Arthur? It looks kind of deserted."

"That's the whole point, Agent Arias. If Sebastian's holding a ceremony to open the Gates of Chaos, he isn't going to want any witnesses, is he?"

"Point taken."

"Pull in here," Arthur motioned. "Let's drive around back."

Analia did as instructed.

As they turned the corner, the driveway opened into a large empty parking lot. Except that it wasn't entirely empty. On the far side, they saw Lillian and Nigel loading Sebastian's van with a variety of boxes, while Howell stood by watching.

At the sound of Analia's car, Sebastian jerked his head up. He immediately recognized Analia and Arthur.

"Get in the van now!" he yelled at Lillian and Nigel as he jumped into the driver seat, turned the ignition, and headed to the backside exit.

Analia floored the gas pedal and tried to make up the distance.

As she closed in, Howell angled the van toward her, and slammed into the side of the petite European sedan. The impact was so intense that it pushed the lighter vehicle several feet to the side and right into a concrete wall.

While Analia cleared her head, Sebastian threw the van into reverse and drove out of the lot, tires screeching the whole way.

Relieved the car was still drivable, Analia pulled around to pursue Sebastian, until Arthur stopped her.

"No. We're not following them. We have to get Michael first."

"What? This might be our only chance. Are you crazy? Michael's probably in that van."

"No, he's not."

"How do you know? We couldn't see inside."

"Because I feel his energy inside of the church, and he's in trouble."

"No, Arthur, I'm done listening to you. You lost the rod, you lost Michael, and now you're about to lose Howell. We're going," she said as she started to pull away.

"No, Analia. Michael will die if you go after Howell," Arthur pleaded.

"You better be right about this."

# Chapter 64
# Somewhere Near Bath

Michael shut his eyes and pretended to be out cold while Jameson made his way to the small room.

There wasn't much he was going to be able to do to stop the man, but he was sure going to try. If Jameson decided to shoot him from the doorway, then it would all be over quickly.

His stomach lurched as he heard the Irishman's footsteps getting closer.

Fortunately for Michael, it turned out that Jameson's idea of intimacy is to look directly into the eyes of the people he murders. Michael learned this as Jameson stood directly above his limp body.

As soon as the red-haired man reached for his gun, Michael lifted his legs, and in one powerful motion kicked the Irishman where it hurts a man most.

With a whimper, Jameson crumpled to the floor.

———————

"I don't see anyone, Arthur. He's not here."

"He's here, Agent Arias. I'm sure of it. Come on, we still haven't checked all of the rooms."

As they neared the back of the old small chapel, they heard a strange sound and rushed down the aisle.

———————

Michael was fighting for his life as Jameson had now recovered from the blow to the groin, and he looked *mad*.

"Oh, shit," was all that Michael could say as he lay helplessly on the floor.

Jameson stood up with his gun in hand, eyes and lips fuming with anger. "You're going to pay for that, Richardson. I had planned to kill you with one bullet to the head. But now I think I'll just puncture your gut in a few places so you can watch your own intestines ooze blood and bile for hours while you die," he spat with vehemence as he holstered his gun and pulled a switch blade from his pocket.

"I don't know, that doesn't sound fun. Can we go back to the quick-and-easy idea?"

"Too late, asshole. I guess it is true what they say about good guys always finishing last. You know, the meek are destined to inherit the earth. Except that by the time they get it, no one will want it anyway. So don't feel bad," he said as he leveled the blade at Michael's torso.

Jameson's knelt to pierce Michael's skin. He stopped when he heard a voice.

"Remember, vengeance is mine, sayeth the Lord," Arthur said as he prepared to take Jameson out with a Hapkido straight punch. But before he could land his intended jab, Analia struck the Irish brute with a deadly roundhouse kick to the left side of his head.

If they had all been starring in a movie, Jameson would have shook off the blow and started a five-minute fight scene. But this was reality, and Analia's kick had hit him squarely on the temple. So while sliding into a state of unconscious, Jameson simply murmured a very un-dramatic, "huh."

"Nice kick Analia, Tae Kwon Do?" Arthur questioned.

"Ten years of training, old man. I wasn't sure that Hapkido punch of yours was going to get the job done."

"Who would have thought you could kick that high, Agent Arias? I guess I'll have to be more careful what I say to you," Arthur retorted.

"Do you guys think maybe you could stop one-upping each other long enough to untie me?" Michael asked from the floor as he held up his rope-tied hands.

While Arthur helped Michael to his feet, Analia cut the ropes with Jameson's knife.

"I'm glad you're alive, Michael," Analia said as she looked at Arthur with a knowing grin, "so what are we going to do now? We have no idea where Sebastian is headed."

"I sort of know where they're going," Michael offered.

"Where?" Analia questioned enthusiastically.

"I don't really know exactly, but I heard Howell mention something about a cave up the coast."

"Great. Thanks. That's really narrows it down," Analia returned, her excitement now fading.

As she looked over at Arthur in the hopes that he might have a suggestion or two, she saw that he was standing still and his eyes were glazed.

"Arthur, what's wrong? You look kind of strange."

"I'm fine. I was just trying to remember. Something about a cave sounds familiar, I just can't remember why right now." While actively searching the files of his mind, Arthur's phone signaled that he had received a text message.

As he touched the screen, Analia looked over his shoulder.

"It's from Josh Erskine at the Institute."

"What does he say?"

Arthur laughed.

"Come on. What is it?" Analia prodded.

"OK, Agent Arias here's what he says."

> Arthur,
> How's the weather?
> Is it *c*old *t*here in *t*he UK?
> It's *s*unny again here, no surprises!
> You remember my **m**om Joyce don't you?
> She just called and asked me to say **hi** for her.
> She also wants to know if you will **have** dinner with us sometime soon.
> *B*ye for now,
> Josh

"What? Is he joking?" Michael asked.

"No. This is a game we used to play in college. Sometimes we used to code our communications just for fun."

"A code?"

"Yes. If he's using it now, he must be concerned that someone is monitoring our communications."

"I don't understand. What's the key? Why are some letters italicized and some highlighted in bold?"

"They refer to information found on a particular set of Tarot cards."

"You mean those things fortune tellers use?" Analia asked.

"Sort of, but not all decks have the same pictures and information. And we don't use them for divining the future. We developed this code using a deck with Hebrew letters. Each italic letter in the message stands for the first letter of the English transliteration of the Hebrew word associated with a specific card. And each one of the cards has a particular numerical value. The bold letters in the message signify the first letter of the name of a specific card, which then corresponds to a letter of the English alphabet. Thus any italic letter is associated with a *number* while the bold letters correspond to a *letter* of the English alphabet."

Shaking her head, Analia decided to pass on any further explanation. "Whatever. Just tell me what it says."

"Give me a minute."

Analia tapped her feet impatiently on the stone floor while Arthur scribbled a few notes on a small spiral bound pad he kept with him at all times.

"I've got it. It's an address, 246 Belgrave Rd. #18"

"Wait a minute, Arthur. You must have made a mistake. Your message has 16 characters in it and there are only 13 letters in the code."

"How astute of you, Agent Arias. The Hebrew alphabet doesn't really have a letter that corresponds to our 'e' so I just intuited where they should go. I did the same with the number sign. Also, some of the cards correspond to numbers greater than 10 so his last 'B' refers to the number 18. Since there is more than one card that begins with the letter 'h' Josh's use of 'hi' refers to one specific card."

"So that is all is? It's just an address?"

"No, there's more. We also developed certain key words to add further meaning to our coded messages. The word *surprise* indicates a mystical event. The fact he put an exclamation point after the word means he thinks the event is important. His use of the word *mom* means help."

"Someone at this address must need our help, Agent Arias. We should go right away."

"What about Howell? We can't just let him go."

"I don't intend to, Analia, but if Josh took the time to send me this, when he knows all that's going on, it must be related to what we are doing."

# Chapter 65
# London

Arnie and Moshe sat around the small round dining table poring over stacks of computer printouts.

Moshe had managed to dig up an amazing amount of information on the Internet while Arnie and Jackie had been at the bookstore. They had been puzzling through it ever since the return from their strange visit to Dr. Malowski's. After that crazy event, they decided that they better start finding their own answers.

Hours earlier, a blurry-eyed Jackie had finally succumbed to the need for sleep after being up for almost two days. Arnie and Moshe had continued the quest since then, but were now thinking of taking a much-needed break, when they heard a knock at Moshe's front door.

"Are you expecting anyone?"

"No," Moshe replied as walked to the hall closet and pulled out an old nine-iron golf club.

"What do you think you're going to do with that?" Arnie asked as he eyed the rusted, worn-out shaft.

"It's better than nothing," Moshe answered as he headed for the door and peered through the peephole.

"Who is it?"

"Arthur Alexander. I received a message that someone at this address is in need of assistance."

"What is he talking about?" Arnie whispered.

"I have no idea who this guy is," Moshe responded in a hushed tone.

"We can't let him in, Moshe. For all we know, Marty sent him over and this is some kind of set up."

"Who do you work for?" Moshe asked the stranger in what he hoped sounded like an intimidating voice.

"I am a member of the Pentalpha council. I battle the forces of darkness. We're here to help."

Moshe and Arnie looked at one another as they shrugged their shoulders. Apparently, the Occult Police had arrived.

---

They all sat around Moshe's table while Arnie explained all that had happened over the last couple of days. Arthur was thoughtful as he listened carefully. When Arnie was finished, he shared some of their own experiences.

"What have you found so far in your research, Moshe?" Arthur asked.

"Not that much really. We did find a rough sketch in an old book that bears some resemblance to the black rose design Jackie described. All the reference indicates is that there are fragmented records of such a Grimoire being used centuries ago by a cult of the shadow, nothing more specific than that."

As Arthur reflected on the revelations of their new companions, he realized just how critical the situation was. Their accounts of Marty and their description of the book seemed to confirm what he and his associates had suspected back in France. This new information, coupled with Sebastian's involvement, nearly guaranteed that they must be dealing with an ancient Grimoire dedicated to the Qlippothic Prince, Azarelis. The CEO would never waste so much time on anything of less significance.

"If Marty attempts a conjuration of a Prince of the Qlippoth, under the influence of The Book of the Gates, and he succeeds in opening a portal for Azarelis, your friend will become the victim of a force so chaotic that death would only be the beginning of his horrors. And please believe me when I tell you that I'm not exaggerating. If Sebastian Howell combines that energy with the blasting rod and the forces of darkness gain a foothold in this space-time continuum, humanity will have to redefine all of its traditional ideas of hell."

"I just don't understand, Dr. Alexander. How could Marty be involved in this?" Arnie questioned. "He sometimes has a bad temper and can be a general pain in the ass at times, but he's basically a good guy. I just can't believe that he would be a part of something like what you're describing."

"Marty probably isn't choosing to cooperate. The Grimoire is a very powerful device. It's filled with geometric diagrams and seals designed to brainwash whoever reads it. Marty is most likely being controlled subconsciously by the Grimoire and by the Dark Brotherhood. And the book itself is very seductive. It makes all kinds of promises to its guardians, ones that it has no intention of keeping."

"Are you saying that the book can control anyone who reads or uses it?" Moshe inquired.

"No. No, it can't."

"Why Marty then?" Arnie asked honestly.

"I don't know. Something must have made him susceptible to its powers of persuasion."

The room became silent as they all considered Arthur's words.

"I think we should ask Jackie to join us now so we can develop our strategy for stopping Marty. She's his wife and will be an integral part of pulling him out of the delusion that has such a strong grip on him. I'll do everything I can to bring him back, I promise." *If he isn't too far gone.*

Arnie nodded and left the room to go wake Jackie.

While Arnie walked down the hall, Analia turned to Arthur. "What about Howell?"

"Analia, Howell has the rod. All he needs now is the Grimoire and he can control Azarelis. Wherever Marty and that book are, Howell is sure to be there as well."

Before Agent Arias could respond, Arnie burst back into the room.

"Come quickly. Jackie – she's gone!"

Moshe and Michael ran to the bedroom while Arthur and Analia bolted out the front door to look for her outside.

In the back room, Michael stared at the now-empty bed, cautioning everyone not to touch anything.

Arnie leaned his head out of the window to see if by some miracle Jackie was outside. All he saw was Arthur, who looked up at him and shook his head.

Analia soon returned and indicated that her search of the rear of the building had also yielded nothing.

When Arthur came back in, he stopped abruptly at the bedroom door and wrinkled his nose in disgust. "The scent of the Qlippoth is strong here." Looking around the room for answers, he noticed a small piece of paper on the floor. "What is that?"

"That's the seal I gave Jackie for protection. I copied it from the Sixth and Seventh Books of Moses," Moshe explained. "I guess I didn't help her much," he said sadly.

"Let me see that," Analia said as she bent down to pick up the parchment.

"You have done everything you could have here, Moshe, to help your cousin and his friend. And it won't go unnoticed. A talisman such as this one though isn't really effective unless it is consecrated," Arthur said with sympathy in his eyes. "I doubt if it would have prevented this from happening in any case. Something here isn't right. I suspect Jackie went willingly with whoever entered this room. There's no psychic trace of a struggle."

"For once I will have to agree with Arthur," Analia concurred. "Read the back of the parchment," she finished as she handed the piece of paper to Arthur.

As soon as Arthur touched the seal, his eyes blurred and his hands started to tingle. Instinctively he stood up straight as a beam of energy shot through the top of his head. The current swiftly ran down his body and out through to the floor below, causing his consciousness to shift.

*When Arthur's vision cleared he saw a dark bluish-green ocean on his right and high jagged cliffs to his left. In front of him, about a thousand yards in the distance, he saw the opening to a sea cave.*

*He looked down and was surprised to see that his body was that of a young woman. Realizing that Jackie's talisman had linked his consciousness with hers, Arthur mentally opened all of his inner senses in order to further immerse himself in the vision.*

*He felt the rough sand squish between his toes and heard the surf pound rhythmically on the beach. His wrists were tied tightly behind his back and he felt the same intense pain that Jackie did. At his side, he saw Marty dressed in the brown robe of a monk. In one hand he carried a long wicked-looking sword, and in the other he held the Grimoire.*

*Arthur scanned the surrounding area in the hopes of recognizing a landmark or two. But as they neared the cave, he saw nothing useful. Undeterred, he mentally recited a special prayer he often used when he needed higher guidance. He then closed his eyes and took a deep breath of salty air. When he opened his eyes again, the beach had vanished. Instead, he was standing at the crest of the Tor. His master stood before him.*

> *"It will be up to you and yours to seek the quarry in a cave on the coast, in order to neutralize his mischief and chaos. Come closer, and I will impart the location."*

*This time roads and street signs all formed clearly on the inner screen of his conscious mind.*

208

When the operation was complete, Arthur mentally thanked his master and then returned to Moshe's British flat.

"Arthur, are you going to read it or not?" Analia asked.

Arthur looked down at the seal and this time he read Jackie's handwriting.

"*I've gone with Marty. I have to save him. Please don't follow us*," Arthur read aloud.

"Oh, no," grieved Arnie.

---

While Analia was downstairs with Michael and Moshe loading the car, Arnie stood near the front door filled with anxiety. This had all been his fault. If he had not come up with this ridiculous idea of an Eastern European tour, none of this would have happened. The sole reason that he even suggested it was to give Marty another chance at success. Now his best friend and wife were in trouble, and he was powerless to help them. All because he had arrogantly assumed he knew what Marty needed.

Arnie was so absorbed in his own thoughts that when Arthur placed his hand on his shoulder, he jumped.

"Arnie, do you still have the seal Moshe made for you?"

"Yes, it's right here."

"Let me have it. I will see if I can activate it."

Arthur held the pouch in his hands while he meditated on the seal's intent. Moshe had made it to control the chaotic energy and unbalanced force of the Qlippoth. The trick now was to find a way to transform that unbalanced force to serve the forces of Light.

He started by activating his own spiritual center just above his head. One stage at a time, he then drew the energy down through corresponding centers in his body. At each juncture he concentrated on a specific power, enhancing it through visualization and internal chanting.

When the operation was complete, he transferred the harmonized energy to the parchment, impelling its etheric molecules to vibrate at a higher, purer, more rapid frequency.

"The seal is now a consecrated weapon. It should *only* be used to serve the Light," Arthur explained as he returned the talisman to Arnie. Equilibrium is the secret of the Great Work. If you align yourself with the current of the One Will, the One Will that set the galaxies in motion, then that current will spin through you. Then you will have the power of the universe on your side."

# Chapter 66
# Burbank, California

"What is this supposed to mean Erskine?" Agent Stone roared as he barged into Josh's office.

"What does what mean?" Josh threw back at him.

"This," Agent Stone answered as he threw a single sheet of paper onto Josh's desk.

The IIRPP chief looked down at a hard-copy of the message he sent Arthur earlier that day.

"So you *are* tapping my phone. I knew you were. Why do you think I sent this is the first place?" Josh accused as anger washed through him.

"I want to know what it means. And I want to know *now*!"

"I'm not telling you anything. You're totally out of line here and I'm done cooperating."

"If I have to take this to the NSA, Erskine, I swear I'll have Homeland Security here in an hour scrutinizing everything you do. Hell, I'll tell them this place is a terrorist shelter."

"Go ahead," Josh challenged with fury in his eyes.

# Chapter 67
# The Carpathians
# 1429

The Dark Brothers gathered around the altar. A circle of flame burned around them. Marie lay on the floor, her limbs bound tightly. The look in her eyes and on her young face were evidence of her growing fear. As the monks moved closer, a single cry escaped her lips.

"Marie," Stefan shouted from the gallery above.

Her sullen eyes looked up at the familiar voice.

Stefan rushed forward.

The villagers poured down the stairs behind him and attacked the surprised monks. Their fists and weapons pummeled the brothers who, unused to physical combat, fell easily.

Stefan, brandishing a sickle, looked like the avenging Angel of Death as he swept down toward his daughter. As he neared Marie, one courageous brother stood in his way. Stefan sliced the foolish monk's throat and then scooped up the girl before the splattered blood reached the floor.

"I have her. Let's go," he commanded.

Their task complete, the victorious villagers reversed their course and headed back to the stairs. The remaining monks looked to Viktor for direction. "Go after them!" he shouted.

The monks raced after the villagers.

Peter saw them coming. He turned and ran back toward the altar.

"Neither you nor your friends will survive this farmer," Viktor promised as he held his sword high above the altar. A vortex opened above their heads and a mangled green form with venom-dripping fangs emerged.

Peter stared in disbelief. Then, despite the fact that his left hand was shaking, he centered the monstrosity in his sites and shot a silver bullet right into the middle of the swirling mass.

The blast was deafening as it resonated through the vaulted chamber. The beast cried out in agony as it withdrew into the whirling clouds. As the vortex closed Grigor leapt at Viktor, dagger in hand, just as a continuous volley of lightning struck the monastery and the altar within.

Screams echoed up the tunnel as Stefan, Marie, and the other villagers ran out into the cold night air. As they looked up at the sky, they saw the moon and the stars. The clouds had vanished, the night was clear, and still the lightning struck.

# Chapter 68
# The Northern
# Coast of England

The ride up the coast passed in strained silence.

Before they left, Arthur asked Moshe to remain in London and notify the police if they didn't check in by morning. Arthur had then contacted the McLain's and asked them to organize a second wave of defense against Azarelis, should his efforts prove unsuccessful. Of course, if Sebastian succeeded in using the blasting rod to usher the Dark Prince of the Qlippoth into our world, there wasn't going to be much anyone could do to stop him.

Analia sat poised on the edge of her seat while she looked out the window and gazed sightlessly at the dark English countryside. All she could think about was Howell.

According to Arthur, he was on the verge of calling down some kind of super-evil being to enslave all human life. But all that she could think about was how Howell had kidnapped them all, rammed her rental car, and almost killed Michael. It was time the corrupt arms dealer got what he had coming. Sebastian Howell had to be stopped, and Analia was burning with anticipation.

In the back seat, Arnie alternated between reading Dion fortune's "Psychic Self-Defense" and Moshe's "Sixth and Seventh Books of Moses." And each time he switched books, he prayed, a new experience for the life-long agnostic.

Michael was driving and closely following the instructions Arthur had received from the Inner Plane Adept at the Tor, while next to him, his fellow initiate prepared mentally and spiritually for the battle to come. Arthur knew it could be a fierce one, and he methodically rehearsed possible scenarios while meditating for clarity and inspiration. He still felt a little woozy since Jameson hit him over the head, and secretly he hoped that his reactions would be as swift as usual.

Arthur also knew that he was still forgetting something.

He had remembered the Tor and the location of the cave, but he felt certain that his inner teacher had imparted another significant piece of information during sleep.

When they arrived at their destination, Michael stopped the vehicle a few hundred yards from the coast at a car park next to a memorial commemorating the fallen heroes of a World War II naval battle. The sky was dark and threatening, with the hint of a late-season squall riding on the winds that blew in from the ocean. The entire site was deserted and there was no sign of Sebastian's van.

Without exchanging words, the group headed out and followed a narrow trail down to the sand, warily trekking their way and trying to use their flashlights as little as possible. They were all wearing very dark colors and their shapes were nearly invisible in the deep shadows of the early predawn hours.

As they neared the prophesized location, they began to hear the faint sound of chanting on the night breeze, barely audible above the sound of the rolling surf. Knowing they were heading in the right direction, they picked up their pace.

Together they topped a small ridge that led down to an isolated stretch of beach about 50 feet below. Down the shore to the south, Arthur spotted the entrance to a small cave.

"That's it," Analia whispered. "Let's go," she directed quietly as she started climbing down.

"No. We can't enter from the front of the cave."

"Why not?

"It's not safe."

"What do you mean? The cave isn't even guarded."

"No, not yet it isn't. Come on, I've got a better idea," Arthur said as he filled his nostrils with a whiff of sulphur-based incense.

Staying on top of the ridge, Arthur hunkered down and made his way toward the top of the cave while the others followed behind. As they neared it, Arthur turned to Michael and asked him to stay behind.

"Come on, Arthur, I want to get these guys just as much as you do," Michael pleaded.

"I'm sure you do. But we need someone to stand guard and go for help in case we fail in there. I need you to do this friend. Someone has to be here to pick up the pieces, if necessary."

Michael nodded reluctantly and the rest of the group continued toward the cave. As they neared the apex, they saw puffs of smoke and the reflected light of a fire streaming from a natural chimney in the roof.

"That's how we're getting in," Arthur whispered. "It looks big enough that we should easily be able to slide down and keep to the sides of the opening."

Analia and Arnie looked at Arthur dubiously, but indicated through facial gestures that they were willing to follow.

As the group of three peered down and readied their descent, they saw four monks wearing the habits of the Dark Brotherhood. They were positioned around the fire below and in the center stood Marty, also wearing the vestments of a brother. In front of him, the Black Grimoire of Azarelis was open and working its magic.

In a dry, commanding voice, Marty recited a long formula of summoning as he gazed down hypnotically at the large leather-bound book. Sounding the words from somewhere deep within his subconscious mind, he spoke in a language he had never formally learned. In his right hand, he held Viktor's cross-hilt sword, while the other hand rested lovingly on the first-page seal of the open book.

At his feet, her eyes wide with terror, was Jackie. Tears cascaded down her cheeks as she stared in shock at her husband.

"Where are Sebastian and his crew?" Analia whispered to Arthur.

"I don't know. Something must have held them up."

"Why are the monks performing this thing without him? I thought you said they needed the blasting rod to usher in this Dark Prince of yours?"

"They do. Without it, Azarelis can never completely enter our world."

"Do the monks know that?"

"I don't know, maybe they're just prepping for Sebastian. Let's not waste any time waiting for him to show up."

Analia nodded. She would never have a better chance to get this close to Howell and she was actually disappointed at his absence. At the same time, the woman down there appeared to be in real danger, and this guy Marty was obviously a loose cannon. She knew it was her duty to pursue regardless.

Cautiously they worked their way down a cleft in the rock wall. Arthur was now holding a short ritual dagger at the ready while Arnie held the large brass ankh Arthur had asked him to carry. Analia trailed the other two with Jameson's pistol snug in her hand.

As they crept noiselessly down the small shaft, Arnie looked longingly down at Jackie and felt like a guard-dog restricted by a short leash. He still could not believe that Marty would harm her, even though the evidence of his friend's intention was right in front of him.

As they neared the sandy cavern floor, Marty finished his long lyrical speech as a green-colored cloud formed in space above the altar. Steadily, the transparent form grew larger and denser until it nearly overshadowed the ring of brothers below. Then slowly, stage by stage, the glowing, pulsating fog began to take shape as fangs and tentacles broke the outer surface.

Arthur jumped the remaining few feet to the ground and leapt to a place next to the ring of Dark Brothers.

*"Procul, o procul, este Profani!"* His voice thundered off the sides of the rock walls.

The effect on the four monks was instantaneous. Arthur's words released a backlash of their own evil power, which now whipped around them like a miniature cyclone tearing at their skin like a thousand tiny pricks. The monks grasped their heads and doubled over in agony.

Frantic for Jackie's safety, Arnie ran toward her bound form and shielded her body with his. Enraged, Marty snarled at Arnie and shouted, "Judas!" just as three figures ambled through the mouth of the cave. Their bodies formed a triangle and in the lead, Sebastian Howell proudly displayed the blasting rod of Hermes, now activated and blazing with force and energy.

"Alexander, I see you've come to the show. Too bad you've lost your ticket," Howell bellowed as he leveled the rod at Arthur.

"You can't really expect that the wand of light will answer your dark call, can you Howell?"

"The rod is neutral, Alexander. You know that. It reacts to the thoughts of its operator. It can't distinguish between light and darkness. I am now its Master and it will do as I command!" Sebastian shrieked.

The growing sphere above the altar shot out a beam of green light that ricocheted off the tip of the rod. The result was a magnified beam of life-taking energy that locked on Arthur as though impelled intelligently by Sebastian's thoughts.

With all of his strength, Arthur jumped to the side, narrowly escaping the deadly beam.

While Arthur repelled the attack, Analia worked her way around the edge of the darkened cave, careful to stay out of the firelight as she inched toward Sebastian's blind side. She had planned to shoot at him through the strange holographic form, but just as she was about to pull the trigger, she changed her mind. Something about the shot bothered her and so she had decided to move closer.

While Sebastian continued to direct the deadly ray at Arthur, who now appeared to be tiring somewhat from his repeated dodges, Analia made her move and pointed Jameson's pistol at Sebastian's outstretched arm. As she centered her target in the gun's sights, Nigel moved behind her and pushed her full force to the side.

The bullet landed squarely in the sand beneath Sebastian's feet.

Recovering quickly, Analia returned Nigel's attack with a kick to his gut and a blow to the back of his neck. He bent over in pain and then ran at Analia like a wounded animal. She expertly pivoted away from his hurling form. Unable to stop his forward motion, Nigel landed on top of altar, right next to the book of Azarelis.

Seduced momentarily by the ensnaring power of the Grimoire, Nigel reached hypnotically toward the treasure.

Marty was quick to react. He thrust Viktor's sword toward Nigel and roared, "Azarelis!"

In a blur of motion, the creature stretched out a tentacle, seized Nigel by the neck, and slammed his body to the ground with a crushing, sickening thump.

Nigel was already dead as the beast swung his limp form back and forth like a bloody, broken doll.

The monks scrambled back to avoid the flaying appendages while Arnie helped Jackie to her feet and dragged her slowly to side of the cave. Howell, still completely absorbed in his assault on Arthur, paid no attention to the macabre spectacle.

Blinded by his desire to destroy Arthur, Sebastian didn't see Nigel's bleeding body coming toward him until it was too late. The Black Rose CEO stared in disbelief as Nigel's form collided with his arm and the blasting rod flew through the air.

It landed right at Arnie's feet.

Without hesitation, Marty's life-long friend quickly picked it up and tossed it to Arthur like a baton.

"Here, Doc, catch."

Arthur caught the wand and aimed it directly at Marty's unholy conjuration. This time a clear, bright, white stream of light shot forth, driving Azarelis back toward his own space and time.

The creature howled.

While Azarelis retreated, Marty ran at Arnie, sword outstretched, ready to run him through. Arnie braced himself, and then ducked and countered while Marty swung wildly. As he fought for his life, all that Arnie could think of was how much he loved Marty and Jackie and how much he was going to miss spending his life with them.

Marty drew back the sword and with all of his might, eyes blazing, aimed the ancient weapon at Arnie's heart.

The tip of Marty's sword punctured the pouch that hung from Arnie's neck. An invisible shield flared around Arnie as a current of energy flowed through Viktor's sword. Marty was propelled backward with tremendous force. As the magician's body fell to the ground, standing in his place, now separated from his body, was the dimly luminescent etheric form of a burned and scarred Viktor.

The ghostly monk snarled wickedly as he moved again toward Arnie.

Arthur stepped in between them and sketched a pentagram in the air while chanting an ancient word of power.

The malevolent monk stood his ground and grimaced. Frustrated, he turned back toward the creature of chaos still hovering, half in this world and half in some outer dimension of darkness. In desperation, he shouted a command in Arabic and the gruesome being, still struggling for life, advanced toward Arthur and Jackie, tentacles flying.

Arthur readied the rod to retaliate when one of the other monks recovered, moved forward, and pushed his hood from his pale haunted face.

Analia immediately recognized him as the man from Heathrow airport and the theatre alley, the same one who had disappeared, *twice.*

"Grigor," Marty whispered, still in a daze on the ground.

"Viktor, I should have done this hundreds of years ago," Grigor declared vehemently as he plunged his silver dagger into Viktor's chest. The monk's eyes bulged in their sockets as his corpulent form dropped to the ground.

Unfortunately, Grigor's actions had no effect on Azarelis.

As Arthur raised the rod in defense, he heard his master's voice ring in his head.

His eyes relaxed while the dream he had while flying over the Atlantic played again on the inner screen of his mind. When Arthur saw the graceful form of an eagle fly into the morning sky, he looked over at Marty and knew what to do.

"Marty, remember, 'He shall lift you up on eagle's wings.'"

The effect on Marty was miraculous. Arthur's words triggered an unconscious memory. One that now gave him the strength he needed to break the spell of the book. He looked at Arthur and grinned.

He reached for the Grimoire, lifted it high above his head, and flung it into the fire.

Confusion erupted as the blaze exploded. The creature cried out as its body burst into flames. As it struggled to withdraw back through the inter-dimensional portal, it reached out and pulled the dying etheric form of Brother Viktor with it. As the Gates of Chaos snapped shut, the cavern reverberated with a loud thunderclap.

Arthur looked toward Grigor who smiled in triumph as he and the other three monks slowly dematerialized in a pool of light. As their forms faded, the cave filled with the brilliant rays of a golden dawn.

# Chapter 69
# The Northern
# Coast of England

Analia stood triumphantly over a handcuffed Sebastian while a British medic tended to the long jagged cut that bled down the side of his cleanly shaven face.

Analia hadn't wasted anytime once Arthur had taken possession of the blasting rod.   While everyone was distracted by the glowing green *thing* over the altar, Analia came up behind the crooked arms dealer and knocked him unconscious.

Analia had then pinned Sebastian down easily and cuffed his hands behind his back just as Marty threw the Book of the Gates into the fire. The resulting shock wave had loosed several medium-sized rocks from the cave ceiling and one had sliced open Sebastian's face while he lay helpless on the ground.

The Black Rose CEO scowled now as the young paramedic tried to dab the blood with a sterile piece of gauze. "You inept fool.   Do you even know what you're doing?  If you screw up my face, I'll see to it that you become intimately familiar with the concept of pain."

The medic looked to Analia for help while his face turned a pasty-white color. To keep Sebastian quiet, she checked him with a hard kick to his shin while she continued explaining the events of the night to an agent of the British Secret Service.

After apprehending Howell and making sure everyone else was alive and safe, Analia's next order of business was to call Banes. She herself had no legal authority in the UK, and for two good reasons she had no intention of calling in local law enforcement. First, she had no idea what she would say.  How would she ever be able to explain why they were there and what had happened in the cave?  Secondly, there was no way she would entrust Howell to a small village constable.  Sebastian had endless financial resources and contacts.  Within hours he would no doubt have some high-ranking official bailing him out.

Banes had moved swiftly. In less than an hour, a helicopter carrying three British agents and two medics approached the coast and landed in the isolated parking lot. For the last several minutes, two of the agents had been combing the area looking for Lillian, who had managed to run from the cave during all of the commotion, while Analia debriefed Agent McAllister. Amazingly, the man seemed unruffled by anything she said, including the more esoteric happenings during their stay in the UK.

While he wrote out her statement, Analia looked over at Arthur who was surrounded by a worn-out looking Marty, a relieved Jackie, and a confused-looking Arnie. Analia knew that Marty's manager was delighted that the ordeal was over. She also noted by the way he spoke about his friend's wife that he definitely had deeper feelings for Jackie than friendship. Analia suspected that Arnie was happy that his friends were reunited, but at the same time he wished Jackie was giving *him* a long warm hug of appreciation instead of Marty.

"I don't know, Dr. Alexander, ever since I opened that damned book I felt like I was standing by and watching my body do things that I couldn't control," Marty explained as Jackie's eyes misted over.

"That's how the book works, Marty. It seduces and paralyzes your subconscious through a complicated design of geometric forms. Then it slowly uses your subconscious mind to infect your objective consciousness. Once that link is made, it is able to gradually take over all of your voluntary functions," Arthur explained.

Marty then went on to recount what had happened on the road to Ostrava and then during his stay in London. Marty described the monastery, Viktor's initial friendliness, and then the monk's strange reference to Marty being *expected*. He described the Chamber of Conjuration, Grigor's assistance, and even how he had returned to the monastery only to find burned-out rubble and the modern-day Grigor.

As Arthur listened to Marty's story, he tried to connect what he heard with all of the other information he had already uncovered. When Marty finished, everyone looked to Arthur for interpretation.

"Well, I can't say for sure exactly what happened. These monks you ran into, Marty, were most likely some later form of a group of Left-Hand Path adepts who migrated to the Carpathians sometime after the crusade. What's most interesting is that the monks were no longer there when you returned. Did any of you notice anything unusual about how they looked back in the cave?

Arnie offered the first suggestion. "Yeah, it was like they were made out of shadows."

"Exactly, they didn't seem quite real. I've never seen anything like it. They must have been caught somehow in between the world of form and the world of images. I suspect that the lightning storm, of which you spoke Marty, must have had something to do with it. If Viktor was attempting to bring in Azarelis and something went wrong, like the monastery being struck by lightning, perhaps the vortex closed before he was able to properly send Azarelis back to his own time and place. The entire monastery might have been inadvertently stuck in some kind of inter-dimensional loop."

"So how does that explain what happened to Marty?"

"Well, they were no doubt looking for a way to get back to the manifest world and I guess they figured Marty here was their ticket."

"Why me?" Marty asked. "I mean I'm sure that in the last few hundred years many other people must have stumbled on that monastery."

"Maybe, and maybe not. The astral world doesn't follow the same laws as ours does. You all were able to see the monks here because Viktor already had a hold of Marty and the book, which fortified their material forms. When Marty stumbled on them, they were most likely still on the astral plane. Only someone who is psychically open would have been able to *see* the monks and the monastery. Marty here must have some talents he doesn't know about. Perhaps that's why he is so drawn to magic?" Arthur finished with a smile.

Marty returned Arthur's smile, happy to have control of his body again.

"I just have to know, Dr. Alexander. Why did these monks want to open the gates in the first place?" Arnie asked.

"Oh, who knows, probably to gain power. Viktor must have figured he could use the influence of Azarelis to bend the mind of whoever he wanted. What he didn't understand is that the Grimoire only has the power to open the Gates. The blasting rod is needed to usher in Azarelis and control the power of the Dark Prince. That's why Sebastian wanted it so badly."

"I still don't understand why they needed me," Jackie asked.

"The use of blood in rituals is an ancient practice. Most people don't have a proper understanding of why. The chemical composition of blood enhances the power of any dark ritual with its very special etheric life-giving properties. And the purer the blood, the better."

"Dr. Alexander, what made you, back there in the cavern," he hesitated, "what made you quote the first line from that old hymn?"

223

"I'm not sure I can fully explain that Marty. The words just came to me. They certainly seemed to have a strong effect on you though."

"Someone I know loved that song. I'm pretty sure he gave me the strength I needed back there to break the spell," Marty shared as he reached for Jackie and gave her a giant hug.

"One last thing Dr. Alexander, remember how I said I locked my keys in the car before I walked up to the monastery?"

"Yes."

"Well, when I ran back out with the book, my key was in my pocket. How could that be? I mean, what could have happened?"

"I don't know, Marty. The human imagination is capable of all kinds of mischief," Arthur said as his eyes danced.

"And now if you will excuse me, I have a few words I'd like to say to our CEO over there before the British Secret Service takes him away."

———————

Sebastian looked up from his uncomfortable seat on a very hard sand-covered rock and noticed that Dr. Alexander was on his way over.

Anger coursed through his body. It was bad enough that he had lost the rod and then been tackled by a woman. Now he would have to endure the taunting of his sworn enemy.

At that moment, Sebastian pledged that the next time he ran into the occultist, Alexander wouldn't walk away alive. Sebastian had no respect for any of Arthur's skills, and he considered him weak prey that simply just caught a break today. He would never make that mistake again, and he was certainly not going to show Alexander that he was defeated. He straightened his back until it became rigid, and then looked at Arthur maliciously.

"Hello, Sebastian," Arthur greeted with a wide cheerful grin. "It seems things haven't quite turned out as you planned. Soon the rod will be back safely where it belongs, *and* your precious Grimoire, has been destroyed."

Sebastian laughed at his words. "You think you have me beat, Alexander? Is that what you think? Let me assure you that this is far from over. It's only a temporary setback. Whatever charges they trump up against me will never stick. I'll be back at work within days. You and I will meet again soon. And next time I'll enlist help that won't be so incompetent."

"Is that what you think in that twisted mind of yours, Sebastian? That you're sitting there and I'm standing here because of someone's incompetence? All you see is what you want to see, Sebastian. You think everyone else is corrupt just because you are. That's why you think that humanity isn't worth saving. You are deluded, Howell. The world only appears evil to you because you view it through the lens of your own twisted heart. You should try seeing life through my eyes."

"Your plan didn't succeed because evil only begets evil. Ego reigns supreme for those that submit to the Left-hand path. In the end, Dark followers are always out for self and unity can only be achieved for very short periods of time. Corruption inherently breeds disloyalty and self-interest. Darkness is unstable. Hostile forces are always looking for ways to bring followers down."

"The universe is always on the side of good. Each one of us is guided by an inner knowledge of this inherent good, whether we choose to acknowledge it or not. Humanity is naturally attracted to the Light, even if individuals turn away at times. God is always there guiding and helping each one of us. Not through miracles, but by the natural law of unity. Crisis has a tendency to strengthen our feelings of oneness, and that is what you witnessed today. People with a common goal working together are strengthened by their group desire."

As Sebastian sneered at his words, Arthur moved closer.

"Eventually, Howell, the darkness will swallow you up."

# Chapter 70
# Burbank, California

As they drove toward the Institute, Analia had mixed feelings about the conclusion of this frustrating case.

On the one hand, she was certainly glad it was over. This had been the strangest assignment she had ever had in her career with the Agency. She still didn't understand most of what had happened, as much of it seemingly defied rational explanation.

On the other hand, she was pleased that this case had led to the arrest of Sebastian Howell. The guy was bad news, and Analia was thrilled that she was able to take him down. That alone made her work here worthwhile. But, she would also have to admit, that she was going to miss these crazy occult guys just a little bit.

After arriving back at LAX, they dropped Michael off on campus for an afternoon class, and then headed back to the Institute. Arthur wanted to finish everything up there before taking the rod back to the foundation, and Analia, of course, couldn't return to her own office until the weapon was safely returned to the vault. Banes had been very clear about that particular part of this assignment.

As they drove to the IIRPP, Arthur asked Analia a question she didn't expect.

"So why didn't you shoot at Sebastian through Azarelis when you had the chance?"

"You saw that?"

"Yes, I did. What stopped you?"

"I'm not sure. The shot felt wrong. I decided to wait."

Arthur nodded to himself.

"It's a good thing you did. Azarelis only ignored you because you weren't a direct threat. If you had shot through its body, it would have considered you dangerous, and retaliated. Most likely you would have suffered Nigel's fate."

Analia looked back impassively at Arthur as he continued.

"Your ammunition would have had no effect on Azarelis. Other than the blasting rod, only a silver bullet has any debilitating effect on a creature such as Azarelis."

"A silver bullet? Are you kidding, Alexander?"

"No. I'm serious. Where do you think the legends about werewolves and vampires and silver come from? These kinds of creatures are more etheric than real and silver disrupts their matrix."

"Are you telling me that you believe vampires and werewolves really exist?"

"I didn't say that, Agent Arias," Arthur corrected as he pulled into the IIRPP parking lot.

As Arthur and Analia exited the car and entered the lobby doors of the tall glass-paneled building, they ran into Agent Stone. He greeted them briskly as he hustled a handcuffed Stan Myer to a vehicle waiting nearby. Confused, Analia looked back at the retreating pair.

"What's that all about?"

"I have no idea."

As soon as they entered Josh Erskine's office, they knew that something significant had happened at the Institute during their absence.

"What happened, Josh? You seem kind of subdued." Arthur asked hesitantly.

"You won't believe it. I'm not sure I believe it."

"Try me," Arthur prodded.

"Do you know that Stone actually burst into my office demanding to know what that message I sent you meant? He even threatened to take it to the NSA for decoding, if you can imagine. Obviously, I knew for sure then that he was tapping my phone, and we kind of had it out. When I threatened to hire a lawyer and sue his ass for invasion of privacy, Stone finally decided to take me into his confidence and tell me everything."

"Apparently neither Stone, nor the FBI had any interest in the experiences of our psychics or the alleged astral breach. He just used your presence here, Agent Arias, as a cover."

Analia raised her eyebrows. "That's interesting, how dare he?"

"Evidently he and his partner have been monitoring the IIRPP for weeks, trying to build a case against my colleague Stan Myer. And up until a few hours ago, they suspected I might be in on it, which is why Stone was hacking all of my communications."

"I guess that explains the handcuffs," Analia commented offhandedly.

Arthur nodded in agreement.

"Anyway, when you showed up on Saturday, Agent Arias, Stone figured it was a perfect chance to get into the Institute and poke around without tipping Stan off."

"That explains a lot." Arthur acknowledged.

"Yes it does, doesn't it? Stan's only worked here for a few months, but apparently he's been very busy for the last few years swindling rich widows using an advanced form of hypnosis. Stone said he's defrauded women in more than ten states and he has cleared nearly four million dollars. The Feds have been tracking him for a while. Anyway, Stone was able to gather enough information here off Myer's computer and files to put him away for a while, I guess. According to Stone, it's all admissible since I invited him in, even if it was under false pretenses. I don't know if his search was legal or not, and I don't plan to ask. It's bad for business to have someone like Myer working here."

Analia and Arthur exchanged surprised glances.

"You haven't heard the best part yet," Josh continued. "When Stone confronted Myer, he broke down and started sobbing. He even tried to bribe the G-man with information. Too bad Stan started blabbing before the Stone agreed to listen to him, so no deal was made."

"What he told him should be of particular interest to you Arthur. Stan informed Stone that the whole psychic message thing was a fake. He confessed that someone paid him a bundle to hypnotize the psychics into believing that they had received some kind of important communication."

"I guess that explains why I didn't receive the psychic warning," Arthur observed.

Josh smiled in agreement.

"Why would someone do that?" Analia questioned.

"Myer said he didn't know but suspected it had something to do with the blasting rod. Whoever paid him, made an offhand comment about some ancient artifact."

"I told you, Agent Arias. Many people want that blasting rod. Whoever master-minded this must have been desperate to get his or her hands on it."

"And I told you, Alexander there's always a logical, rational explanation for everything. There was no mystical message about a space-time continuum breach."

"Really, Agent Arias? Everything has a rational explanation. Have you been able to figure out how to explain the accuracy of the pendulum in London, or my vision of the location of the sea cave, or the presence of Azarelis over the altar?"

"No, Dr. Alexander, not yet I haven't.  I'm still working on it," she said with a smile.

"Wait. If the message was a fake, how did Myer know about the psychic breach in the UK? "

"I don't know, Agent Arias.  It's quite a coincidence though, don't you think?"

# Chapter 71
# Burbank

As they rode the elevator down to the first floor, Analia looked over thoughtfully at Arthur.

"So how come when I saw the tall pale-faced monk at the airport he was dressed in regular clothes and not a monk robe?"

"You saw him, Analia, exactly as you expected to see him."

Analia looked blankly back at Arthur while he quickly changed the subject.

"Well, Agent Arias, don't you think you might miss all of this excitement?"

"Right, Alexander. What I actually was thinking was that I can't wait to get assigned to a project that doesn't involve psychism, beings from astral worlds, or any hint of inter-dimensional travel," she retorted decisively.

Then Analia looked playfully at Arthur and added, "You know, you really do move quickly for a guy your age. How old are you anyway?"

Arthur just grinned.

# Epilogue
# Los Angeles

Analia walked purposefully down the long hallway, toward the one light that was still shining on the otherwise darkened floor.

While everyone else had gone home hours ago, Analia was betting that her new boss would still be working. He seemed like the type to be married to his job, and sure enough, even at this late hour, Assistant Director Banes was still at his desk in the downtown high-rise.

What she really wanted to do was go home and unpack some of the boxes that still littered her new apartment. But, this had been an emotionally trying case, and Analia was ready to move on to something a little more grounded in reality. So, she decided to work late in order to finish debriefing Banes and make her written report. Tomorrow would be the start of a new monk-free day.

As Analia knocked lightly on his door, she reflected again on his knowledge of the blasting rod. All day she had tried to decide whether or not she should ask him about it. After puzzling repeatedly over his connection to the rod, Analia was hoping to get some kind of closure.

"Come in Agent Arias," I had a feeling you might drop by tonight."

"Yes sir, I wanted to see you before starting my report."

"I like your work ethic, Agent. Please, sit down. Tell me everything."

For the next hour, Analia relayed all of the pertinent details and events of her travels with Dr. Alexander and his supporting cast of characters.

"You are to be commended Agent Arias, I knew you were the right person for the job."

"Thank you, sir. There's also one more thing I would like to ask."

"Go ahead."

"How did you know about the blasting rod?  I never told you what we picked up at the Foundation."

Banes looked appraisingly at Analia before responding. "Agent Arias, I'm glad you're paying attention, but there will be some details of the cases you're assigned to that you will not be privy to. The rod, at least at this time, is one of those details."

Analia nodded. A certain amount of secrecy usually surrounded the cases she worked on, and she had long ago accepted the fact as a necessary evil of the work she generally found rewarding.

"I understand sir. Unless you have some more questions I better get started on my report, it might take me a while to explain all about Dr. Alexander's *astral journeys*."

"No more questions for now, but Agent Arias you are not to submit or show that report to anyone other than me. When you're finished, you need to destroy all other copies. The details are all classified and you may not talk about this case with anyone else in this office, or any other. Do you understand what I am telling you?"

"Yes sir, but that's not standard procedure, is it?"

"Agent, you're going to find that many of the things we do around here don't conform to standard procedures. You are now part of a special division that follows its own set of rules."

"I don't understand. What exactly do we do here, sir?"

Banes paused before replying, choosing his words carefully. Then, with a wry grin, he answered her question. "Agent Arias, have you ever heard of a television show called the X-Files?"

CPSIA information can be obtained at www.ICGtesting.com
Printed in the USA
LVOW060330300911

248458LV00002B/4/P